Right then and there, Jack. **And that could**

"I've had a wonderful time," she said, jumping to her feet. "Thank you so much. But I have a stack of papers waiting to be graded."

"Then get to it, Teach." With a grin, he shook her hand. "See you around."

She nodded and fled, trying to look as if she weren't fleeing. This was going to be bad. Very bad. A neighbor who cared enough to save the tiniest creature and wasn't offended when she shot holes in his worldview. Someone she could appreciate and also talk to. Yes, this was going to be very bad.

At home she plopped into a living-room chair and drew a deep breath. She was alone.

Alone was good.

She could handle alone.

Right?

Also by Sue Civil-Brown

Sue Civil-Brown

the Life of Reilly

HQN™

ISBN-13: 978-0-373-77204-9
ISBN-10:   0-373-77204-1

THE LIFE OF REILLY

Printed in U.S.A.

To Buster, who spent some time in my koi pond and didn't eat the fish. The fish thank you.

To African gray parrots everywhere. You talk, but we don't listen. Well, except for a handful of scientists... And thanks to *Discover* magazine for teaching me that African grays really *do* talk intelligently, although not as rudely as a certain bird.

And thereby hangs the tale.

the Life of Reilly

CHAPTER ONE

"I TAKE IT YOU weren't satisfied to be quantum consciousness dispersed through eleven dimensions?"

Lynn Reilly stood in the living room of her little bungalow, the tropical breeze of Treasure Island blowing through open windows and screened doors. The furnishings, though sparse, were wicker with brightly colored pillows. Curtains matching the pillow covers—which Lynn had made herself—tossed gently in the breeze.

It should have been an idyllic evening scene: tropical breeze perfumed by exotic flowers, the sound of the surf in the distance, the sun settling low in the sky and casting a golden glow everywhere it touched.

Should have been being the operative phrase.

Lynn had forgotten all that beauty because she was standing in the doorway of the room staring at her Aunt Delphine.

Delphine looked pretty darn good. As if she'd

had a face lift. Nothing exaggerated, just enough to take a few years off. Her skin tone was great, too. Lynn would have given her right arm to achieve that particular satiny rosy look.

So Delphine looked great. The only problem was, she shouldn't have been standing in Lynn's living room.

Because Delphine had died five years ago of a stroke.

Delphine smiled. "You could at least say, 'Hi, Aunt Delphine. It's been a while.'"

Instead, Lynn said, unable to wrap her mind around what was happening, "You're supposed to be dead."

"Pah!" Delphine replied, frowning. "Death is far overrated, dear! And by the way, you're wrong about the number of dimensions."

Lynn's knees started to give way and she sagged onto the nearest chair. Was she really discussing quantum physics with her dead aunt? Shaking her head in shock, she asked, "Okay, so how many are there?"

"Sorry, dear," Delphine said. "You'll have to earn your Nobel Prize on that one."

And that was Delphine, as enigmatic in the after-life as she had been in life. Wasn't she supposed to be playing harps with angels or something? How could God have let her escape from heaven to come to Treasure Island?

But then, given Delphine's nature, the better question might have been: How could God have *prevented* her?

"You're not supposed to be here," Lynn said lamely.

"Probably true." Delphine said. She was wearing her favorite green dress which was covered in huge red cabbage roses, and settled onto the other wicker chair. Well, not settled, exactly. She almost…floated. "But I thought I'd drop in anyway."

"How soon can you drop out?" Lynn asked pointedly.

God, this was impossible. She loved Delphine. How could she not? The woman had raised her from the age of ten, when her parents had died in an accident. But she *shouldn't be here.* Lynn was a scientist. Reality didn't behave this way.

Did it?

"Lynn, honey. You and I need to talk."

Uh oh, Lynn thought. Whenever Delphine said that, she was in for the Lecture.

"I can't understand why in the world a young woman your age, with your training and credentials, would move to a tiny island to teach little kids. You should be at Stanford or MIT. There are hardly any eligible *men* here!"

"Delphine…" But then Lynn bit her tongue. She had had this discussion with Delphine before. Too many times. When she'd decided to major in physics and mathematics, Delphine had told her she would alienate men. When she had graduated *summa cum laude* and decided to pursue a Ph.D rather than a Mrs., Delphine had told her she would surely end up a lonely old woman.

"Oh, don't purse up at me," Delphine scolded. "Do you have any idea how *blessed* you are?"

Blessed? Lynn sat up straighter. *Blessed?* Blessed to have the world's most interfering and manipulative aunt returned from the grave? Not that she didn't love Delphine to pieces, but the last five years had been undeniably…calmer. More rational. Because nobody had been trying to make Lynn over into her own image.

Even as she thought it, Lynn realized she was verging on tears. Interfering and manipulative, yes, but so, so loving. Part of her wanted to fly across the room and try to hug her aunt just one more time.But the scientist in her erupted in a state of armed rebellion. This could not be real. It had to be an hallucination, and giving in to it would be dangerous to her sanity.

"I'm going to take a walk," Lynn said, clutching frantically at the straws of her mental health. "I expect you to have vacated the premises by the time I return."

"But we're not finished!" Delphine said.

"Oh yes, Aunt Delphine," Lynn said. "We are. Go juggle some comets, or pick a star to send into supernova...or whatever else you might have to do. But let *me* live my life, okay?"

Without waiting for an answer, Lynn rose and stormed out, tamping down irritation and fear, pondering the inevitability of what had just happened.

Of course Delphine would do this. Even if she *was* an hallucination.

REVEREND JACK MARKS was in his driveway, washing the ancient, cranky Jeep that was his emergency transportation. The island's salt air made rust a constant problem, and keeping the Jeep clean was a near daily chore, at least when they weren't having a drought. At the moment, car washing was limited to once a week.

But it wasn't really a chore, for it gave Jack time to think about life, God and his place in the universe, time to meditate as he went through the repetitive, mechanical motions of scrubbing and rinsing, scrubbing and rinsing.

Nearby, the island's pet alligator, Buster, waited on the grass for a spray from the hose. Buster, who'd lately been spending most of his time up at the airport, had apparently been driven into town by the island's recent lack of rain. Jack obligingly hosed him from head to tail, listening to Buster's groans of pleasure.

"Oooh, that feels good," Jack said to the gator. Grinning, he hosed the beast yet again, even though he was well aware that he was wasting precious water. Even Bridal Falls had shrunk some for lack of rainwater. The pool beneath looked smaller, too. But Buster was a living being who needed his share of water, too, and as Jack thought about it, he decided Buster needed the water more than the Jeep. So he turned the hose back on the gator until the beast was in the midst of a muddy puddle.

Buster approved, rolling in it. So much for the scrubby lawn.

Jack was not the stereotypical image of a clergyman. He eschewed clerical garb for Hawaiian shirts, khaki shorts and leather sandals, even when he was leading worship. It wasn't that he disrespected God. Far from it. He simply knew that God looked beyond what clothes a man was wearing, and was more interested in the cleanliness of the soul than the cleanliness of the suit. Treasure Island suited his view to a T: liberal and laid-back.

He glanced up as his new neighbor, the pretty dark-haired schoolteacher, emerged from the front of her house. So much for cleanliness of the soul. He fought down the urge to take a third glance, because upon the second one, he realized she certainly was fetching in bicycle shorts and a sports bra. He told himself not to notice, that women on Treasure Island often exercised in such garb, as the tropical heat would permit little else. And to be honest, with most of the women he saw dressed in that way, it wouldn't have disturbed him.

But there was something about *this* woman that made his heart skip a beat. Maybe it was the dark eyes that seemed at once placid and deep, or the smile that could easily have substituted for the island's power plant or even—so much for cleanliness of soul again—the long legs that seemed to carry her with such effortless grace. Whatever it was, this woman was certainly worth a fourth and fifth glance, if not an outright stare. Not the sort of thing a man of the cloth ought to do. But then, he was a man like any other, and he had the sneaking suspicion heaven would understand.

He was about to call out a friendly hello—having convinced himself that he meant nothing by it beyond the sort of neighborliness that typified the community here on Treasure Island—then hesitated when he realized she was not moving with her usual, casual grace. She was almost stomping, which, he could not help but notice, gave ever the slightest bounce in her...pectoral region. She was upset. Even angry, maybe. Certainly disturbed. Not the time for a friendly hello.

His first instinct was to mosey over that way and ask if something was wrong. But before he could make up his mind about a proper approach to something which might prove to be delicate, Lynn Reilly turned around and walked back into the house. Looking, Jack thought, rather like a woman determined to face a great unpleasantness. She disappeared inside and the screen door slapped closed behind her. Shrugging, Jack started washing his Jeep again.

A moment later, his head snapped up as he heard Lynn Reilly's voice float clearly through her open windows.

"*You,*" Lynn said loudly, "were supposed to *dissipate!*"

TREASURE ISLAND RESIDENTS rarely minded their own business. Indeed, on this island, if you suggested that someone should mind own business, he was likely to look at you as if you had inquired about the marital status of a tuna sandwich. It was one of those places where, if you didn't know what you were doing, someone else surely did. Jack had only a few more scruples. In short, if he learned something in confidence, he held it in confidence. On this island that rarely happened.

Still, he hesitated. He hadn't yet met the schoolteacher. She'd arrived just before the opening of the term, and he'd been away on a rare vacation. Bursting into her house demanding to know if something was wrong seemed hardly likely to endear him to her.

But curiosity had sunk its teeth into him, and if Jack had any significant flaw, it was his curiosity. Since his childhood, people had been saying that curiosity killed the cat, but that hadn't slowed Jack any. Piqued, he stepped over Buster with a muttered apology and strode straight toward the new schoolteacher's house. Behind him, Buster lifted his head from the mud curiously.

After all, he told himself, the sanity of one of the island's very few teachers was a matter of concern. So was her safety. Either one constituted ample excuse to butt in. Especially on Treasure Island.

He supposed he didn't look very reputable, pretty much wet as he was and covered with soap stains and grime from scrubbing the Jeep's wheels. His nails would have shamed a coal miner. So as soon as he rang Lynn Reilly's bell, he shoved his hands into his pockets.

She appeared on the other side of the screen door, looking harried and maybe even a tad frightened. "Yes?"

"Ms. Reilly, I'm your neighbor, Reverend—"

"Yes, I know," she interrupted. "Jack Marks. I'm sorry, but this isn't a good time for a social chat."

Give her points for being blunt, he thought. He always liked that in a person. "Social chatting can wait," he said, giving his best ministerial smile. "I understand that just dropping by can be inconvenient, although on this island it's hard to escape."

"Then what?" she asked.

Maybe she was a little too blunt. And there was something about the way she was standing, as if she were trying to block something from his view. "I'm sorry. It's just that I heard you while I was washing my car, and I thought you sounded…distressed."

To his amazement, color rose to the roots of her hair. Had he interrupted some kind of tryst? But no, he was absolutely certain that she had sounded as if someone were bothering her.

"I…uh…" Words appeared to have utterly escaped her, surely a strange state of affairs for a middle-school teacher. Her color deepened even more, reminding him of a freshly boiled lobster... although he had long since sworn off eating anything that had to be cooked alive.

"Unexpected quantum field collapse."

He gaped at her. What language was she speaking? She made a visible effort to gather herself.

Then a recognizable word burst out of her. "Telephone," she said.

"Telephone?"

"Telephone."

"What about the telephone?" he asked.

"Someone was bothering me. I hung up on her."

He nodded. "I'm sorry to have disturbed you then."

"No. I mean, it's okay, it's just that, well, I have an interfering aunt." She gave him a weak smile.

"I have an interfering mother," he said with genuine sympathy. "Treasure Island is just far enough away."

Her smile was sickly. "Aunt Delphine is...never far enough away."

"She can afford the international long distance, eh?"

She nodded. "It's as if she were right in the room."

He chuckled. "I'm more fortunate. My mother insists that I call *her.*"

"I wish Aunt Delphine would learn the same manners."

"Well, I'm sorry to have bothered you. I'll just go back to washing my car then."

"Thanks for caring."

"Sure." More polite smiles. He was halfway back to his Jeep when something made him look around. Lynn Reilly still stood in her doorway, behind the screen, watching.

Some impulse, born of the devil he later thought, caused him to say, "Why don't you come over for dinner tonight? Just a simple salad and grilled fish, but I have plenty."

"Thank you! I'd love that."

He thought her acceptance sounded awfully relieved for the circumstances, but he shrugged inwardly and returned to his car.

Then, through the open window, he heard Lynn Reilly say, "Just leave me alone!"

He winced, hoping she didn't mean him.

CHAPTER TWO

"GOT A LADY COMING over tonight?"

The voice came from the yard next door, and it belonged to Zedediah Burch, aka Zed-the-Bait-Guy. Not that there were that many other Zeds on the island. None, in fact. But somehow it was always Zed-the-Bait-Guy, run together into a single word. He caught and sold fresh chum for the commercial fishermen and the few sport fishing boats the island boasted. You could always count on Zed-the-Bait-Guy for exactly what you needed to entice the kind of fish you were looking for.

Jack paused in the process of spreading out a tablecloth on the slightly rusted wrought-iron table on his small brick patio, a patio that rippled and dipped a bit because his predecessor hadn't thought to make a level bed of sand to support the bricks, all of which looked like castoffs from a brickyard.

"What makes you think that?" he asked.

Zed-the-Bait-Guy shrugged and moved a wad of

chewing tobacco a little more firmly into his cheek. "Tablecloth."

"Oh." Jack looked at the oilcloth he was spreading, a sheet he'd bought from Hanratty's general store a couple years back. It was already cracking along the folds. "You think this is fancy?"

"I think you wouldn't bother for me."

Jack had to grin at that. "You're right, Zed. For you I'd let the rust show."

"Rust adds to the taste," Zed said. "So who is it?"

"The new teacher. I thought I'd be neighborly."

Zed nodded and turned to spit into the spittoon he kept on his side of the property line. The wad landed with an audible *ping* that sent a shudder up the back of Jack's neck. He had to remind himself that millions of viewers watched baseball players do exactly the same thing, dozens of times during each game. In glorious full-color close-ups, too. The reminder didn't help.

Jack swallowed hard, then spoke. "Could you move that a bit farther away while we're eating tonight?"

Zed shrugged. "Won't be here. Big game tonight."

"What are the stakes?" Jack asked. He didn't have to ask what kind of game. Poker was *the* game on Treasure Island.

"Me and Fred Hanks are facing off with Mick McDonald and Joe Cranston. Winner gets to ask Hester LeBlanc out to dinner."

"Ahh."

Hester had been widowed nearly two years ago when her fisherman husband had gone overboard during a severe squall. There was some talk that he'd gone over on purpose, rather than face Hester's anger, since she'd just learned he was sparking around with Camille Danza. Some went so far as to suggest that Hester...arranged...his untimely demise, although Jack saw nothing in her that would hint at such a possibility. Even on Treasure Island, sometimes gossip was just that—gossip.

Regardless, thus far the island's middle-aged, would-be lotharios had respected her mourning. Apparently they had decided that long enough was long enough. "Good luck."

Zed shrugged philosophically. "Winning only means you get to ask first. Doesn't mean she'll say yes."

"True."

"That schoolteacher though..." He smiled. "Quite a looker."

"I hadn't noticed." *Liar!* Jack felt instantly ashamed. He was a preacher for heaven's sake. He had no business lying.

"Maybe you'd better get Buck Shanahan to fly you into Aruba to get your eyes checked then," Zed suggested, with a twinkle in his eye that made clear he did not believe Jack one iota. "Whatcha making?"

"Just salad and grilled fish."

Zed shook his head. "No dessert? No taters? Look, I got a couple of bakers you can have. They're pretty good cooked on the coals. And I have some rum cake I picked up in Aruba. Ain't been opened yet."

Before Jack could say anything, Zed was hurrying toward his back door.

Jack shook his head smiling and finished spreading the oilcloth. That was one of the things he loved about this island. On Treasure Island, being neighborly wasn't merely a phrase; it was a way of life.

When Lynn Reilly arrived, he had the potatoes wrapped in foil and baking on the hot gray coals, the salad tossed and ready, and the fish seasoned with dill and on the rack, prepped for grilling.

He'd even dug into the church's supply of communion wine for a bottle of passable red, although he knew he ought to serve white wine with fish. Unfortunately, his budget didn't allow for buying wine from the only supplier on the island, the casino.

"Smells delicious," Lynn said appreciatively as

she took a chair at the table and accepted a goblet of wine. She had changed into a white sun dress that caught the red of the setting sun and reflected it back as pink. The sky overhead seemed ablaze tonight, probably heralding rain for tomorrow.

"I hope you like dill," he said, reaching for the wire fish basket.

"Love it."

The potatoes were done, so he put the fish over the heat. It would cook fast, even though the coals had burned low and gray.

"It's nice of you to ask me over," Lynn said. "I've got a grill out back and a patio, too, but every time I think of actually grilling, it seems like a lot of effort for just one person." She leaned forward, resting her elbows on the table. "It's funny, when I moved here, I was sure I was going to do all those things that come to mind when you move to the tropics. Cook and eat outside, spend hours on the beach or in the water."

He chuckled. "I know. It turns out you have to make a real effort to do it, just the way it was back on the mainland. I fight the battle every day."

"Do you?" She looped her fingers and rested her chin on them.

"Yep. I don't know if I feel lazy because of the weather and the lifestyle, or if it really *is* too much trouble to bother for one person."

She laughed, her brown eyes sparkling. "The air is so soft it's almost tranquilizing. And when the breeze starts in the evening, I just want to sit and enjoy it."

"Yeah, I have the same problem. The longer you live here, the easier it gets to function, but at first you just want to go on a permanent vacation."

"School keeps me busy, thank goodness. Some things can't be ignored, like teaching a class or grading papers."

He flipped the fish over. "How many students do you have?"

"All the younger ones, from first grade up, then high-school physics one and two, calculus and applied math." She held up a hand. "It sounds like a lot, but I have a total of sixty-three kids."

"So lots of individual attention."

"That's what attracted me to this island in the first place. With so few students in each class, we can explore more. And I can get some of them hooked on science, so maybe they'll stay with it after they graduate."

"You're passionate," he said.

She shrugged. "There's a big universe out there. The better we understand it, the better we'll know our place in it. Maybe we'll stop acting as if it's our garbage can. In fact, I'm thinking about taking some of the classes for a day trip to see an island in its pristine state. One of the parents was telling me about a small island where the only fresh water is in a rain pool."

Jack nodded and tested the fish. "Just another minute." Looking back at her, he continued. "I don't think our kids appreciate just how important rain pools are to our survival. This island would be dead without rain, and we've had to dig cisterns in the rock up on the volcano to ensure a steady flow. It doesn't just magically come out of the tap."

"It doesn't do that anywhere," she smiled. "But yes, I agree with your point. It's especially critical on these small islands. Rain is truly the gift of life."

"Just ask Mars." He removed the fish from the grill and gently pushed a piece onto each plate. Then he forked the potatoes out of the coals and set them on a separate plate. "I'm afraid I don't have sour cream, but I have—"

"I have sour cream," said a voice from the deepening dark next door. Zed stepped out of the shadows. For once tobacco didn't create a bulge in his cheek. "You must be the new schoolteacher."

Jack rolled his eyes. "Lynn, this is Zed."

"Zed-the-Bait-Guy," Lynn said quickly.

"Hi." Zed extended a hand in greeting and smiled broadly, a mistake considering what the chaw had done to his teeth. "Let me get that sour cream for you."

Jack put his hands on his narrow hips. "I thought you had a poker game?"

Zed smiled. "Was just getting ready to leave."

Right, Jack thought. And people complained about *his* curiosity.

Zed returned in thirty seconds with a carton of sour cream. "Keep what you don't use," he said. "Seeing as how I can get more when I buy more spuds."

"Thank you," Lynn said.

"Yeah, thanks," Jack said. "Your game?"

"My game?" Zed blinked. "Oh, yeah, my game. Wouldn't want somebody else to get at Hester first because I didn't show. See ya later."

After his footsteps vanished into the sound of the surf that was only a few blocks away, Lynn asked, "Does Hester know they're playing for her?"

Jack reached for a spoon to use with the sour cream and passed both to Lynn. "Probably. There aren't a lot of secrets around here."

She nodded. "Makes sense."

He lifted an eyebrow. "You think so?"

"Why not?" she asked. "Human attraction is largely random anyway. It's a matter of phero-mones—whether the other person smells like a viable reproductive partner. And we don't even know it. At the most basic level, it's about whether proteins in our brain are open or folded, a largely random function of precisely where the potentiality wave collapses into a point particle. So why not turn it over to the deal of a card?"

Jack looked at her, trying to find words. "Umm…"

She laughed. "Sorry. I go over the top sometimes."

"It's just that I've never heard love spoken of in such…cold terms."

"Noooo," she said. "It's not cold at all. It's quite beautiful, in fact. The universe deals to each of us in turn, random shuffling at the Planck scale, and yet we're responsible for how we play every card we're dealt. It's a mathematical and ethical symphony beyond imagining."

"Planck scale?" Jack asked, then shook his head. "Never mind. How's the fish?"

"Fantastic! I don't think I've ever had fish this fresh."

"It came in on the boat this morning. One of the perks of living here."

For a little while they were quiet, enjoying the food and the deepening tropical evening. As the last of the daylight faded, two citronella candles in clay pots provided the illumination. If there were any mosquitoes on the island, Lynne had yet to run into them, but the candles drew the attention of an equally successful pest: moths.

With her chin resting in her hand, she watched as Jack gently waved them away, saving them from death by fatal attraction. She couldn't help but find it touching; surely he was the first person she'd ever met who actually cared what happened to a moth.

"These fellows," he said as he waved them away, "are harmless, though not particularly pretty. It won't be long though before the real butterflies start emerging. The colors are glorious."

"That would make a great class project for my younger students."

"Just don't kill them to examine them."

She sat up a little straighter. "Observation without interference?"

"Exactly," he said. "You can catch them alive, look them over, then let them go."

"You realize, of course, that observation without interference is not even theoretically possible," she said. "Heisenberg? Schrödinger? Wave-particle duality? Double slit experiments? Any of this ring a bell?"

"Umm...you've gone into that other language again."

"That was English," Lynn said. "Well, Heisenberg and Schrödinger are German names, but still…it can't come as a shock to you that we change the universe whenever we look at it."

"When you stare into the abyss, the abyss stares back into you?" Jack asked.

"Well, that's Friedrich Nietzsche. He was a philosopher, not a physicist."

"Is there a difference anymore?"

Lynn smiled. "Touché. When we start to look at the most fundamental building blocks of the universe, we do tend to blur that line, don't we?"

Jack shrugged. "I really couldn't say. I don't know all that much about it. But listening to you…well, I'm reminded of some of our more esoteric conversations back in seminary. How many angels really *can* dance on the head of a pin, and the like."

Lynn felt the flush rise to her cheeks. Maybe it was the wine. Maybe it was the shock of a dinner invitation on the heels of Delphine's visitation. "I'm sorry, Jack."

He held up a hand. "No, don't be sorry. I have to say, I'm fascinated. Truly."

Fascinated. That was a word that could mean a lot of things. Some of them purely intellectual. Most of them not. The latter could be…dangerous. Very dangerous.

She sighed.

"Something wrong?"

Lynn shook her head. "Just tell me to hush when I start babbling about things that sound too weird."

"On Treasure Island?" he asked with a wink. "Trying to define *weird* here is like stepping into a tar pit."

"But—"

"Lynn," he interrupted, "just be yourself. Don't try to impress me, because you already have. And don't try to play to my expectations, because I don't have any. If I'd wanted to be surrounded by staid, ordinary, never-risk-looking-weird people, I'd have stayed in Connecticut."

He waved his hand over the candles again, sending a few more moths back to the safety of the shadows. She took the opportunity to study him, really study him. She'd spent most of the evening avoiding directly looking at Jack except in brief glimpses. The interface of observer and observed was never more apparent than in human interaction. All her life, she'd had a strong tendency to watch people, to examine every movement, every facial tic, every shift of the eye or the posture, looking for cues to their thoughts. It had consistently made people uncomfortable, to the point where she'd trained herself not to look at people directly. That had grown into a shyness that had plagued her through childhood and into the present day.

Right now, however, she decided he was an attractive man. Person. Not a movie-star type, but handsome enough in a laid-back sort of way. His face seemed to want to smile, and laugh lines decorated the corners of his eyes and etched the edges of his mouth. The sun had bronzed him, nothing surprising here in the tropics, and left his brown hair streaked with blond. Almost a surfer look in a way, except his eyes held so much more depth.

That was when he realized she was staring at him. To her astonishment, he didn't squirm. Instead, he smiled, revealing great teeth. "You look like you've never seen anyone push moths away from flames before."

"I haven't."

He nodded. "I actually find it an interesting paradox. God gave most creatures a desire to live and the means of survival. Then we have the moth, who seems willing to immolate himself just to approach the light. One would think the heat would warn him off."

"Not if he can't feel it."

He nodded. "Or…if the light is so beautiful the moth wants to approach at any cost."

Instinctively, she looked into the candle flame. "It *is* beautiful."

"And for the moth it is at once a desirable goal and a deadly trap."

She glanced his way. "Are we talking metaphor here?"

"Why do people always think I'm speaking in parables?"

"Maybe because you're a minister."

He laughed at that. "Sorry, I was just marveling at one of nature's oddities."

"There certainly are a few of those. Although…"

She leaned on her elbows on the table. "Well, I shouldn't I guess."

"What?" he asked.

"The moths aren't attracted to the flame."

"Is that a fact?" His eyebrow lifted.

She nodded. "It's actually the warm candle wax that's the attraction. The infrared signature of warm candle wax coincides with that of the sex-attractant chemical emitted by female moths. Light-conducting spines on their antennae carry that signal to their brains, and they think there's a…well…they think there's a horny female moth there."

"That would certainly explain the self-immolation," Jack said. "Huh. So it's not the flame at all."

"I didn't mean to spoil it for you."

"Not at all! Why would you say that?"

She shrugged. "People are more comfortable with the familiar. The assumption is woven into the fabric of our language—'Like a moth to flame.' Then science comes along and shows something else entirely. People resent it when science turns their beliefs upside down."

"Some people do," he said. "I'm not one of them."

Lynn nodded, wondering if his casual smile were covering something else. In her experience, discussing science with religious people tended to end very badly.

He paused for a moment, then continued, "Lynn, I've always felt that we miss so much if we don't realize that the entire universe around us is full of wonders. Every breath of air, every beat of our hearts, is a kind of miracle. A beautiful, beautiful gift. Understanding why it happens, at a scientific level, doesn't disprove the miracle. It helps us to appreciate the miracle even more."

Right then and there, Lynn decided she liked Jack. And that, she reminded herself, could be a serious problem.

She jumped to her feet—not too quickly, she hoped—and said, "I've had a wonderful time, Jack. Thank you so much. But I have a stack of papers waiting to be graded."

He rose immediately. "Then get to it, teach." With a grin, he shook her hand. "See you around."

She nodded and fled while trying to look as if she weren't fleeing. This was going to be bad. Very bad. A neighbor who cared enough to save the tiniest creature from its own urges, and wasn't offended when she shot holes in his worldview. Someone she could appreciate and also talk to. Yes, this was going to be very bad.

To her great relief, she found her living room empty of Delphine. She plopped into a chair and drew a deep breath, taking a moment to look into every dark corner of the room, making sure Delphine wasn't hiding in the shadows before letting out a deep sigh.

She was alone.

Alone was good.

She could handle alone.

Right?

CHAPTER THREE

"YOU DIDN'T HAVE ANY papers to grade at all."

Lynn rolled over in her bed with a groan and pulled the pillow over her head. The first roseate light of dawn was seeping between the Bahama shutters, far too early for rising. On Treasure Island, school started at ten in the morning because so many students went out early to fish with their parents.

"Go away," she mumbled and tried to reach for the strands of a really lovely dream she had been having. "It's too early."

"You lied to get away from the nice preacher."

Lynn groaned again, rolled over and closed her eyes. "You're not here. I refuse to observe you and thus the quantum wave does not collapse and thus you are not here."

"Don't be silly, Lynn," Delphine said, now a warm presence beneath the covers. "You know it doesn't work that way. You're not the only observer here. And if the pheromone scent under here is any indication, you weren't the only observer last night either."

Lynn threw back the covers in horror. "Aunt Delphine!"

Delphine, now sitting primly on the side of the bed, garbed in some diaphanous thing that Lynn remembered from years past, simply smiled. "I'm not going anywhere."

Lynn scowled. "Stay *out* of my bed, Aunt Delphine!"

"Oh please," Delphine said, patting Lynn's foot. "I would never dream of doing something so tawdry. I may be a ghost, but I'm not like *that*."

"Pffft. Don't eavesdrop on my dreams either."

Delphine put a hand over her eyes. "I didn't see a thing, dear. But it doesn't take a bloodhound to tell that you had some nice ones."

"Arrgh!"

Lynn leapt out of the bed and headed straight for the shower. When she emerged, Delphine was buffing her nails at Lynn's vanity table.

"Feel better?" Delphine asked.

"I feel less like a broadcast antenna at least."

"That's good, dear," Delphine said. "And I'm sorry. That was a bit...forward of me. You must understand that in my state of existence, privacy is simply not a relevant concept anymore."

Lynn found it impossible to imagine in detail, even while she could understand the theory of superposition and interconnectedness that underlay Delphine's new experience. Still, the idea of not having a truly private thought was unnerving, to say the least.

"You look younger," Lynn said, giving in. Hallucination or not, she found an odd comfort in Delphine's presence.

"I can look any age I want to now. In fact, I don't even have to look human. However, I've chosen a younger version from your memories…from back when you thought I was the coolest aunt ever."

"How old was I then?" Lynn asked, trying to towel the moisture from her hair and fighting a losing battle against the ever-present humidity. "Three? Four? It must've been before the age of reason."

Delphine laughed. "I always loved you, Lynn."

In spite of her irritation, Lynn felt a pang. "I know, Aunt Delphine. I loved you, too."

"Past tense?" Delphine asked, shaking her head.

Lynn hung her towel over a rod and considered the question. It was customary to speak of the dead in the past tense and yet… "No. I guess not."

"Would you like to know what happens when we die?" Delphine asked, looking away as Lynn shrugged on her bra and panties. "You should wait until your skin dries, dear. It will be much easier to get dressed then."

"That would mean waiting until January," Lynn said, now reaching for a pair of capri pants and a flower-print blouse. "I never really feel *dry* here. And yes, I would love to know what happens when we die."

Delphine smiled. "Nice outfit. Not what I'd have worn to teach in my day, but it's practical here. I can't tell you all of it—that would spoil the surprise—but let's just say I have unfinished business."

Lynn shook her head as she picked up a brush. "I refuse to be your unfinished business."

Delphine shrugged. "Sorry, kiddo. Not your decision."

"Oh, God!"

"Precisely."

Lynn headed for the kitchen and her prized espresso maker. How many shots? Two? Four? *Twelve?* How many would it take to wrap her brain around Delphine's intrusion into her life? And why didn't they have a Starbucks on this island yet?

Four shots, she decided. An Americano over ice with just enough cream to take the bitter edge off. She needed to be buzzing high on caffeine to deal with this.

"I *do* miss Starbucks," Delphine sighed behind her.

"What? They don't have them in heaven?"

"Don't blaspheme, dear." Then, "Hmmm. Ahh! That's much better!"

In spite of herself, Lynn whirled around to look. Her aunt was now seated at the dinette with an iced latte in her hand.

"It's so hot in the tropics," Delphine remarked.

This was too much. "Where did you get that from?"

"I thought about it and there it was." Delphine smiled beatifically, then sucked delicately from the straw. "Oh, that's the best I've ever had."

"It's not fair."

"What isn't?"

"That you get to think one into existence, but I have to make mine." Petulance, Lynn thought. Now she was being petulant with a ghost.

"Well, Lynn, you live in a cause-and-effect world. You have to effect the cause to cause the effect. So start brewing so we can chat before you leave for school."

She didn't want to spend her usual quiet coffee time with a dead aunt. This was *her* time in the mornings, time to sit on her back porch and sip her coffee, taking in the fragrance of bougainvillea and dew before they evaporated and left behind only the tang of salt air. However, she had no choice in the matter, so reluctantly she walked out to the porch and sat with Delphine. Besides, she didn't *really* want Delphine to go.

"That's so much better," Delphine said approvingly.

"So are you going to tell me the mysteries of the universe?"

"Don't be silly. You have to find them out for yourself."

"Then *why* are you here?"

"I can't tell you that," Delphine said. "I just have to finish something."

"Oh, lovely." Lynn put her chin in her hand, her elbow on the table, and stared at her favorite aunt. "You know you could cost me my job."

Delphine appeared appalled. "I wouldn't do that!"

"You will if I keep talking to empty air."

Delphine pursed her lips. "I hadn't considered that. I was only thinking of my mission."

"I'd appreciate it if you would keep that in mind."

"Of course I will."

"Thank you." Bargaining with the dead. Lynn closed her eyes, surrendering briefly to a sense of surrealism that Dali and Kafka might have conspired to create.

She lifted her coffee and sipped, considering how bizarre it felt to look across at a dead person. Common sense said this could not be happening, but then again what was reality? When she considered her former colleagues at Princeton investigating the effect of consciousness on the underlying quantum field of the universe, reality became a tenuous thing.

But there was nothing at all tenuous about Delphine's appearance. She looked solid enough to touch. A thought occurred to her. "You're not cold."

Delphine arched a brow. "Why would I be cold?"

"Ghosts are supposed to create cold spots. You draw energy from the matter around me in order to materialize. I should experience that energy drop as coldness."

Delphine laughed. "That old tale. Well, I suppose some do. But I'm not exactly a ghost."

"Then what *are* you?"

"A non-physical manifestation of my consciousness."

"A ghost."

"Not the same thing at all, Lynn. Not at all. A ghost is merely an imprint left on the quantum field. Like a footprint left in the dirt. The footprint is there, but the person who left that footprint has passed on."

"Really."

"Don't sound so dubious. Remember, I've graduated ahead of you."

Lynn had the worst urge to roll her eyes. "Graduated what ahead of me? Death? Yes, I'll give you that much. But physics? Oh Auntie, let me assure you that physicists are working on things you only imagined when you were still teaching."

"You think I don't know that? My point is—I *have* the answers now. You don't." Delphine sipped her latte then frowned. "Which reminds me. Why in the world did you leave Princeton and your research to come to this place and teach youngsters, of all things?"

"Do you really want an answer?"

"Yes."

"Because I got sick of the underhanded competition," Lynn said. "Not with my peers, but with my students. I'm sure you heard about it. Students were stealing books and papers from the library to prevent other students from reading them. Buying their term papers on the Internet. Fudging their experimental results. I felt as if I were teaching a generation of cheats. Not that I should have been surprised, given how some of my colleagues behaved."

"Your work was stolen."

"Yes." Lynn scowled. "And I hope Donald Farthing enjoys his new-found fame."

"He was that professor you were dating, right?"

"Unfortunately."

"And he's the one who stole your work?"

"Two years of research on 11-dimensional Calabi-Yau shapes, trying to prove my theory of quantum space-time. I had to develop a new mathematic to solve it, Auntie, just as Newton had to develop calculus to fashion the equations of classical mechanics. Then one morning I wake up and find he's published my research on the Internet, under his name. He'd copied my files to his computer and even backdated them. And since he was a tenured professor and I was just a Ph.D candidate…"

Delphine nodded and took another sip of her drink. She sucked loudly at the straw just as she sometimes had in life. "I never really cared for Donald," she said finally. "I'm so sorry he proved me right."

"You're not the only one."

"Well," Delphine said, suddenly brisk, "this *is* a nice spot for a change of pace. Almost like a vacation. Is that why you chose this place?"

"Yes, it is. Just let me get on with it, will you?" But a vacation was not the reason she had chosen this island. A vacation had been the last thing on her mind. She'd needed to escape, yes—especially from the academic world that was looking at her like a bug under the microscope—but Treasure Island had been an accidental discovery on the Internet.

She'd been browsing around, looking for various teaching jobs, when this one had popped up. She might have passed it by, except that her mathematical mind had immediately calculated the thousands of miles this job would put between her and Donald.

The lure had been irresistible.

"But of course!" Delphine arched a brow as if surprised. "I'm not here to hinder you."

"No?" Lynn felt entirely dubious, with good reason. Delphine's help had often caused more problems than it had cured. "But, um, I really should handle my own life on my own."

Delphine smiled benevolently. "You only think it's your own life."

Lynn didn't know how to react to that. She wanted to throw something, but that wasn't her nature. She could have told her aunt to stop playing the sphinx, but she'd never told Delphine to do anything except butt out. Which she had just tried to do.

"Look, dear," Delphine said kindly, "you know you're part of the Unity. Nothing affects only you. Others are involved. But, I promise to stay in the background as long as my work here if unfinished."

At that, she dissipated. Lynn felt anything but reassured. Delphine in the background could be as every bit as disastrous as Delphine front and center.

Groaning, she sat on the back porch, drank coffee and watched the remainder of the sunrise. Before long, despite everything, peace began to fill her again. That was why she had come to this island, and the sun's early rays seemed to bathe her with it.

Forget Delphine, she told herself. The worst she could be was a nuisance. The best....

Well, the best that could be said was that Delphine had just confirmed a lot of current theories in physics. She smiled at that and raised her coffee in a toast to the sun. The world was an amazing place.

It even included an alligator staring at her from beneath a shrub.

She blinked and peered more intently. God, it *was* an alligator. It must be Buster, she realized. He was the only crocodilian on the island and more a celebrity than any of the human inhabitants, even World Series of Poker champion Bill Anstin. Buster was not quite wild, not quite a pet, not dangerous but neither to be trifled with when he set his mind to something.

Rather like Aunt Delphine.

"Tell me you're not in league with her," Lynn said.

Alligator physiology made it impossible to shrug, but somehow Buster conveyed a shrug regardless.

"Aren't you supposed to be with Hannah?" Lynn asked. Buster was smitten with Hannah Lamont, a pilot who lived with Buck Shanahan up at the airport. Island legend said that Buster had played a prominent role in getting Hannah and Buck together and thus ensuring that Hannah stayed on Treasure Island.

"Mmmhhhhmmm." It was a wordless groan and yet Lynn had no doubt what Buster meant.

"She'll be back soon, I'm sure."

"Mmmmmhmmmmm."

"So you're lonely and hanging around with me?"

"Mmmmmhmmmmm."

"Delphine's going to make trouble for me, isn't she?"

"Mmmmmhmmmmm."

Lynn sighed. "You have to understand, Buster. She was the stereotypical spinster schoolmarm. When she was a girl, guys didn't like girls who were too smart. And she was way, *way* too smart. She never found anyone who could put up with that, and for as long as I can remember, she's been bound and determined that I should not end up alone."

"Mmmmmhmmmmm."

"What she can't understand," Lynn said, "is that

I would rather be alone for the right reasons than be with someone for the wrong reasons."

"Mmmmmm?"

"I don't want to be with someone just for the sake of being with someone. I'd rather be alone than be with the wrong person again."

"Mmmmmhmmmmm."

"You think I'm crazy, right?"

"Uhmmmuhmmmm."

"No?"

"Uhmmmuhmmmm."

"Will you do me a favor, Buster?" Lynn asked, looking into his saurian eyes.

"Mmmmmm?"

"When Delphine makes things nuts—and we both know she will—will you remind me I'm not crazy?"

Buster blinked and seemed to be assembling the parts of the thought before he replied.

"Mmmmmhmmmmm."

So okay, Lynn thought. At least she had an ally. An ally-gator. She laughed at the thought as she rose to get ready to leave for school. Maybe Buster was wrong. Maybe she *was* crazy.

But she could still laugh at herself. She laughed even harder when she realized her aunt had done it again: she had her niece talking to alligators.

Delphine tended to have that effect.

CHAPTER FOUR

THE NEXT AFTERNOON, just as he was about to set out for his daily jog on the beach, Jack stepped out of his house to find Buster waiting in the now-dry wallow they'd made together yesterday.

Jack stared at the gator, wondering why he was hanging around here when lately he'd preferred to be up at the airport. But the obvious plea was just too much to ignore, especially since he couldn't see even the smallest puff of cloud in the sky.

"Okay, Buster," he said. "I'll get the hose."

"Mmmmmmmmhhhhhh."

This gator talked. Of that Jack had not the least doubt. Admittedly the beast was limited by lack of lips and proper vocal chords, but somewhere during his long gator-solitary life on this island, he seemed to have learned English.

Jack turned the hose on Buster, and a stream of water ran over the rough hide, causing the gator to groan ecstatically.

"It might," Jack said to Buster, "be ecologically more sound to put you in my bathtub."

Umum, Buster answered, shaking his head.

"No, I guess not. I'd have to change the water anyway to keep it clean."

Buster groaned happily, wiggling in the dirt until it mixed with the water and became mud.

An amused voice came from next door. "Does watering him make him grow?"

Jack looked up to see Lynn standing in front of her house, backpack slung over one shoulder, a stack of file folders in her arms.

"I don't know," he said truthfully. "But since the drought it sure makes him happy."

She laughed. "I agree. A happy gator is desirable. Do you feed him, too?"

"That's one thing we avoid. We don't want him too comfortable around us."

"So what does he eat?"

"Well, he was eating fish and birds at the pool but now..." Jack shrugged. "I suspect it may be time to dump a few dead chickens and fish waste somewhere near the pool. He can't be catching a whole lot right now."

"I was thinking that, too." She walked to her porch and set down her folders and backpack before coming toward them. She remained a respectful distance from Buster, though. "He and I had a visit this morning. A very nice conversation."

"You didn't run shrieking? Most newcomers do the first time they meet him."

"I'd heard about him from my students. No point in becoming terrified, from what I heard."

"None really. If he ever attacked a human, it was One-Hand Hank Hanratty, the guy who brought him here. The local myth is that Hank lost his hand to Buster, who wasn't real happy about being the only gator here. Or maybe he wasn't happy about being brought here. Whatever, he's certainly adapted."

"Quite well it seems. He's even gotten you to do his bidding."

Jack laughed and looked at the gator, who was happily rolling in the mud. "I guess that's enough. We don't have water to waste." He turned off the spigot and Buster made a sound very like *awwwwwwwwww* but kept on rolling happily.

"I swear," Jack said, "I'm never again going to refer to the reptilian brain as the cause of most of the bad in human nature. This reptile is both smart and a good guy."

"I see your point."

He wiped his hands on his shorts and flashed her a grin. "Wanna come jogging with me on the beach? It's the best time. Great breeze, beautiful water…"

She hesitated, just long enough to make him wonder if he had something green caught between his teeth. But then she smiled. "I was going to go in early, but... Just let me change. Although I warn you, I'm used to jogging on pavement, not sand. I don't know how far I'll get."

"Not a problem. I'll just leave you in my dust."

She grinned. "We'll see about that." Then she whirled, scooped up her school things, trotted back to her house and disappeared inside.

Jack found he was still smiling. He glanced at Buster. "She's pretty unaffected and charming, isn't she."

Buster lifted a muddy eyelid. "Mmmmhmmmmm."

"I thought you'd agree. And don't worry, I'll rustle up some chickens from the general store and some fish offal from the docks after my run and I'll drop them off for you up near the falls."

Buster made a disappointed groan.

"Look, you know it's against the rules to feed you in town. Although, I have to admit, after all this time, we ought to trust you more."

Buster seemed to nod.

"And, I'd be awful surprised if no one has ever fed you in town."

Buster winked, as if to say, *I'll never tell.*

"Yeah, that's what I thought. Well, I'll see what I can do."

Buster rumbled something and worked his way deeper into the mud.

Less than five minutes later, Lynn, clad in a jogging outfit, met Jack on the cracked pavement. They stretched a bit, then loped at an easy pace down toward the beach. "It's easier if you run on the wet sand," Jack told her. "The water has it pretty much packed."

"Yes. The electrolytic effect of the water increases the charge interaction between the sand particles, forming a more stable soil matrix."

"That means the water has the sand packed, right?" Jack asked, staring at her.

"Umm…yes. I guess I've spent more time in laboratories than I have at beaches."

"Living here ought to remedy that."

From his mud wallow, Buster watched them go, apparently content to let the stupid humans run around in the heat by themselves.

THEY RAN AWAY from the town, to avoid the fishing boats and piers, along a wide expanse of spun-sugar sand. Lynn felt her calves straining in a new way, even on the harder wet sand, but she hardly cared. She was still utterly enthralled by the Caribbean blue water, a color that defied description. She could have scientifically explained that incredible blue-green down to the last grain of sand on the ocean floor, the exact depth of the water and its refractory abilities, but for once the scientist in her just wanted to shut down and let her senses drink it all in.

Besides, however far she had gone at Princeton working with the quantum universe and the observer effect, the reaction of the observer remained un-quantifiable. In short, there was no scientific way to explain her reaction to the sheer beauty around her.

And at the moment, she didn't care.

She was breathing deeply and her calves were screaming when finally Jack slowed to a halt, the tiki-hut roofs of the casino in sight.

"Are you okay?" he asked. He was hardly out of breath.

"My legs are complaining about the sand."

He flashed a charming grin. "Let's walk back then."

She glanced at her watch and saw that she still had plenty of time. "At least part of the way," she agreed. "You're a bad influence, you know."

"That's the first time I've been told that." He cleared his throat, indicating he was joking, as they turned and started back.

"I'm sure," she agreed dryly.

"What did I influence this morning?"

"Well, like I said before, I was going to school early. I wanted to prepare some projects to do with my students."

He looked at her with an arched brow. "Not a volcano, I hope."

"Why not?"

He pointed to Big Mouth, the towering volcanic cone that had birthed the island. "Because we live with the real thing."

"And it's going to erupt for the benefit of my class?"

"Gee whiz, I hope not."

She had to laugh at his pretend look of horror. "No, not volcanoes," she finally said. "Isn't there a volcanologist on the island?"

"Yeah, Edna. I'll introduce you, if you like. She could probably tell the kids whole bunches of fascinating stuff. Maybe even take them on a walk up to the lava tubes."

She nodded, trying not to grimace as her legs tried to knot up on her. "I hope I can walk to school. Darn, that was a punishing run."

"You'll get used to it."

She looked askance at him. "You're awfully sympathetic, being a minister and all."

He shrugged, a wicked twinkle in his eye. "Absolutely heartless, that's me. Try walking backward instead."

"Huh?"

"Trust me."

Uggh. The last time she'd heard those words.... But she decided to let go of the memory and pivoted, glancing over her shoulder as she walked, feeling how the reversed motion stretched and soothed her calf muscles.

"Don't look," he said. "You'll make your neck ache. Just trust your muscle memory to guide you."

"You sound like Obi-Wan Kenobi from *Star Wars.*"

He laughed and shook his head. "Nah. Just an old, broken down, church-league basketball coach."

She wished she wasn't imagining him out on a basketball court. She wished she wasn't dragging her gaze away from an awesome pair of runner's legs, close enough to touch, muscles rippling with a controlled power that made his stride seem utterly effortless. She'd thought he was attractive before, but somehow this morning, he'd passed attraction and hit the top of the scale at ten or so. Perfect ten. She almost giggled at herself.

"My class," she said, in a tone meant to remind herself of important matters. Instead she came off sounding stern, as if corralling recalcitrant five-year-olds.

"Yes," he agreed, looking suitably solemn. "Your class."

She cleared her throat and made herself look away from him. The water was more beautiful, after all. Wasn't it?

"One of the things I've been learning from my students is how little they know of anything off this island."

"Is that bad?"

"Depends." She still refused to look at him. "I don't want to bring in the big, bad world, if that's what you mean. It's not my job anyway. Besides, they *already* gamble. How much harm could I do?"

He threw back his head and laughed. "Point taken," he said finally, wiping a tear from his eye. "Sin and degradation, all the way down to kindergarten."

She eyed him. "Why do I think you're making fun of me?"

"It's just the way you said it. There's nothing inherently wrong with gambling. It becomes a problem only when you bet more than you can afford to lose, when you forget that the game is played for the pleasure of the game itself and not for the profit from it. Kids here learn from very early that you can enjoy the game within the limits of your resources, that you don't need a bigger risk in order to experience the pleasure. It's not a forbidden, secret passion. It's just something fun to do, and a good way to learn about the ups and downs of life."

"And here it's a civic duty. I know. And frankly I don't care. If that's how people here want to govern, by the outcome of card games, that's their business."

"Then why did you say what you did?"

She thought back to her words. "I guess that came out wrong."

He merely smiled.

"I guess what I'm trying to get at is that these kids know a lot about cards, a lot about fishing, a lot about every little nook and cranny on the island. But they don't know a lot about how the ecology works or how different it is in other places. Or how much impact man has."

"Those would be good lessons."

She stopped walking and leaned forward, grasping her toes and lifting gently.

"Cramping?"

When she looked up, his gaze was a blend of concern and something else...open admiration for the way her pose highlighted her...assets. She quickly stood up.

"A little. It'll wear off."

She forced away the thoughts of how she must

have looked a moment earlier, and instead scooped up a handful of wet sand and let it slowly slip over her tilted hand. "Don't you see it, Jack? At first it barely moves. Then, as the water seeps down to contact my skin, it forms a lubricating layer. Friction decreases. The sand slides faster, and…" It fell to the earth with a *plop*.

She looked at him. "Every molecule is a miracle. Every atom, every quark. Even the most ordinary activity is part of the flow of mass and consciousness through space-time, ripples of potential talking to one another in a language so subtle and beautiful that even now we're only beginning to understand parts of it. I want my students to see that beauty, to see that magic."

He smiled broadly now, nodding. "That would be great. So what project were you thinking of?"

"I want to start first by showing them the interconnectedness of the ecosystem. How everything depends on everything else, and nothing is too small or insignificant to consider. Then I want to move on to a contained ecology, like an unpopulated island."

"Well, I know of the perfect island, although I'm not a hundred-percent certain it's never been contaminated."

She waved a hand. "Contamination is inevitable. So long as the wind blows and the waves wash ashore, things will travel—from seeds, to microbes."

He nodded. "You're doing good, teach. Maybe you can even tell us what impact Buster has had on this island."

She looked at him. "Buster *is* part of this island now. And I suspect he's done less damage than the casino."

"Shh. He's a very self-important alligator."

She laughed then, feeling better than she had since Delphine had first appeared in her living room.

Delphine. Oh, lord, there was trouble coming. Lynn could feel it in her bones.

CHAPTER FIVE

LYNN BEGAN TO FEEL she was making genuine inroads into her new life and new job. She had learned each student's name and was settling into something of a comfortable and even normal routine, if such could be said to exist on Treasure Island.

Then, of course, Delphine returned. The timing was just *too* perfect. In another world, she might have thought it an accident. But the way things were going lately....

Coming down the short hallway in the white panties and men's T-shirt she slept in, she entered the kitchen with no thought except coffee. She hadn't even waited to put her contacts in, and she'd lost her glasses in the move, a mistake because without them she needed to make the coffee by touch, since the world was utterly out-of-focus.

Not that she had a chance to practice, because just as she stepped toward the sink with the coffee carafe in her hand, the under-sink cupboard doors blew open and water spewed forth with all the ferocity of a fire hose.

Lynn shrieked. "Delphine!"

But Delphine apparently had decided to remain invisible this morning, even though it was totally obvious to Lynn that nothing short of diabolical intervention could have sprung that leak exactly at that instant.

Slipping on the suddenly flooded floor in her bare feet, trying not to drop the glass carafe, she continued her way to the sink and counter. But despite her best efforts she fell.

"Delphine!" she cried again as she hit the floor on one side, cradling the carafe to her breast as if it were a baby. "I'm going to kill you, do you hear me? You'll be deader than dead!"

Rising to her knees, she began crawling toward the counter, getting sprayed now directly in her face. She wondered if it was possible to hit a deceased aunt with a pipe wrench. If she could even find one.

JACK MARKS HEARD the shriek as he was watering the herb garden he tended on the side of his house. He wasn't especially domestic, but he loved to cook, and he loved truly flavorful food, which here on

Treasure Island meant growing your own herbs or impoverishing yourself to have them flown in.

Fresh was better anyway, he thought, humming as he watered. From time to time he turned the hose to hit Buster, who had for the time being taken up permanent residence in the wallow in front of Jack's house. The neighbors were even beginning to remark on it. Jack, of course, knew the secret: water. He was the only one who cooled Buster off.

"Delphine!"

Who was Delphine? And why did Lynn sound so distressed? Jack felt the urge to go help, the white knight in him coming to the fore, then reminded himself to mind his own business. He sprayed Buster again, then bent over to shut off the water.

Another shriek and a thud. Jack straightened and looked toward Lynn's house. The screen door to her kitchen might as well have been made of wood for all he could see.

"I'll kill you, do you hear!" she shouted. "You'll be deader than dead!"

O-o-o-kay, he thought. A life hung in the balance. Time *not* to mind his own business. He dropped the hose onto the ground, wiped his wet hands on his shorts and strode toward Lynn's door.

As he came closer, he heard a rushing sound and Lynn's voice erupting in language blue enough to dye the entire Caribbean. He winced, then felt an unwilling grin tug at his mouth. He didn't know many people who could swear like that.

He reached the door and cupped his hands around his eyes so he could see past the screen into the dim kitchen. "Lynn?"

"Go away!"

Was she talking to him? Or to the Delphine she'd been shouting at earlier? Either way, she sounded stressed to the point of breaking, so he opened the door and stepped into the kitchen.

The flood wasn't the first thing that caught his attention. Oh, no. He might be a preacher, but in that instant he was *all* man. With water spraying everywhere, Lynn was scrambling to get under her sink, tossing bottles and cans in every direction. She was also an extremely tempting sight in a white T-shirt that was nearly transparent from the water, clinging to her every curve like a caress. And that cute little rump, cased in white bikini panties, up in the air....

"Ooof!" Shock and pain hit him at exactly the same moment as a can of white enamel spray paint, flung across the room, hit him in the family jewels. For an instant, fiery pinwheels blinded his vision. He doubled over and lost his balance, falling face-first into the flood.

Shock retrieved him from pain long enough to

turn him once again into a man of the cloth, one with a white horse and a lance. Another can flew, but he dodged it and crawled forward through the water.

"Damn it!" she said, twisting her face to one side as she tried to feel for the water cocks.

"Here, let me," he said, sliding up beside her. It did not help to realize that cold wet clothes between two warm bodies was surprisingly sensual. He gritted his teeth and reached in for the cocks. Moments later he had shut them.

Lying side by side on the floor, looking into the cabinet, neither of them moved or spoke.

Finally he cleared his throat and said, "Who is Delphine?"

He might as well have touched her with an electric prod. She stiffened, jerked away and glared at him. "What are you doing here?"

"Trying to be helpful. I heard you scream."

"You think I can't turn off the water by myself?"

Lying there, soaking wet, with his privates throbbing in pain, he wondered if he had lost his mind. Surely his help shouldn't have elicited that kind of response.

"Of course I think you can turn off the water by yourself. I was just trying to be helpful."

"You and Delphine both!" She pushed herself farther away. "I can live without this kind of help."

"Who's Delphine?" he asked. "I heard you yelling at her."

"My aunt!" She sat up, looking thoroughly and utterly disgusted. Sitting up, however, gave him a wonderful view of her bobbing breasts. He closed his eyes.

"Your aunt is visiting you?"

"No."

His eyes popped open and he sat up. "Just passing through?"

She scowled at him. "Quit giving me the third degree."

"Well, you *were* threatening to kill her."

Her jaw dropped, then a moment later snapped shut. "She's *not* here."

What was going on? There was suddenly something furtive in her eyes, as if she were hiding something. All of a sudden Jack had a truly uneasy feeling about this woman. Was she crazy? Was she hiding this Delphine somewhere in the house and planning to kill her?

The last idea he immediately batted away like a gnat as being highly unlikely. Crazy seemed more in the ballpark, especially on this island. Only slightly crazed people lived here and moved here. Himself, for example. He could have served in some nice wealthy church, driving a nice expensive car, eating at restaurants and all those other glorious things you got to do if you landed among well-to-do congregants. Instead he'd chosen to come here and live like a beach bum where at last he could be himself.

Most everyone here was a little bent. Why not the schoolteacher? On the other hand, she was charged with looking after the children....

Deciding he needed to keep an eye on her, he pushed himself to his feet. "Let me help you clean this up. I'm good at swabbing decks. Did it for four years in the navy before divinity school."

"No. No!" Looking horrified, she jumped to her feet. "I'll do it. You've got better things to do."

He ignored her and bent down to look at the copper tubing. "I've never seen a pipe split that way. Look at that tear. It's like someone slashed it."

She started to bend to take a look, but at that instant appeared to realize her state. Looking down at herself, she turned bright red. "Get out of here," she said hoarsely. *"Now!"* Then she turned and fled, slipping a bit on the wet floor.

Jack hesitated, unsure whether to laugh, swab the deck or just flee before he got sucked any further into this woman's life. Then he realized he really had no choice; he'd been told to leave.

Turning, he marched out of her kitchen, ignoring the way water slopped over his feet and sandals. The woman was an oddball, he thought. She talked to herself, threatened to kill a woman who wasn't even there just because she was frustrated with a burst pipe and then refused help with the cleanup.

That latter, he thought, was downright unneighborly. The least you could do is accept freely offered help when you had a bit of a catastrophe. Even if you were a woman, half-naked and exposed in a now-transparent T-shirt and panties. Heck, *especially* then!

He shook away the thought as stepped out the door and found himself face-to-face with Buster.

"Why aren't you in your wallow?" Jack asked.

The alligator opened his mouth just enough to show all those huge, gleaming teeth and moved toward Jack.

Instinctively, Jack backed up. "I'm not your dinner."

Buster groaned and shook his head, still showing his teeth.

"This is ridiculous," Jack said. "You've never eaten anyone on this island."

Buster appeared unimpressed, as if to say, *there's always a first time.*

Jack moved to step around him, but Buster, moving with that always amazing reptilian speed, blocked the way.

"What is going on here?" Jack demanded. He stepped the other way and again was blocked.

"You devil," he said to the great beast with the huge gleaming teeth. "You don't want me to leave."

"Mmmmhmmmmmm," came the response.

Well darn, Jack thought. Here he was, stuck on a cement stoop, caught between the house from which he'd just been evicted and an alligator that appeared to have every intent of biting him if he moved in the wrong direction.

The choice between the slightly crazy virago inside and the slightly crazy alligator outside was hardly a choice. How long was he going to have to stand here?

For a moment he thought of trying to dart past Buster—after all, the alligator had never harmed a soul in recent memory—but he was intelligent enough to realize that if he moved fast, he might well evoke a predatorial instinct that not even Buster could control.

So what now, genius? he asked himself.

Buster settled the issue by opening his mouth to a gaping maw and darting toward him again.

Jack jumped back through the screen door and let it slam shut between them. "Now what?" he asked the empty kitchen as Buster grinned at him.

GRIPING BENEATH HER breath, both horrified and embarrassed beyond words, Lynn threw her soggy clothes into the bathtub and toweled herself dry.

"You're gonna get it, Delphine," she muttered. "I don't know how, but you're gonna get it. I've got enough problems without you bursting my pipes."

"Whatever makes you think I did that?" All of a sudden, Delphine was sitting on the edge of the tub.

"Because I know you," Lynn said. "There is nothing beneath you when you want something."

Delphine arched a brow. "Really?"

"Really," Lynn answered, even though Delphine's response had been more one of disapproval than question.

"Well, dear," her aunt said, "I'm a woman on a mission from above. Sorry. I can't leave. But I really don't understand what makes you think I'd flood your kitchen. Did I ever treat you so abysmally in life?" Delphine patted her hair, which somewhere between her last appearance and this had gone from gray to bright red. Cherry red.

Lynn felt a pang of conscience. "No."

"See? What makes you think I'd do it now that I'm an angel?"

Lynn frankly gaped at her, clutching the towel, forgetting about the terry robe on the back of the door that she'd been about to reach for. "An angel? *You?*"

Delphine sniffed. "I succeeded at life."

"In your own extraordinary way," Lynn agreed

sarcastically. She draped the damp towel over the bar and reached for the thick terry robe the weather was seldom cool enough to wear. Right now, however, she felt unpleasantly chilled.

"You'll have to excuse me, Delphine, but I have a kitchen to mop."

"Oh, don't worry about that. There's a nice young man doing it for you."

Lynn gaped. "I told him to leave!"

"He tried to."

Lynn's hands settled on her hips and she frowned at the apparition sitting on the edge of her tub. "What have you done now?"

Delphine assumed a look of utter innocence. "*I*," she said firmly, "haven't done a thing. But some of the local fauna seems to have…reached a decision."

"And you had nothing to do with that."

"Not a thing. I'm quite sure of that."

Lynn *wasn't* so sure about that, but then she remembered that, while Delphine had mastered the art of misleading through misdirection or omission when necessary, she had never out-and-out lied about anything.

Which made this even more perplexing.

"Do go out and help the lad," Delphine said. "He shouldn't have to clean the mess all by himself."

"I was going to clean it by *myself.* I didn't ask for help."

"But he was feeling so bad about not being able to give it!"

"I'm capable of taking care of myself!"

Now Delphine frowned. "That may be so. But take it as a little whisper from heaven—allowing others to help you from time to time is merely *polite.*"

Then, in an eye blink, Delphine vanished, leaving Lynn alone in her bathroom. Which, when she thought about it, was one place she *ought* to be able to be alone.

Grabbing her robe off the hook, she slipped it on and belted it tightly. Then she went out to find out what kind of chaos was *now* occurring in her kitchen.

She stopped at the doorway as she saw Jack Marks mopping steadily away at her floor. He seemed to sense her, for he looked up, then paused.

"Don't blame me," he said. "I know you threw me out. But Buster wouldn't let me leave."

Being reminded that she'd thrown him out embarrassed her, but curiosity about what he said grabbed her even more. "Buster?"

"Take a look out your door."

Jack had already managed to clear a large swath

of floor enough that she could cross it without sloshing. "I doubt," she said by way of apology, "that this floor has ever been this clean."

He actually grinned. "I guess there's a silver lining in every flood."

She couldn't help smiling back. Then she looked out her door and saw Buster sitting at the very edge of her stoop, grinning with all his alligator teeth. "He stopped you?"

"Quite forcibly."

Her heart skipped. "Do you think he's suddenly gotten dangerous?"

Jack came to stand beside her. "Somehow I doubt it. But frankly, I wasn't going to try and test him."

"I wouldn't either. My gosh, look at all those teeth!"

"The better to eat you," he replied wryly.

It should have been impossible, but Buster managed to look wounded around the edges of his gaping maw.

"Awww," Jack said sarcastically. "*You* were the one who kept threatening me when I tried to leave, and now you want me to believe you're innocent?"

Lynn decided that seeing Delphine might not be as totally weird as she had initially thought. After all, she had talked to an alligator, and now Jack was too, and darned if the gator didn't look as if he understood.

She spoke. "This could get us committed anywhere else in the world."

He looked at her. "That's what I love about this place. So, since I can't leave, can I finish the floor?"

She decided not to mention the front door as her cheeks reddened. "I'm sorry about the way I acted before. I was rude when you were trying to help."

"You were upset. But someday you have to tell me about Delphine."

Lynn's flush deepened. "Maybe. We'll see."

He nodded, wrung out the mop into the sink and went back to work. Lynn couldn't figure out anything else to do except grab handfuls of old towels to wipe up the dampness and suck water out of crevices.

"Nothing on this island ever really gets dry," Jack remarked as he swept the mop around. "The heat will evaporate the excess, but the humidity will remain."

"That's one of the first things I noticed here, the humidity. It's odd though because even though it's there, it's not real troublesome."

"Unless it turns really hot. Most of the time, though, it just seems to soften the air."

"Well, I haven't needed any moisturizer since coming here."

He flashed a smile. "One of our many money-saving benefits."

"Does the island have a plumber?"

"We sure do. I already put in a call to him."

"Any idea when he'll get here?"

Jack leaned on the mop handle and grinned. "Well…he said as soon as he could."

"And that means?"

Jack shrugged. "I guess it depends on whatever else he needs to do."

"Oh, great."

"Relax. All things come in their own time on this island."

Harv Cullinan's time proved to be about a half-hour. "Caught me just before I left for a day of fishing," he told Jack as he stepped into Lynn's kitchen. "There I was, dreaming of a big 'un. All set to go, me tackle box beside me, waiting for Geordie to pick me up."

"I'm sorry," Jack said.

"Me too," Lynn said a trifle sarcastically. "Next time I'll make the pipe wait."

Harv looked at her. A short, bulky man with a balding head, he might have been a miniature *Hulk*. "Now, now, teacher, nice of you to worry about me, but there's always another day to fish."

Lynn nearly gaped at his response. She'd been churlish and he'd taken it as a kindness. There must be something in the air here. Worse, his response made her aware of how peevish and unpleasant she was being. "Sorry. I'm sorry you missed your fishing."

"Like I said, always another day."

Slowly, as if his every joint ached with monstrous pain, he lowered his bulk to look into the open cabinet beneath the sink.

"My, my," he said, his voice sounding hollow as he put his head inside the cabinet. "That's a beaut."

"We thought so," Jack agreed.

Slowly Harv eased back and sat on his heels. "It's not gonna be easy."

"Why not?" Lynn asked.

"Because pipes don't split like this. Not copper ones, unless somebody's done something to them." He eyed her suspiciously from beneath bushy brows.

Lynn felt as if she stood accused before a jury. "I swear I didn't do anything to it."

"*Someone* did," he said darkly.

Lynn had a pretty good idea who, but she hadn't gone far enough over the edge to say so out loud. "Can you fix it?"

"Oh, aye. I'll need me helper and some other tools. Back shortly."

She hoped shortly *was* shortly.

"He'll take good care of you," Jack said. "I've

gotta run. I'm meeting a couple planning a wedding. I'll check back later."

Buster let him pass this time and slowly returned to the wallow where he settled in with contentment.

As she changed into more suitable clothes, Lynn wondered if she'd come to this island to teach for real, or if she was in some mental hospital totally lost in delusion.

What happened next would only increase her questions.

CHAPTER SIX

THE HULK AND COMPANY returned an hour later, shortly before Lynn needed to leave for school. To Lynn's horror, a backhoe and two trucks pulled into her yard. The Hulk and three helpers appeared, all of them carrying battered tool boxes.

She jumped out her front door and barred the way. "What do you need all this stuff for? It's just a little broken pipe."

"It's a broken *copper* pipe," Harv Cullinan answered, as if that explained it all. His three minions all nodded sagely.

"Wait," she said again. "Why the backhoe?"

"Because," the Hulk said patiently, "we need to check all the pipes."

"But why?"

"Do you want one to split inside your wall?" He shook his head. "Substandard materials. I've seen the mess...."

Somehow Lynn couldn't halt the tide. Four

beefy men pushed past her into her kitchen. She followed them.

"I'm not sure about this," she said.

"We are," Cullinan answered. "We don't do jobs halfway, teach. No point in it. Just causes you more trouble and money in the long run."

"But it's just one little broken pipe."

"It's a sign of worse. I told you earlier, copper don't split that way."

One of the men had crawled under the sink while she was protesting, and when he re-emerged, he looked as glum as if he'd just been told life had ended. "It's bad, Harv," he said. "Wrong gauge. Too thin."

Cullinan looked at her. "See? You got a big problem, teach."

Just then the backhoe started digging up her front yard. "What's that for?" she asked desperately.

"Gotta check it all out. These places is old."

"But I can't afford…"

"Don't be worrying your pretty little head. We'll take care of you."

Yeah, thought Lynn. To the tune of thousands of dollars she didn't have, most likely. And it was all Delphine's fault. Her aunt had broken that pipe, sure as she was standing here.

"What if I want to run the risk of just fixing the one pipe?" she asked desperately.

The Hulk shook his head. "I wouldn't be an honest man if I let you do that."

With that he ushered her out of her own house, leaving her helpless to do much except watch her front yard being trenched. A few of the neighbors came out to watch, too.

"It's okay," said the woman from across the street. "Hi, I'm Betty Denton. I work nights over at the casino."

Lynn shook her hand. "I just had one little pipe under the sink burst. This seems a bit...much?"

Betty shook her head. "Trust me, Harv is a damn good plumber. He's had to do most of these houses over because people originally built them themselves, and a lot of them cut corners. He did my place last year."

"He dug up your yard, too?"

Betty hesitated. "Well, not quite. But he had to rip out a few walls."

"Walls? *Walls?*" Rendered speechless, Lynn stared at her bungalow, wondering what she'd have left of it by nightfall.

Betty patted her arm. "Dil Stedman does great drywall. You'll never know."

"I'll never know." Lynn repeated those words all the way to school, all the way through the day and on the way back home. As she approached her block, however, her trepidation grew so great that her feet dragged. She half expected to find nothing but a hole in the ground where her bungalow had been.

As she rounded the corner, the first thing she saw was the heavy equipment, then the trench running through her front yard and the fact that not a working soul was in sight.

Trepidation gave way to a nub of anger. They couldn't have left her in these straits.

But they had. The backhoe had dug down to the sewer and water lines, exposing them. Inside the house a tangle of tubing, none of it connected to anything she could see, stuck out from her beneath her sink.

"Gaaaaah!"

She dumped her book bag on the now-dusty table and on leaden feet went to survey her bathroom. The tile wall holding the shower head and faucet had been pulled out, leaving an exquisite view of two-by-fours and pipes.

Hanging from the shower head was a sticky note. She pulled it down and read, "Betty says you can shower at her place. We'll be back as soon as we have all the parts. HC."

Slowly, note in hand, Lynn sat on the edge of the tub. "Delphine," she whispered, "I'm going to get you. Somehow."

At that, Delphine appeared, sitting on the commode. Her hair was still cherry red, which clashed nicely with the orange dress she was wearing. "I'm not responsible for this."

"It would have been nice if you had appeared and scared them out of here before they tore my house apart."

Delphine patted her hair and sighed. "It's just a minor hiccup, dear. When the plumbers are done, you'll never have another problem. At least not of this kind."

That seemed foreboding. "I better not have any more problems at all!"

Delphine sniffed. "You expect too much from life. There are *always* problems. Plumbing and a ghost are the least of them. You need to alter your perspective."

"What perspective? How could anyone living in this madhouse have a perspective?"

"It's really quite easy. Take a deep breath, then laugh. You'll see."

At that moment they were interrupted by Jack's voice calling from the kitchen. "Lynn? Lynn, would you like to go to the tavern with me?"

Lynn was off the edge of the tub like a shot, headed for the kitchen. "Look what he did to me, *your* plumber."

"You're welcome," Jack said, clearly irritated.

"He tore up my whole house!"

"He must have needed to."

"I'm not so sure about that."

Jack hesitated, then turned a sharp about-face and headed for the door. "Buy your own beer," he said shortly.

"There," said Delphine from behind her. "What did I tell you? You really need to learn some manners. People here are at least trying to be friendly, unlike the other places you've lived." She sniffed again. "Ungrateful girl!"

Lynn turned to glare at her, too, but caught only a glimpse of rainbow hair as Delphine faded from view. There didn't seem to be anything else to do. Lynn kicked the wastebasket.

What the hell did she have to be grateful for?

SOME EVENINGS JACK WENT to the tavern on the edge of town. It was a great place to socialize with the folks of Treasure Island. Men of the sea tended to be a God-fearing lot, as were their wives, so he saw most of them in his church on Sunday. But that wasn't the same as befriending them, and Jack had long felt he could do a lot more as a friend than as a preacher. Hence, he spent some evenings at the tavern and some evenings at the ever-running poker tournament on the upper floor of City Hall. And every Saturday he shot hoops with the island's children, male and female. Between the three, he socialized with nearly everyone.

On this particular evening, he chose the tavern where he was warmly greeted and invited to sit at a table with six of the biggest—literally—fishermen on the island. He felt dwarfed among them, but that didn't especially bother him until one of them punched him in the shoulder. Jack was no wuss, far from it, but these guys' idea of a friendly tap would have knocked down sheetrock and two-by-fours.

Before long the conversation turned from the day's catch to the new schoolteacher.

"There's something whacked about her," said Jazz Bingle, a guy tall enough to play for the NBA if he hadn't also weighed close to three-hundred pounds. "The wife says she's teaching them about global warming."

Jack's interest perked. "What's wrong with that?"

Jazz shrugged. "Nothing. But it's kinda weird when your kid comes home as says the earth getting hotter could cause an ice age. Now how do you figure that?"

Bart Abernathy nodded. "Don't add up, do it? How does hot make cold?"

"That's what I asked my kid," Jazz agreed. "He weren't none too clear about it."

Cal Hiller spoke after he wiped beer foam from

his mouth. "I don't see what difference it makes. A whacked teacher just fits with all the other wackos around here."

"But what if my kid wants to go to college?"

Cal nodded. "That's a point."

Bart agreed. "But," he added, "what difference does it make in the long run? Nothing we can do about global warming, if it's really happening. And if there's an ice age, we'll just be sitting real pretty."

"How do you figure that?" Jazz wanted to know.

"Cuz it won't freeze down here on the island," Bart said, clearly enjoying the role of authority on the subject. "Ice won't get down this far. So nothing will change for us."

Jack wasn't quite certain of that, but didn't want to get into an argument. Instead he said, "Why don't you just ask the teacher about it?"

All of a sudden, six huge grown men looked like uneasy little boys. Clearly, none of them felt quite old enough or wise enough to take on a school-marm. Jack had to hide a smile. It was like nuns, he thought. To this day he felt a quiver of apprehension when he saw a nun. Even though he was not Catholic, his parents had sent him to parochial school for a "better" education.

"I'll ask her about it," he said finally. "I'd like to know the answer myself."

"Well don't mention my kid," Jazz said. "I don't want him in no trouble."

"I don't think she's that kind of person, Jazz."

"You can't tell about somebody who claims that when the planet gets too hot everything's going to freeze."

Jack found that a hard statement to argue with.

Barrel-chested Nat Simmons broke the silence. "Did you hear about that marlin Jeffries brought in today?"

Thus turning the conversation from the frightening prospect of questioning a teacher to one more comfortable. Jack was willing to go along for the ride. When these guys started telling fish stories, it was a load of fun.

But he made himself another mental note to keep an eye on Lynn. Something there wasn't right, and when the locals started commenting, it was time to take heed. He was sure that behind the comments about global warming was some other kind of concern or they wouldn't have bothered to bring it up.

Because, as folks around here like to say, everyone on this island was at least one sandwich shy of a picnic. For them to comment on Lynn meant they felt she might be a sandwich, a pickle and a bowl of potato salad shy.

Talking to herself wasn't a crime. Offhand he knew of several people who commonly talked to the air. Even her screaming at an aunt who wasn't there didn't exactly constitute a crime.

But he had to admit he was wondering about her himself.

He sipped the beer he had no intention of finishing and wondered how to handle the situation. If it needed handling at all. Yet he'd been on this island long enough to know when he was being told something through the side door.

He pushed his icy mug around on the table, watching it smear the water that had dripped off it. "Hey, guys," he said finally. "For real here. Are you worried about more than just the global warming?"

"I'm not even worried about that," Jazz said.

Jack almost sighed. He knew they were being deliberately obtuse. So he came out and said it baldly. "So what's your worry with the new teacher?"

A chorus of *nothings* answered him. If there was a problem, they weren't going to tell him. He was, as was so often the case, on his own. Finally he got up and challenged one of the guys to a game of darts.

Unfortunately, once these guys clammed up, he might as well try to get the sphinx to talk.

IN THE MORNING, JACK stepped out his front door with a mug of coffee in his hand. He carefully avoided looking in the direction of Lynn's house.

In the event, that proved to be a rather easy thing to do, because he was faced with the oddest sight: Buster was lying in his wallow, still faintly muddy from yesterday's spray. But it wasn't the gator that caught his attention as much as the African gray parrot that stood facing Buster, not inches from his nose.

Jack held his breath, wondering if he were about to witness the bird's last moments of life. Lord, and African grays were so expensive! Where could it have come from? No one on this island could afford any pet so expensive, except perhaps Bill Anstin, the casino owner. And if he'd gotten a bird with that kind of prestige—read cost—everyone on the island would have heard about it.

He had the worst urge to shoo the bird away, but feared that if he did, Buster's predatory instinct would have taken over in an instant, and bye-bye birdie.

The bird had its head cocked to one side, of course, because it could only see Buster with one eye at a time. Buster probably wasn't doing much better with the bird that close.

Taking care not to make a sound, Jack sat slowly down on his top step.

Then, totally flooring him with amazement, the parrot, with a little flutter of wings, leapt up and settled right on Buster's head. Buster never even blinked.

"Hey you!"

Shaken from his astonishment, Jack looked around to see who had called. It sounded like a woman, but wasn't a voice he recognized.

"I'm talking to *you,* stupid."

Jack's head snapped back around as he realized the bird was doing the talking. And there was no mistaking the fact that the bird was looking right at him. "You're just a parrot," he said, reaching for the last shred of reality.

"Yeah, and you're *just* a human," the bird said. "But *you* can turn on the hose. And the crocodile wants a bath."

CHAPTER SEVEN

AS THE TIME GREW closer to leave for school, Lynn's frustration built to the boiling point. She'd been washing in the bathroom sink—at least she still had some running water—but not a single plumber had showed up yet. Her house was a wreck, her life was a wreck, and nothing was being done. *Nothing*.

Finally she decided she could not wait any longer. Grabbing her book bag, she stepped outside, determined to get the plumber's number from Jack. This island had neither a phone book nor directory assistance, nor even a human voice she could talk to on the phone for Harv and the Destroyers. But Jack had known how to call them.

Jack, she decided, was the root of all evil.

Once outside, however, she froze. Looking across the trench in what used to be her front yard, she saw Jack sitting on his porch with a cup of coffee. Nothing unusual in that. What *was* unusual was that there was a parrot perched on Buster's head.

And Buster didn't seem to mind.

Well, why would he? she asked herself. After all, people made sure he was well-fed. But wasn't that an African gray? She'd heard tales of their brilliance and ability to learn to speak. Not merely imitate, but to actually *speak.*

Despite herself, curiosity caused her to walk around the trench, toward Jack's house.

"Careful," Jack called out quietly. "I still haven't figured out the dimensions of the situation."

So she moved slowly, aware that both Buster and the bird watched her as she rounded them and came to sit on Jack's step beside him.

"I've been watching for the last hour," he said. "So far the bird has called me stupid and told me the crocodile wants a bath."

"Oh." She stared at the pair. "I've heard about African grays. They don't just mimic speech."

"Yeah, I've heard about it too."

The bird made a brief clicking sound then said, clear as a bell, "Idiot male. You could at least get her some coffee."

Lynn had to clap her hand to her mouth to smother the laughter.

"I don't like being called names," Jack retorted.

"Then don't act like one of those names. Get her some coffee."

Jack looked at Lynn. "Wait until it starts picking on *you*." But there was merriment in his eyes. "Would you like some coffee?"

"Thorazine might be in order, but I'll take the coffee. Thanks."

He rose and went inside to get it.

The bird said, "*Men*. No amount of training is ever enough."

Lynn giggled. "What's your name?"

"I don't like my name. So I won't tell you."

"Where are you from?"

The bird cocked its head, glaring at her from one eye. "If I tell you that, you'll try to send me back. I don't think so!"

Jack returned with the coffee, handed her the cup and resumed sitting beside her. "Quite a conundrum," he said.

"How so?" Lynn asked.

"Is this as real as it seems? Is that bird really communicating?"

"It seems to be," Lynn said. "Of course, I talk to my walls, so I'm not a good judge."

Jack looked at her. "I didn't say that."

"No, but you've been thinking it. Anyway, with regard to the bird, I don't see why it has to be anything at all. I mean, if it wants to stay here and sit on Buster's head, what harm can it do?"

"It hasn't insulted you yet."

Again she giggled. "I'm sure it will. It's a very outspoken bird."

"To say the least."

"The shower," the bird said. "The crocodile wants his shower."

"Buster is an alligator," Jack said.

"He *thinks* he's a crocodile," the bird retorted. "Get the hose and take care of him."

"Why," Jack asked musingly, "do I resent being ordered around by a birdbrain?"

The bird fluffed its feathers. "Do you want me to drop a load on your head?"

At that, Lynn rose swiftly, draining half her mug of coffee as she did so. "I've got to run. I'm going to be late for school."

Suddenly she turned toward Jack. "That reminds me. When will those plumbers be back?"

"I'm not sure. When they have all the parts."

"That's not good enough. Call them for me, since you called them in the first place. My whole house is torn up."

Turning, she marched away, hearing the bird say behind her, "Uh-oh. You made her mad."

Jack answered, "So what's new?"

TODAY WAS THE BIG DAY. Lynn and her classes began to set up the glass aquarium in which they were going to build a self-contained ecology. The kids were enthused, and the schools had arranged for all the science classes to meet together for one entire day to get the project rolling.

They had brought their little bags of things they had gathered around the island: dirt, moss, rocks, seeds, some small plants. In one corner they placed a bowl of water, trying to make it look like a pond surrounded by pebbles, and then, with great excitement, they placed the glass top on the thing, sealing it.

"Now," Lynn told them, "it should rain in here. Sometimes you won't be able to see inside because the glass will fog up, and other times, if you watch, you'll see water drops coming down from the top. Just like real rain. I think we probably have some insects in here from the plants and soil, so we'll have to watch and see what we can find."

One boy was practically hopping up and down. "So it'll live all by itself?"

"Eventually." Lynn smiled. "Right now I can't say for sure. We may have to add some things or maybe take some out until we get a balance that makes the plants happy. So we'll have to check every day, keeping an eye on how things look. We want to catch problems before they ruin our terrarium."

"But that's not like the real world," a girl said. "It's too tiny. And we'll need to add stuff."

Lynn pulled up a chair and sat beside the terrarium. "Let's think about that. What is our planet?"

"A terrarium," someone answered.

Lynn smiled.

"Yessss," a couple of the smaller kids yelled.

Lynn spoke. "A very big, very complex terrarium, with lots of different climates. But even Earth gets stuff added to it, sometimes from deep inside when a volcano erupts, and sometimes from space in meteorites and other space dust. So even Earth isn't a closed system. Are you following me?"

The nods and intensity of interest pleased her. "Treasure Island was once an erupting volcano on the sea floor, building and building until it emerged from the sea and came to be the island we know. When it emerged, it was bare rock and ash. But can anyone tell me how there came to be so many plants and animals?"

Hands flew into the air and answers started popping out. "Birds came and brought seeds." "Some things came on the ocean waves." "Some animals swam here and brought other stuff with them!" And so on.

"Okay," she said finally. "This island is a terrarium too. Everything here came from some other place. Like Buster. And just as we talked about in class, some things thrived and others died until a balance came into being."

More nods.

"But our little terrarium is even more fragile than the island because it's so small. So we'll have to tend it carefully until it finds its own balance. Then it will stay happy and healthy until...what?"

"Until we do something wrong," a teenage boy answered. "Like we're doing to our planet."

Lynn nodded. "So what we have here is what scientists call a microcosm, a small model of a much bigger system. It's like a garden. And we have to be good gardeners."

There was some more discussion, then she stepped back to let the children look and talk. Some of the other teachers had joined them and seemed to be enjoying the project as much as the children.

"Great job, teach."

Startled, she turned at the sound of Jack's voice. She had to bite her tongue to keep from asking about the plumbers.

"Thank you, Reverend Jack," she said, remembering all the kids in the room. The parents, she saw, were beginning to arrive, too, and as they did their child or children would grab them and drag them to the terrarium, talking excitedly about what they had learned.

"It seems," Jack remarked as he leaned back against the wall and folded his arms, "that these kids have been hungering for this kind of experience."

"Thanks. I just hope I can keep coming up with ideas that excite them."

"You will." He winked. "And if you start to feel brain-dead, plenty of folks will be happy to jaw with you to work out more ideas." He jerked his chin toward the kids and the growing number of parents. "Those parents are as happy about this experiment as you are. Every one of them will want to help maintain it."

She looked back toward the huge cluster around the terrarium. "You think so?"

"I know so. And if you ever run dry, try getting one of these folks to turn fishing into a lesson. These guys know the sea in ways no oceanographer ever will."

"That's a great idea."

His smile broadened. "There'll be a picnic on the beach tonight. We have one every few months. Complete with a bonfire. You should come."

She realized that sounded absolutely wonderful. "Am I invited?"

"Would I have mentioned it otherwise? Bring a

towel, wear your swimsuit under your clothes. There's nothing like a moonlight swim in the Caribbean."

A tingle of delight shivered through her. "What time?"

"I'll get you at five, okay?"

Before she could answer, one of the parents had come over, wanting to talk with her. As she turned to the parent, she glanced at Jack. "At five," she agreed.

LYNN WAS EXCITED about the beach party. She hadn't done anything like that since college. When she got home, she plunged into her closet to dig out her blue one-piece bathing suit…she thought it a rather attractive one with a matching sarong, and a white cover-up to wear over it all.

Picnic meant she should bring something, she supposed, so she made some turkey sandwiches on homemade bread and wrapped them carefully. She probably ought to bring her own soft drinks, she thought, and pulled a six-pack of colas out of the cupboard.

Finding something to carry it in was another matter. She was rummaging around in her living room to find something that would serve as a reasonable basket when Delphine popped in again.

Literally popped. Lynn heard the sound before she turned and saw her aunt.

"Hi," Delphine said, smiling her best. Her hair was now green—a green that could never have existed in nature.

Lynn wondered if refusing to answer would cause her aunt to give up.

"I can't give up," Delphine said.

"Stay out of my head!"

"I'm not *in* your head. But you're broadcasting, dear."

"Broadcasting?" The thought was horrifying. Lynn felt her cheeks heat.

"Relax. Most of us on this plane don't have time to listen. We have other things to concern us."

"Then maybe you shouldn't be here."

"I *told* you," Delphine said patiently, "you are my concern. For now."

"What did I do to deserve this?" Lynn asked the question looking up at the heavens, but Delphine answered anyway.

"I *could* get offended," Delphine said. "After all, I thought I was always your favorite aunt."

Lynn felt a pang. "You are! Were. Whatever."

"Then you should be glad of this opportunity to see me from time to time. It won't last forever, you know."

Lynn instantly felt her heart squeeze painfully. She hadn't been looking at matters that way. "I'm sorry," she said, dropping disconsolately onto a chair. "I *do* miss you, Auntie Delph."

"Thank you." Delphine managed to move instantaneously to the other chair. "I know you do, Lynnie. I shouldn't be so hard on you."

"Why *are* you being hard on me?"

Delphine merely looked secretive. "Did you like the *pop* when I arrived?"

"What *was* that?"

"Well, being a Princeton genius as you are, you called me a wave collapse. So I thought you might like to hear the wave collapse."

In spite of herself, Lynn giggled. "That's a first."

Delphine wagged her finger. "But you'll never be able to measure it when I do it. Now go finish your packing and have fun tonight."

Another *pop,* surely Delphine's way of making Lynn smile, and her aunt was gone.

"Do you always talk to the curtains?"

Jack's voice startled Lynn into jumping off the chair. "What…?"

"Sorry," he said. "The door was open, I heard you talking and I let myself in rather than disturb your conversation."

Lynn's face burned. "You shouldn't do that."

"Apparently not." His brow furrowed. "Are you all right?"

"I'm fine, really."

"Really? I'm the island's only preacher, and you're a teacher. If you escaped from an asylum, I need to know."

Lynn gaped at him, then started laughing. "I'm ready. Let's go to this party."

Jack shook his head. "Did you escape from an asylum?"

"Most definitely," she said, still chuckling. "I'm sure you heard of it. It's a very famous asylum. And all the inmates are as odd as I am. The Princeton Engineering Anomalies Research Lab. Otherwise known as PEAR."

The preacher facing her blinked. "PEAR? What did you study?"

"The effects of consciousness at the quantum level."

He held up a hand. "I won't be able to follow you into that territory."

She nodded. "It's been said that anyone who claims to understand quantum physics…obviously doesn't. So don't feel alone there."

"You understand it, though," he said.

"Ha!" Lynn shook her head. "No way. I live in a world where human thoughts can flip a bit in a computer. My research proved that. But I can't explain it. I can predict how often it will happen, and to what degree, but I can't tell you *why* it happens. Do I understand it? Maybe my dead Aunt Delphine does, but I surely do not."

Now *his* jaw dropped. "You're talking to your dead aunt?"

She started grinning again. "Give me a reason why I shouldn't."

His mouth opened, then closed. After a moment he said, "I can't. I'm a man of God. I believe in life after death. So yes, you can talk to your dead aunt."

"Good. Because that's what I'm doing." The words hung there like an indictment, and she waited, smiling, for his judgment. It felt so *good* to acknowledge what was happening.

"No problem," he said after a moment. Then he reached out and touched her forearm with his fingertips, sending an electric shock straight through her to her very center. For an instant she feared she was going to collapse into his arms, overwhelmed by a need she'd been ignoring for years.

"Let's go," he said. "Or we'll miss all the fun."

When they arrived the bonfire was already big and burning, a couple of poker games were under way at folding tables and kids and adults of all ages were playing in the surf.

Jack selected a patch of sand near the fire but not

too near, among people who welcomed Lynn warmly. He spread a blanket for them to sit on.

"We do this every so often," he repeated. "No special occasion needed. When you live in a tropical paradise, you should enjoy it."

"Even the guys playing cards?"

He laughed. "For some folks that *is* paradise."

A woman nearby scooted across the sand and stuck her hand out to Lynn. "Hi, I'm Billie Jensen. My son Carr is in your science class. I'm sorry I couldn't get over today to see the terrarium. It's all Carr is talking about."

Lynn smiled at the pleasant looking redhead. "We've sure been having fun with it. Carr's been a great help."

"I couldn't get away from the casino today. Could I come by on Monday?"

"Of course. Any time you want."

"I'll take you up on that then. I get so annoyed when I can't get off for an hour or so for important things like this."

"I can understand the feeling. But don't worry. You're always welcome."

Everything continued like picnics anywhere in the world would until people were through eating. Then, in the all-too-brief tropical twilight, several games of beach volleyball broke out. Lynn, despite her protests that she didn't have a foggy idea how to play, wound up on Jack's team.

"I can't do this," she warned the other players. "I'm a geek."

"That's fine," Jack said with a supremely confident grin. "I'll play for both of us."

The other couple laughed. "Yeah, right," Barney Lowe said. "Just get ready to lose, preacher man."

Jack bowed. "I shall do so humbly."

"Oh, sure. You'll be preaching against the sin of my pride come Sunday."

"You? Proud?" Jack laughed, a wicked twinkle in his eye. "Just because you think you can beat the geek and me? What you have in brawn, we have in brains."

"Ho-ho," Barney said, his tone a jibe. "We got the preacher's goat, Lu. We'll beat him to a pulp."

The game started almost immediately. In fact, it seemed to Lynn there was no warning at all before the volleyball was coming right at her face. She was sure she was about to get beaned in the nose when Jack's fist suddenly appeared right in front of her and sent the ball flying back.

"That's the general idea," Jack said quickly. "Hit the ball back over the net."

Easier said than done, but after a few volleys she began to get the hang of it. She'd rather have been chasing quarks in a particle accelerator, she supposed, but this was okay. It was hell on the legs though.

And the elbows, she discovered when she slipped. Sand suddenly became sandpaper.

"Ow!"

At once the game stopped and Jack hurried to her. "What's wrong?"

Lynn sat up and grabbed the ball, heedless of her skinned elbows. "Not a thing," she said as she punched the ball back at Lu. Now she was annoyed enough to feel strength surge into her limbs. Not annoyed at the others, but annoyed at herself for being a klutz.

All her life she'd been a geek and a klutz. And suddenly she didn't like that. The adrenaline surge did wonders for her.

"Hey, whoa," Barney called across the net. "I thought you didn't know how to play?"

"I don't!" She hammered the ball back.

"Then I want some of what you're taking," Lu said just before she slipped, reaching for the ball, and managed to slide onto her bottom.

"It's just physics," she heard herself say. She wanted to wince, but didn't have time before the ball came flying at her.

"Physics?" Jack asked. He was panting.

"Yeah, vectors, ballistics…" And it was. In her mind's eye she found she could see where the ball was bound to go if she hit it just right. But she also wished she hadn't made such a geeky remark.

The others hardly seemed to care though. All of a sudden the game was fast and furious. She and Jack eventually lost, but they were gasping with laughter as they fell exhausted to the ground.

"Darn, woman," Jack said. "Next time I think we'll win!"

"Not tonight." Wincing, Lynn looked at her elbows. The were reddened and bruised, but not scraped. "Some other time. I need more practice."

"Oh, really?" Barney asked sarcastically. "For the last few minutes I thought I was in the Olympics."

Lynn laughed. "I don't know what happened. I just know that I probably won't be able to walk for the rest of the weekend. My legs are already killing me."

When they caught their breath, Lynn limped with Jack back to their blanket and fell happily on it. Lu and Barney brought their blanket over so they could continue talking.

Night was beginning to settle at last, in the stunningly rapid way of the tropics. Since moving here, Lynn had noticed the huge difference in twilight from New Jersey, but she was still amazed every night to watch it happen.

Lying back on the blanket, she watched the earth's shadow blacken the sky behind the thin band of twilight until an immense number of stars appeared, more stars that she had ever imagined it was possible to see when living in the Northeast where city lights never really permitted total darkness. Then, just as she felt that she would get dizzy from the night, the silver rim of the moon poked up to the east, so huge and brilliant that it lit the few clouds around it.

"It's so beautiful," she murmured.

She glanced at Jack and found him staring at her. "Yes, it is," he agreed.

She looked quickly away, but there was no escaping the heavy warmth she now felt throughout her body. He thought she was beautiful.

It was the perfect end to a perfect day.

CHAPTER EIGHT

THE FISHING BOAT LOOKED rather beaten to Lynn, but she was growing accustomed to that. Salt air constantly corroded everything, and she was beginning to understand that trying to keep up with it would have kept the locals too busy to support themselves.

So that somewhat-rusty bucket was sounder than it looked. Its skipper, Leo Beacham, assured her the rust was superficial.

"She's due for a scrape and paint in about a month," he said, patting the boat's metal side. "I know folks keep saying it'd make sense to go to a fiberglass hull, but who has the money for that? So I scrape and paint Ol' Tessie here, and she runs like a dream the rest of the time. Got more to worry about with the engines than with this old hull."

"The engines?" Lynn felt a lurch in her heart.

"Seeing as how I'm using them all the time," he said, patting the boat again. "But not to worry, me and Artie can fix anything that goes wrong."

"Does it go wrong often?"

Leo scratched his stubbly beard. "Nah," he said. "And I'll make sure everything's tuned up before we take her out with the kids. But...are you sure you want the dry run first? Cuz Artie and I can't go next weekend."

"I'll be just fine. I'm familiar with boats. My dad used to take me out every weekend on the Atlantic."

Leo nodded. "Much rougher water. Well, if you can handle that, you can sure get this girl over to Empty Island."

What a name for an island, Lynn thought. Apt, since no one lived there, but unoriginal. Or maybe in its own way it *was* original.

"I just need to see the island first," Lynn explained. "If I'm going to take all those children over there for a lesson on an untouched habitat, I have to make sure it's pristine."

Leo nodded. "Makes sense. Far as I know, nobody's been there except to look around and decide not to stay. Nothing wrong with the place, except it's small and the only water is in a small rain pool, too small to count on."

"That's what everyone tells me. Have you been there?"

"Once. It's like every other island, just small. And it doesn't have a bar." He winked.

Lynn laughed. "Maybe I should open one."

"I think you're doing better teaching," Leo said seriously. "My Ginny thinks you're the best teacher ever."

Lynn blushed. "That's so nice to hear."

"You make it come alive for 'em, Ms. Reilly."

"Lynn, please."

He touched the brim of his seaman's cap and grinned. "No one's ever old enough to call a teacher by her first name."

She laughed again and tossed her head, loving the way the gentle, warm breeze caught her hair and lifted it. She was definitely getting addicted to this crazy island. "So it's okay with you if I take the boat next weekend?"

"Sure enough. I'll clean her up a little, but we'll be fishing in the meantime, so..." He shrugged. "No promises."

"That's fine. I don't want to inconvenience you. I think I can stand the smell of fish."

"It does kind of get into every seam. As for how many of the kids you'll be able to take at one time..." He looked at the boat. "A dozen, maybe. Artie and me will go with you when you take them. Might have to do a couple runs over the next few weeks."

"That's not a problem if you're willing. I didn't think we could take all the students at one time."

Leo shook his head. "I don't think anyone on this island has a boat big enough. But tell you what, I'll ask around. Maybe we can get four or five boats to go over there at one time so all the kids can go together."

Lynn clapped her hands excitedly. "That would be wonderful!"

"No promises," Leo said again, and grinned. "But I reckon we can get enough of the guys to take a day off from fishing."

"Oh, that would be perfect. But meantime, I need to go make sure it's the right island."

He nodded. "I think it is. No large animals except for birds. The mosquitoes are hell though. You'd better wear some repellant." He paused. "While you're at it, maybe you can give these kids some appreciation for how we manage to survive here. They think coconuts grow on trees."

Laughing at his own humor, he tipped his cap and jumped aboard his boat, ready to go out fishing. Lynn waved after Leo and Artie as they pulled away from the dock.

The sun was just coming up now, behind her, and the water took on the look of shiny blue metal. Lynn sat on a piling and watched the morning claim Treasure Island. Boat after boat set out, some of them tooting to her as they pulled away. She waved again and again, and thought she had never lived in such a friendly place. Not even the campus and her coworkers had made her feel this welcome.

Her brow knit at that, as she recalled her ex-boyfriend. Sometimes she still wished she could boil him in oil. But then, if he hadn't stolen her research, she wouldn't have come here, and she really didn't have any complaints about this place.

She sighed, and let herself relax into the peace of the morning. She'd been too angry for too long, she realized. Snapping at everyone and everything as if she were a rabid dog, and all because Donald had stolen her work and made her look like a liar before the academic community.

Yes, it was an injustice, and injustice hurt like hell, as did betrayal. Everyone knew that. But it was time to grow up and get over it.

In fact, she thought as she sat watching the dappled waters slowly brighten, she had allowed Donald's actions to turn her into a person she didn't like very much. Crabbed and snappish, and generally ugly.

He'd hurt her enough. Was she going to let him ruin her character and her life?

She shook her head slowly, making a vow to shed the bitterness that had driven her for so long. So what if Delphine was meddling? She loved that woman and ought to cherish every moment she could speak with her aunt, instead of being irritated by it.

Turning a little as the last boat pulled out, she watched the arc of the sun rise over the water to the east, near the casino. Right now it looked metallic, too, orange and brilliant. The few wisps of clouds glowed the same orange, a color no painter, no camera, could ever truly capture. Seagulls rose from their night perches and began to wheel in the sky over the water, shrilly calling to one another as they rose, then dove at fish. Some settled on the water to placidly ride the waves for now. Others followed thermals way up so that she had to tilt her head back. The majority followed the boats out.

A few others came to hover within a few feet of her face, staring at her, letting her know they wanted a handout. She wished she'd brought some bread.

When she tossed out nothing, the birds flew away. They'd probably get their best meal later today, she thought, when the boats came home and the fish cleaning started.

So, she thought, the seagulls had been affected by human habitation. She wondered if there would be any gulls on Empty Island, and if so how they would behave. The island wasn't so far away that they would have been truly isolated.

But was anything truly isolated anymore? She sighed, then shrugged the thought off. Of course nothing was truly isolated. She knew that from her studies at Princeton. What she was hoping to show the children was an illusion of separateness. Part of her wished she could explain that to them, and part of her knew it would be a waste of time to try.

First the ecology lessons. Physics would have to wait.

When the sun's full globe rose above the horizon, still looking metallic, but now emitting a sharp light that seemed to cast everything into high relief, she rose and began the walk back to her bungalow. Other than the fisherman who had already pulled out of the harbor, few people were yet about. Toward the south end of the docks, a small knot of tourists prepared to board the sport-fishing boats that would take them out to hunt for marlin where the waters turned bluer and deeper.

Lynn paused, closing her eyes for a moment, envisioning the map of the Caribbean in her mind. Every detail wasn't perfect, of course, but she remembered enough to think it might make an interesting lesson to show the students how all these islands were linked beneath the water and to talk about how a lowering of the seas would reveal one long body of land.

Maybe she'd do that today, since they were working on earth sciences in general.

"Hey, teach," said a familiar voice. "You always stand around with your eyes closed?"

"Only when I'm trying to think." Opening the aforementioned eyes, she looked at Jack. "You're up early."

"No, I'm *out* early. There's a difference." He pointed to a plastic bag. "I'm going to go throw some chickens in Bridal Falls. Wanna come?"

"I hope they're dead," she said, eyeing the bag suspiciously.

"Squeamish, are we? But, yes, they're goners. Val wrung their necks for me."

"Good," she said unrepentantly. "I know all about prey and hunters, but part of me would find it cruel to throw those birds to Buster alive."

"Buster wouldn't agree. He and the birds are the main reasons you won't find any rats on this island."

"I hope you mean the big ugly kind."

"Well, white lab rats aren't exactly a gift of nature."

"No," she laughed, finding herself walking beside him on the path toward the falls.

"We did that to them." Jack continued, seeming to take a bit of glee in leading this conversation to some point she couldn't yet figure out.

"Yes." She waited.

"But the big ugly ones are self-reliant," Jack went on. "They don't need us to feed them."

"No...."

"Or torture them, either."

Ta-da. There it was. "I never tortured a lab animal. Never used one, in fact."

"Did I say you had?"

"No."

He grinned at her. "Just pointing out that what Buster needs to do to survive isn't quite as cruel as some of the things our species does."

She winced. "I know."

They walked for a bit. After a few moments Lynn asked, "How do you know he'll find the chickens?"

"That gator can smell chicken from the other end of the island. And there isn't another creature around here that will be able to do more than peck at them before he gets here. Give the old guy credit, though. As long as we put chickens in the pool, he stays out of the coops."

"There is something very odd about this island's relationship with that gator. Or vice versa."

He winked. "There's something very odd about this island, period."

"Maybe it's not the island. Maybe it's the people."

He rubbed his chin thoughtfully. "You may have something there. But since we're all odd, we'll never know for sure."

Laughter escaped her. "The worst part is I feel comfortable with that."

"Don't tell me you weren't comfortable with your fellow geeks at Princeton, cuz I won't believe you. And geeks are *truly* odd."

"How would you know?"

"When I was young and sinful, I used to pick on them."

"You were one of *them?*" She feigned horror.

"Sorry to say."

The path emerged abruptly from thick growth to the pool and waterfall. Lynn froze in her steps, staring at the kind of beauty she thought you could only see in a movie or a *National Geographic.*

From high above, over the lip of black volcanic rock, water fell in a rushing sheet to foam in the pool below. All the plants around the pool seemed to be in full bloom with huge, colorful flowers. She hardly heard the plops as Jack threw chicken after chicken into the pool.

"It's so beautiful," she said finally, raising her voice to be heard over the rushing water. "Where does the water come from? Isn't the drought affecting it?"

"Some. The falls have thinned a bit. Edna, the volcanologist, says it's coming from somewhere inside the volcano. She's trying to find where it's stored, because she said it could weaken the side of the cone if there was an eruption. But nobody really knows. We only know it's not coming out of our reservoir."

"Wow. Wow. Wow." She repeated herself, turning slowly to take it all in.

"It's worth the walk," he agreed.

"It's worth ten times the walk. Why does everyone call this Bridal Falls?"

"Because some tourists from a cruise ship decided to get married here." He pointed across the pool to a flat ledge of black rock. "And since then, it's become a kind of advertising for the cruise ships that dock here once a week. We have maybe three weddings a month here. And local folks like to attend to make it more festive."

"Do you perform the marriages?"

He shook his head. "The captain of the ship does."

"I thought captains could marry people only at sea."

Jack shrugged. "Who around here is going to get fussy about a little detail? They want the guy with the fancy uniform, not me with my Hawaiian shirts and shorts."

"Does that bother you?"

He laughed. "Why would it? I have my hands full with the local people."

He pointed to a rock that looked as if it had been made into a bench by God's own hand. "Have a seat. If Buster comes while we're still here, it won't keep him from eating."

Lynn looked at her watch and saw she still had plenty of time before school, so she sat beside Jack on the bench. "This is paradise," she said.

"That's what I think sometimes," he agreed. "In fact, when I sit here, I wonder how Adam and Eve could have been so stupid as to eat the apple."

She looked at him. "Maybe God knew they'd eat it."

His brow lifted, but he said nothing.

Sensing his eyes on her, Lynn shrugged and leaned forward, resting her elbows on her knees. She should have, she realized, sat on his other side, because the breeze was stirring just enough to fill her nostrils with the scent of clean, soapy man. Delicious. Too delicious.

"Well," she said, trying to distract herself, "at Princeton we pretty much concluded that everything is one and that consciousness is at the root of all."

"Did you?"

"Simplification, but yes. So you and I aren't separate, nor are we separate from this beauty around us."

When he said nothing, she glanced at him and found him looking at her, an odd glint in his eye.

"I prefer separate," he said.

"Why?"

"Because it creates so many possibilities."

She knew exactly what he meant. Every cell in her body seemed to explode with heat. No, she told herself. *No.* She'd been burned before. She'd vowed never to let herself be burned again.

Quickly, she looked away, hoping he didn't read her reaction in her face. This was too much. She had come to this island for a few years' escape to lick her wounds. Not to get all tangled up with a handsome preacher. Not even for the sheer joy of sex.

"Lynn."

She refused to look at him. Then his hand touched her shoulder and she felt once again that electric *zap!* Part of her wanted to leap away, but the rest of her remained frozen.

"Lynn," he said again. "Should I apologize?"

That astonished her. She swung her head around and looked at him. "Apologize? For what?"

"I get the feeling I scared you."

At once she reached for whatever toughness she

could find and draped it around herself. It was a thin coat at best, but it was a coat.

"You didn't scare me. What ever gave you that idea?"

He looked as if he wanted to say something, but thought better of it. Why did she have the feeling he could read her mind, that he knew exactly how she had reacted and why?

Instead he shrugged and turned back to look at the beauty around him. Taking the cue, she did the same.

She stiffened a bit as she thought she saw Delphine in the shimmering waterfall, shaking her head at her.

In that instant, Lynn felt sad. Sad for opportunities lost.

And Delphine seemed to be saying that another one was slipping away right beside her.

"Oh," said Jack, pricking the mood as if it were a balloon, "I finally got a hold of Harv. He's waiting for parts from Aruba."

She turned and sighed. "How long is that supposed to take? Do you realize the mess I'm in? I can't use my shower or my kitchen sink. I have walls torn out. I have to go across the street to use Betty's shower. How long is this going to continue?"

Jack lifted a hand. "Darned if I know. Until Harv gets the parts from Aruba."

"I should never have let that man in my house. *You* should never have called him. I could have wrapped duct tape around it or something."

"It wouldn't have stuck for long."

"Shut up and let me enjoy my delusion. I should have fixed the pipe myself." But she was smothering a laugh.

"Do you know how?"

"No."

Jack looked as if he were hiding a smile. "I rest my case."

"Does it always take this long?"

"We're on an island. A small, underpopulated island. Do you think Harv could afford to keep everything on hand all the time? It's the downside. Sometimes we have to bring pollution in from elsewhere."

She knit her brow. "Pollution?"

He gave her a half-smile. "Everything we bring here is pollution, isn't it, teach?"

She'd just been zinged. And now she had to wonder why. She couldn't prevent a giggle.

She'd come here for a simpler life. Instead it seemed to be growing more complicated by the minute. And she didn't mind it one bit.

CHAPTER NINE

"AUNT DELPHINE." Lynn muttered the name.

Jack felt the hairs on the back of his neck rise, effectively quashing the growing sexual desire he'd been feeling. "Where?"

"In the waterfall."

He looked. "Sorry, can't see her."

"No reason you should."

True, he thought. On the other hand, while he believed in the afterlife, the idea of a ghost appearing and reappearing and having conversations with the living, was stretching his belief just a bit. He tried not to look directly at Lynn, because he didn't want her to see the questions rising in his mind.

"Maybe I *am* crazy," Lynn mumbled. "Jeez, I know that what I'm experiencing is possible. We know these things happen. But that doesn't mean I understand it. The way she talks to me, like she's right there, carrying on an ordinary conversation...."

"Well," he said with what he hoped sounded like

confidence, "they say you can't be crazy if you think you might be."

"Old wives' tale if you ask me. I'm crazy. I'm seeing and talking to a dead aunt."

"You weren't talking that way last week."

"Last week I wasn't looking at her standing in a waterfall."

"Is she still there?"

"No. She just blipped out again. Gone."

"What did she say to you?"

"Not a thing." Lynn sighed and put her head in her hands. "You know, Jack, I'm a scientist. Or I was. Regardless, without experimental evidence, I question everything. Why am I not questioning this apparition?"

"Sounds to me like you are."

Lynn shuddered. "Wave collapse. Everything we experience happens as the aggregate of phenomena at the quantum level. Intention pushes potential into event. The question is, is this happening through *my* intent or hers?"

He grimaced. "Sorry, no answer from here. I don't know enough about it. Ask me something theological."

"This would be kind of theological, if it's really happening."

He hesitated. "Actually, my theology is finding it a bit...difficult."

"Yeah." She sighed and lifted her head. "I don't suppose there's a shrink on this island."

"Whoa there," he said.

She looked at him. "Why?"

"Because shrinks aren't always the answer. I mean, I've had members of my various congregations have amazing mystical experiences. Religious experiences that have changed their lives permanently. And those who were seeing psychiatrists then or later were often told not to take it seriously, that the brain can create these experiences in response to severe depression."

"And you don't think that's the case?"

"Sometimes, maybe. But when it alters your life permanently for the better, I'm inclined to think it may be real."

"Well, Delphine isn't altering my life. She's annoying the dickens out of me."

As soon as she spoke, Lynn regretted the words. "No, I don't mean that, not exactly." She straightened. "The thing is, Jack, I love my aunt. When she died, I was crushed. She took me in when I was ten and my parents died, and she was the coolest mother anyone could ask for."

He nodded encouragingly. "But?"

"No 'but.' Not really. Sometimes she drove me to distraction. Apparently she hasn't given up on that. But even when she made me nuts, I knew it was because she loved me. I missed her so much!"

Jack nodded again. This whole Delphine thing was driving *him* crazy, too, though he didn't want to say so. He believed. He didn't believe. Sometimes he thought she was hallucinating, and other times he didn't think so. He could only imagine the roller coaster this had put *her* on.

And frankly, Jack thought, he *was* still wondering about whether Lynn should be allowed to be alone with the island's children. Oh, it was obvious she was a great classroom teacher, but what if she had one of these "Delphine attacks" when she was on Empty Island with the kids? How would that affect them? What if she cracked utterly and completely?

Hmmm.

He didn't like the way his mind was running. He was seriously drawn to Lynn, although he figured being attracted to a former Princeton scientist was probably a mistake for the long haul because she'd get tired of slumming on this island eventually and want to head back to the big labs and facilities she would never find here.

But then he found himself wondering why she'd left Princeton to come here in the first place? Wasn't that in itself a sign of some kind of insanity?

Maybe she'd burned out. Or maybe seeing spooks had begun to get her into trouble.

He hesitated. He didn't want to believe the worst of her, but there were children involved. He knew where his first duty lay.

"Um...did you see Delphine before you came here?"

"Never. She's a new arrival. I keep wondering if there's something in the air here."

"There might be," he said only half-jestingly. "I mean, look at the rest of us."

"But you all aren't seeing dead relatives."

"Maybe only because others don't talk about it. I mean, I only knew because I saw you talking to the air."

"True." She grimaced. "Trust me, I never would have told anyone."

"I can understand that." Not quite sure what his next step should be, Jack did the manly thing—well, actually the thing he most wanted to do—and put his arm around her shoulders. Beneath it, she felt fragile, small. Protectiveness surged in him. "We'll work through it together," he promised rashly. "If it really *is* your aunt, I'd be thrilled to prove it."

"You would?"

"Heck yes. Lynn, I'm functioning on faith. Do you think I'd mind a little proof?"

At that a small smile curved her lips upward and she turned a little toward him. "But what if I'm crazy?"

Something possessed him then. A devil. An imp. Or just plain hormones. Whatever, he said huskily, "I'll kiss you anyway."

And he did.

The minute their lips met, he regretted the impulse. Not because it was bad. Oh no. He'd kissed a few more than his share of women in his life. But never, ever, had a kiss felt like this.

Maybe Big Mouth, the volcano, was erupting. But no, something inside him was. Erupting and melting all at the same time, like lava, making him burn like a torch and soften like putty. He wanted to lay her down then and there and learn all her secrets, and make them one. He wanted to hear her gasp in pleasure and moan, and feel her writhe and then see her smile with stars in her eyes.

He ached to get closer and closer, in a way he'd never felt before. Red warning flags popped up in his brain. No one had ever affected him this way, not even the woman he had intended to marry. And now he was feeling this with a crazy woman who might be just passing through?

But the thunder of his blood drowned common sense, and the throbbing between his legs was so good….

And then she broke free.

Damn.

LYNN JERKED LOOSE and hopped to her feet. Hunger and fear had torn her, but fear had triumphed. One gunshot blast to the heart was enough for a lifetime. She couldn't risk another. Certainly not a dalliance with a man who knew she might be crazy when she *really* might be crazy.

She stood staring at him, breathing heavily, trying to think of something polite to say before she fled.

At that instant someone burst into the pond area and shouted, "Alligator!"

She turned to look and saw a man and a woman running as if death was at their heels. Tourists from the cruise ship, she thought, because she didn't recognize them.

"That way," Jack said, pointing down a path. "That'll take you back to the ship. I'll take care of the gator."

The couple barely waved before heading along the path he'd indicated. Jack, still sitting on the bench, waited a courteous moment or two before he started laughing.

After a second or two, Lynn helplessly joined him.

"That sounded good, didn't it?" Jack said, through his laughter. "I'll take care of the gator."

"So manly," she agreed, a tear running down her cheek as she continued to laugh.

"I should beat my chest."

Just then, Buster emerged from the path recently vacated by the fleeing vacationers. The African gray was still perched on top of his head, going along for the ride.

"Stupid tourists," the bird said.

"Aww," Lynn said, wiping her cheek with the back of her hand. "Buster looks confused."

"Offended, probably."

The bird fluttered up and off Buster's head as he slid into the pond, where his grinning jaws began to grab chickens. Instinctively, he gave them a few swings with his head, but the chickens weren't really big enough to break into pieces. Still, he seemed to enjoy the action. And one by one, feathers and all, the dead chickens disappeared.

The bird, while all this carnage happened, flew over to sit on Jack's shoulder. "I'm too young to see this," the bird said, burying its head beneath its wing.

"They're just dead chickens," Jack said.

"They're my *cousins,*" the bird responded, muffled beneath the wing.

"Better get used to it. Buster has to eat."

"I know, I know." The bird suddenly lifted his head. "Got any barley or suet?"

"I might be able to find some," Lynn answered.

"Good. I'm getting sick of bugs."

Satisfied, Buster burped and crawled halfway out of the water where the sun dappled him. Then with a contented groan, he closed his eyes. At once the parrot fluttered across the pond and settled back on Buster's head and, as if he felt sleepy too, the bird tucked its head beneath a wing and stopped moving.

Then Jack's gaze met Lynn's. Instantly they both looked embarrassed. One of them mumbled something, or maybe they both did. Without another word, they took the path toward town.

Not talking about what had happened seemed a whole lot safer than discussing it. To both of them.

SUNDAY MORNING CAME and went. Lynn attended Jack's early service on Sunday, in a church packed to the rafters. She soon saw why this little island church held four services every Sunday.

Music nearly lifted the roof. Lively hymns filled the air, led by a choir of twenty. Foot-stomping, hand-clapping music. Then, when Jack gave his sermon, he picked something from the Gospel of

John, one of Lynn's favorite Bible quotes. *He who knows not love knows not God, for God is love.*

From there Jack moved on to talking about the island people, their neighborliness, their quickness to help one another.

"But," said, leaning against the lectern on one elbow, "there's something else about folks here that reminds me of our Lord. Tolerance. Now, that's a dirty word in some places, but not here on Treasure Island. Every one of us is a bit daft."

That brought a roar of laughter.

Jack held up a finger. "But the important thing is, we enjoy our differences. I come from a world where folks were always ready to jump to judgment. The thing I love most about Treasure Island is that you folks don't do that. You're amazing. You just love one another, warts and all."

Afterward there was coffee and doughnuts, and an opportunity to socialize. Lynn remained for a while, laughing and talking, before she headed home. Or rather, to what was left of her home.

HALFWAY TO THE school on Monday morning, walking down the main street, Lynn stopped in her tracks. Ever since she'd arrived on the island, one of the storefronts had been boarded up. She'd assumed it had always been that way, but apparently she'd been wrong. It had never occurred to her to ask.

Because now the boarding was gone, windows gleamed, tables sat out front on the sidewalk and a bright, shiny hand-painted sign said, "Buster's Café" over a grinning-green-alligator logo.

She almost laughed because it was so cute, and decided that on the way home, if they were open, she'd stop in for a light snack.

At that moment, a woman stepped out the front door and smiled. Lynn instantly recognized her as the mother of one of her students. "Hi, Mrs. Beacham!"

"Mabel, please." A woman in her late thirties with dark hair and skin, Mabel Beacham had already struck Lynn as a living dynamo. "What do you think?" she asked, turning to look at the café, setting her hands on her hips as she did so.

"I think the name and sign are adorable," Lynn assured her. "And I was planning to stop in on my way home after school."

Mabel nodded, smiling with pleasure. "This is something I always wanted to do. Finally Leo was making enough from fishing that he could refurbish this old place. It used to be his dad's bar, but then Olsen opened his tavern, and with the casinos, business fell off. His granddad just kinda let it go. Anyway, it'll give Leo more time to play poker."

"It'll be a lot of work."

Mabel laughed. "At least it'll be work on dry land, Lynn. I used to go fishing with Leo, but I'm one of those people who never gets over seasickness. Like that English admiral. Can't remember his name."

"Nelson."

"That's him." Mabel shook her head. "Only unlike the admiral there, I don't get over it even after a few days out."

"Eww," Lynn grimaced. "I'm sorry. That's an awful feeling."

"Tell me about it. Leo finally told me I was no earthly use lying flat on my side, sucking on limes all day." She laughed. "'Stay home with the kids,' he said."

"Well, you've certainly done a good job with both of them, so I imagine you'll do a good job with the café."

"Sandwiches and coffee to start. Soft drinks. I don't want to get in over my head. But I bake my own bread. I have a special recipe."

Lynn's mouth started watering. "Special recipe? I'm sold. Especially since my own is boring. Now I'll spend all day thinking about it until I can get here later."

Mabel touched her arm. "Hang on a sec. You can be my advertising."

Three minutes later, Mabel emerged with a huge wrapped sandwich. "Chicken salad, my own recipe. Make the other teachers drool."

"I don't think that's going to be a problem at all. How much do I owe you?"

Mabel grinned. "Not a thing. Just make sure to eat it where everyone can see. And let everyone know that Leo's going to play Hold 'Em every night. No buy in, but the winner gets a free dinner."

Lynn was still grinning as she resumed her trek to the school.

She'd just had a perfectly normal interaction with a perfectly normal person, so maybe she wasn't as crazy as she feared. While Delphine's appearance might be hard to explain with physics, she was still the only hallucination Lynn was having. A person could live with a single hallucination.

In fact, it was a heckuva lot more miserable living without plumbing.

CHAPTER TEN

BY THE END OF THE SCHOOL day, a single hallucination still seemed an okay thing to live with. In fact, she was quite sure she could handle Delphine if Harv Cullinan would just put her house back together. But school proved her salvation. The day had gone well, the students' interest in the terrarium was heartwarming and their eagerness to learn seemed to be growing fast since the first day of school.

On the way home, as she promised herself, she stopped at the café and discovered that all the teachers who had asked about her sandwich at lunch were there, along with quite a few other islanders. A new business opening was not an everyday occurrence on Treasure Island.

All continued to be cool until she was sitting at an outside table and an older woman she had seen around town joined her. "Hi. I'm Jan Miskner."

"Hi. Lynn Reilly."

"I just wanted you to know how much I enjoyed visiting with your aunt today, when I saw her at the store. Will she be staying long?"

At that point a heart attack wouldn't have been unreasonable. Lynn couldn't even speak. Her mouth seemed paralyzed, as did her entire body.

"She's such an engaging woman," Jan continued, as if she were used to people who sat frozen while she talked. And perhaps she was. "Quite a sense of humor. She tells me she's concerned about you, Lynn."

"Oh," Lynn finally managed.

"I know, I know," Jan said soothingly. "You're like all young people. You don't like it when older folks discuss you. But Delphine is such a dear, and she loves you so much. You're so lucky to have an aunt like her."

At that instant Lynn was wondering if there was any way to strangle a ghost. Or perhaps shove a huge cork in her mouth. And she still couldn't think of anything to say that wouldn't have sounded wild-eyed.

"It's a shame," Jan continued obliviously, "that she's only visiting. I'd love it if she could stay here indefinitely. We'd become fast friends, I'm sure of it."

Lynn managed a sound of mumbled agreement, while considering the potential horror of Delphine becoming a permanent fixture.

"Well, dear," Jan said, patting her hand, "I just

wanted you to know that I enjoyed meeting your aunt. You're very lucky."

With that the woman rose and rejoined her original table.

Lucky? *Lucky?* And what did it mean if other people began to see Delphine? Or perhaps it was only Jan.

Either way, Lynn began to wonder if she had ever attended Delphine's funeral or if she had merely imagined it.

She was still staring into space, wondering if she'd fallen through the rabbit hole into another universe, when a hot cup of tea appeared in front of her, along with a buttered croissant.

"Your aunt," said Mabel, "told me you liked a buttered croissant with your tea."

Lynn jerked her head around. "My—my aunt?" she croaked.

Mable chuckled. "That woman is a pistol. She stopped by for lunch. Why have you been hiding her?"

"Ummm…" Lynn scrambled for something suitable to say. "She just arrived."

"Well, bring her by again. She had me laughing until my sides hurt."

Oh God, Lynn thought. Oh God, this can't be happening. Not wanting to be rude, and not sure what she should do anyway, she ate the croissant and drank the tea without tasting a bit of it. She tossed money on the table, complimented Mabel on her culinary skills, then took off like a bat out of hell for her house.

Or maybe, said some little voice in her head, she should go to the island's only church and demand that Jack give her an exorcism.

Except that wouldn't keep other people from seeing Delphine.

Or maybe Jack could sprinkle holy water. Something. *Anything...*

She burst into the white-clapboard church that looked as if it had escaped from New England for a warmer climate sometime in the late nineteenth century. There, to her amazement, she saw Jack using a dusting rag on the various accoutrements.

She closed the door with a bang and leaned back against it, panting for air.

He looked at her with patent surprise. "What's wrong?"

"I need an exorcism."

"A what?" He looked dumbfounded, which she didn't appreciate, given what she'd already shared with him.

"You heard me. Or maybe this entire island needs an exorcism!"

"What on earth...?"

"That's the problem. Not on Earth. This couldn't be Earth anymore. It's another planet."

He dropped his dusting rag and began to walk toward her. Slowly. Looking like a man who felt he was facing an armed stranger.

"Let's talk about this, Lynn," he said soothingly.

"Talk about what? That two other people on this island talked to Delphine today, and they think she's real?"

It was Jack's turn to freeze. She had the momentary satisfaction of seeing him look like a deer caught in headlights.

"They have?" he asked finally, his voice hushed.

"Two of them talked to me about her. Jan and Mabel."

She could see his mind swing into gear, probably mentally evaluating the stability of the two other parties. But he said nothing.

Enough was enough. She'd had it. "I don't care if you have to bless a whole truckload of holy water. I want this over with."

"You think I can get rid of her?"

"Can't you? Aren't you a preacher?"

"Exorcism isn't my specialty. Besides, that's only for getting rid of evil."

"Get out your books, preacher man, because evil or not, I want this stopped."

"But why?" he asked, stepping closer and looking as if he'd made an important discovery. "If others are seeing her, then you know for a fact that you're not crazy."

"It's worse," Lynn said glumly.

"Worse?"

"Yeah. If others see her, then she really is a wave collapse. And if the dead can just emerge into physical reality any old time, what *exactly* is reality?"

"I thought you physicists had pretty much debunked the whole notion of ordinary reality."

She glared at him. "So it's okay that my dead aunt is talking about me to everyone on the island?"

"Two people is hardly everyone."

"Damn it!" She stamped her foot. "I suppose you think you're being reasonable?"

"Aren't I?"

Slowly she sagged into a pew, overwhelmed by a horrible feeling of helplessness. Jack sat beside her and took her hand.

"I love Aunt Delphine," Lynn said, a tear slowly coursing down her cheek. "I love her, Jack. She was the kind of aunt every kid would love to have. She was more of a friend than an aunt."

He nodded. "You were blessed."

"Apparently I'm *still* blessed. But…how can I make you see?"

"Just talk to me," he said soothingly. "Let it come out any old way."

"I felt like a part of my heart was ripped out when she died. I walked around crying and talking to her for weeks. I thought—scientist or not—that part of her still existed, that she could still hear me."

He nodded. "Of course she could."

"Once…once I even smelled her perfume. It was a scent that nobody but she had. Not just the perfume, but the smell of Delphine, if you know what I mean."

"I know." He squeezed her hand.

"And I felt like I was surrounded by her, as if she were giving me a big hug. And I felt better. I know a shrink would say that I was depressed and imagining it, but it was so…so *real*."

"I don't think you were imagining it."

She looked at him, her vision blurred by tears. "No?"

"Very often people feel their loved ones reach out to them after they die. It's actually a common experience, and given my faith, I believe it's real. Delphine was trying to comfort you."

Lynn nodded slowly, more tears slipping over the edges of her eyelids to run down her cheeks. She didn't even bother to dash them away. "That was okay, you know. Real, imagined, it didn't matter to me. I just knew Aunt Delphine was okay."

He nodded and squeezed her hand gently.

"Things settled down. I went back to work and…" She trailed off, looking away. "Never mind what happened when I got back to work. It's irrelevant to this."

"Okay."

She sighed and shoved her hand into her pocket to pull out the small packet of tissues she always carried, as much for her students as anything. She dabbed at her face and drew a deep, steadying breath. Something drew her gaze to the arched ceiling over the altar, soaring high as if to draw the mind upward.

"The problem," she said finally, "is that while I've been able to prove measurable effects of consciousness at the quantum level and some other effects at a larger level, they always…always depend on the intent of the observer."

"The observer effect," he said.

She nodded. "It's been a conundrum for some time in science that the observer affects the behavior of small particles. Over the past thirty years, we've learned that the effects are bigger than anything we'd imagined. I won't bore you with the details, but we've basically shown that consciousness is intimately entwined with the universe down to the smallest bits of space, time and matter. So yes, when someone dies, they're not gone. Part of them will continue. In what form, we don't know."

He smiled gently. "I do, but go on."

"Anyway, Aunt Delphine being able to appear to me, well, that's scary enough. But when she starts manifesting for other people as well…" Lynn shook her head.

"It shakes up your science."

"I guess so. Oh, I'm not explaining this well."

"Take your time," he said. "I don't have anywhere to go at the moment."

"I don't know if I can explain it," she said finally. She looked at Jack, her eyes finally beginning to dry. "Maybe I imagined those conversations with Jan and Mabel." With that, she pulled her hand from his and walked out of the church.

JACK REMAINED BEHIND, sorely troubled. This was not amusing. Not in the least. He'd been thinking she might be crazy or at least a little unbalanced, talking to empty air and seeing ghosts, but that had been…

Be honest, old man, he told himself. You weren't just concerned about the children. You were concerned about yourself, looking for reasons not to like the woman.

But the thought of Lynn questioning her own

sanity in this way troubled him more than he wanted to admit. The thing was, there was nothing he could do about it except keep an eye on her. If Delphine were really appearing to people, it was nothing short of a miracle, one he wasn't sure he was ready to embrace.

But for Lynn it couldn't be a miracle. She was too much of a scientist, and her church of science apparently was crumbling with every appearance of Delphine.

And that would be enough to cause a mental breakdown.

Not knowing what else to do, he headed for town to talk to Jan and Mabel. If they had seen Delphine, he had his work cut out for him with Lynn. Because that could mean Delphine wasn't dead at all.

CHAPTER ELEVEN

"I'M SORRY, LYNN," Delphine said.

Lynn, sitting at the dinette in her kitchen, hands wrapped around a mug of coffee as if its warmth could reach to the chilly places growing deep inside her, didn't even bother to look up. "Why?"

"I thought talking to those two women would reassure you that you weren't imagining me. I never thought that it might affect you adversely."

"Which is why you taught English and not physics."

"True."

From the corner of her eye, she glimpsed Delphine settle into the chair across from her. Today Delphine had chosen pink hair with an amazing number of ringlets to match the pink satin dress she wore.

"I don't really understand," Delphine said. "People have always seen 'ghosts.' It's not as if I'm something new."

"Ghosts like you are pretty new. Trust me."

"You've done a thorough research of the literature?"

Lynn's head snapped up. "I don't read that claptrap."

Delphine smiled gently. "You see? I'm not singular. I'm not an exception. Others have done this. Others have experienced what you're experiencing. Most of them just never talk about it. But you can relax, dear, I'm not violating your precious laws of physics."

"Of course you're not. That would be impossible. But you're certainly making me think about where our version of them goes astray."

"Consider, then. I'm not a physical manifestation. I'm not Delphine the way I used to be Delphine. You can't reach out and touch me. In every way, I'm an apparition."

Lynn nodded slowly.

"I could do the lady-in-white thing, but that's so...so...overdone. And you wouldn't recognize me if I walked around your house like Lady Macbeth haunting Glamis Castle."

"Good point."

"Just think of me like a movie, an image projected on a screen. Does that help?"

Lynn looked at her. "Maybe."

"Good. Trust me, I'm very definitely dead. But my consciousness survives. And you know from your studies that's possible, right?"

"Of course."

"So stop worrying about your sanity. Start paying attention to what really matters. Like that nice preacher next door. He's attracted to you, you know."

"I don't want to be attracted to anyone."

"Fiddle! You'll get over that disgusting excuse for manhood you dated at Princeton. He's not the exemplar, you know. He's a worm."

Lynn felt one corner of her mouth lift. "Lower than a worm."

"Entirely within reason," Delphine agreed. "Lower than a slug. Trust me, Lynn, he'll pay for that. Unfortunately, most of us aren't around to see karma take its toll."

At that Lynn had to chuckle. "I don't expect to be around to see him get his comeuppance."

"Of course not. But I've always thought life would be *so* much more satisfying if we could see slime reap what they sow. And so much more instructive, don't you think?"

Lynn hesitated. "I wasn't raised to be vengeful, Auntie Delph."

"Of course you weren't. Neither was I. But I

am—or was—a mere human, and sometimes one feels a rather unholy sense of glee when someone like that gets what's coming to them."

Lynn could not deny it.

"However, I didn't mean to shock you by speaking to Jan or Mabel. I had no intention of doing any such thing, although this dithering about your sanity was beginning to annoy me."

"Then why did you do it?"

"They *saw* me, Lynn. Those two women are sensitive. It shocked me when they spoke to me as much as it must have shocked you when you heard about it."

"Really?" Curiosity was overtaking Lynn again. "What were you doing?"

"Well, since I'm *required* to hang around here for a while, as my students would have phrased it, I was doing precisely that. Hanging around. Looking the island over. Trying in *some* way to amuse myself. Being non-physical makes that a bit difficult, you know. I can't go swimming, I can't play poker, and this island doesn't even have a movie theater except at that stupid casino, and I don't like that place."

"Why not?"

"Because some of the people in there are *ruining* themselves." Delphine shuddered delicately. "I wish I could knock their heads together. Gambling isn't evil in and of itself."

Lynn almost gasped. "I never imagined you would say that!"

Delphine waved a hand. "I have a much larger perspective on things now. Gambling is quite all right as long as you aren't neglecting the poor and putting your own family into dire straits. But some of those people over there are doing exactly that!"

For an instant Delphine looked so fired up that Lynn thought of Carrie Nation in her historic crusade against alcohol. All that was missing was the hatchet.

Then Delphine relaxed. "Well, *their* problems aren't my concern. Still, it's rather boring around here."

"I don't think so at all."

"Why would you? You can do all the things I can't. Oh, by the way, if you get the volcanologist, Edna Harkin, to come speak to your classes, warn her to tone down her predictions. No point in scaring the children when Big Mouth won't erupt for at least another sixty years. But that poor woman lives in constant expectation of the big moment that will make her career."

"How do you know so much?"

"I told you—people broadcast. No secrets where I am."

Lynn shifted uncomfortably. "I don't like that."

"Of course not. Your world enjoys the illusion of privacy."

"What's wrong with that?"

Delphine shrugged. "Nothing I suppose. But I can assure you, Lynn, the lack of it isn't disturbing. We are all so *very* much alike at heart."

Lynn sipped her coffee, enjoying this brief return to the days when she and her aunt had often chatted over coffee, thinking over what Delphine was telling her. "It's still creepy," she said finally.

"Then don't think about it. Trust me, we're past voyeurism over here. In any event, I shall take great care that no one else sees me, and you can simply say that I went home on the cruise ship. And for now, I shall leave you alone!"

With that, Delphine vanished. The ache of loneliness she left behind in her wake surprised Lynn. Was she becoming attached to a ghost?

Quite possibly. How very unnerving.

"I LIKED HER," Jan said to Jack. "The teacher's aunt is a very nice lady. A bit odd, but nice."

Jack felt something within him squirm uncomfortably. It was one thing to accept the theory of ghosts and deceased family members returning to comfort loved ones through dreams and other means, quite another to hear that someone outside the family had actually seen and talked to a dead person.

He cleared his throat, trying to gather his thoughts. "Why do you say she was odd?"

"Because she walked into the store as if she was invisible. I mean, she came in looked around, didn't say a word to anyone...very unsociable at first. But I wouldn't let that pass, so I went over and introduced myself. She seemed shocked that I spoke to her."

"There are places where people aren't as friendly as here on the island."

"Apparently so." Jan pursed her lips disapprovingly. "How awful to live in a place like that."

"Definitely."

Jan shrugged. "Well, she was certainly very pleasant once I spoke to her. Mabel joined us, and finally we were laughing and joking like old friends. I *do* hope I see her again."

Though extremely unsettled, Jack wasn't sure he believed that the women had talked to the ghost of Lynn's aunt. Any strange woman from a cruise ship could have come into the café, and when approached said something that made these women think she was related to Lynn. In fact, the more he thought about it, the more likely he believed that to be the explanation. Miscommunication and misunderstanding were far easier to believe than that a ghost had talked to two people.

Yes, that was it. Lynn had probably mentioned her aunt to other people around the island. After all, one of the most common subjects of conversation around here was family and friends. And if someone didn't know you, they were going to want all the details.

So Lynn had talked about her family, and something this tourist had said had persuaded these women they were talking to Lynn's aunt. And Lynn had assumed from what *they* said that they had seen Delphine.

Of course. Nothing to it at all. Just something like the game of rumors. As the story passed from one person to the next, the details became more outlandish.

Still, it wouldn't hurt to Google the obituaries, just to be certain.

He was about to head back to the church to finish his cleaning—he had to keep up with it because they really couldn't afford to hire someone to do it—when the new mayor, Dan Heilbaum, shouted out his name.

At once Jack turned to watch the plump man come running down the street. He liked Dan pretty much. Better than the last mayor, who'd found himself out of office after it was discovered he was in league with developers. Pick any reason and the people of the island would have had the same response: good riddance.

"Jack," Dan called again. "Jack, you've got to come and reason with these people!"

"What people?"

"We're having a riot at the poker game."

Jack didn't bother to ask what poker game. On this island there was always a game. As pastimes went, poker beat out satellite television, American football and even soccer.

Tempers sometimes flared, but a riot?

He trotted after Dan down the street and found the melee at a shade-tree game, several folding tables set up under a cluster of palms. Perhaps thirty men were there, and they were arguing fiercely and waving their arms as if they wanted to hit one another. Jack paused, taking in the scene, wondering what he could possibly do about it. He was just the preacher, and the island didn't have a police force.

"Nobody," shouted one man, waving his fist, "*nobody* gets a royal flush two hands in a row!"

Jack tried to calculate the odds of that and gave up. Getting a royal flush once was rare enough in a lifetime.

"Are you accusing me of cheating?" shouted another man, also waving his fist. "I've been playing poker on this island all my life, and I've never once cheated. And so you know, Dil."

"I also know the odds against getting two royal flushes in a row! It's impossible!"

It seemed that two arguments were going on, one about whether it was possible to get that hand twice in a row, and the other about whether Carter had been cheating.

Well, that complicated things, and Dan hadn't exactly been exaggerating. Tempers were heated, and on this island, if there was one thing that *could* cause a riot, this was it.

Since anything was possible, however remote, in terms of the hands that could fall to a person, he feared that soon the entire argument would turn to whether Carter cheated. On this island, cheating at cards was on par with murder. It chipped away at the very foundation of the whole society, wacky though it was.

"Folks," he said loudly.

No one listened.

"People," he said even more loudly.

They kept on arguing.

"Gentlemen!" This time he shouted, his voice just rising above the din. No one heeded him.

At that instant, Buster, emerging from out of nowhere it seemed, let out a bellow in his deep thrumming voice. It made the ground tremble, and for an instant even the parrot atop his head jumped into the air and fluttered before settling.

Suddenly there was silence. Everyone whirled around and stared at the alligator.

"Thanks, Buster," Jack said.

"Mmmmhmmmm."

"Don't," the bird on his head said, "make him do that again. It disturbs my sleep."

All eyes switched to Jack.

"Look, fellas," he said reasonably in his best listen-to-the-preacher voice, "you can argue until doomsday about whether two royal flushes could fall to the same player in a row. Anything's possible and you know it. How many times has one of you gotten a pair of aces on successive hands? You know it can happen, however remote the likelihood."

"What would you know about it?" Sal Vicchio demanded. "You're just a preacher."

"Then let's go ask the best mathematician on the island. But my point is, you know Carter better than to think he would cheat. None of you would cheat. You never play for anything worth cheating for."

"Hey!" said one of the men, apparently not sure

he liked the way that sounded, but unable to put his finger on why.

"What I mean is," Jack said, carefully backtracking from that precipice, the one that implied these men would cheat if the stakes were high enough, "you all know you're honest men."

There was some shuffling and grumbling, followed by rather sheepish looks.

"I still say that wasn't possible," Dil said, glaring at Carter, who glared back.

"Fine," said Jack. "Let's go ask the teacher."

Which was how the almost-mob came to be following Jack down the main drag with its shabby shops on either side. Only Buster's Café looked anything approaching new and shiny, and at that very moment Mabel and her husband Leo were struggling with a life-size wooden alligator, moving it through the door and onto the porch next to the door.

Jack halted, frozen by the sight. Everyone else jammed up behind him. "Wow!" he said.

The wooden alligator was about twelve feet long, and so lifelike it was amazing...until you saw the face. He almost busted out laughing when he saw it.

The wooden alligator had long eyelashes and was wearing makeup. A cupid's bow mouth had been painted right on the front between slightly bared teeth. Eyeliner highlighted the lashed reptilian eyes. A touch of pink rouge, not too much, decorated the cheeks.

Mabel looked at Jack and shrugged. "We wanted it to make people laugh."

"Oh, it will," he said and let loose his laughter. "I just hope Buster isn't offended."

The crowd behind him seemed to shove him forward. "Let's get this finished, preach," one of the men said. "Then you can come back and look at that ridiculous thing."

So Jack led his horde forward toward Lynn's house, hoping she didn't think they were a lynch mob or something.

And behind him, unbeknownst to him and the other men, Buster stopped and looked up at the alligator on the porch.

He wasn't offended. No. He made a deep thrum inside his throat, and rested his head on a step so he could stare dreamily at the wooden gator.

"She's not real," the parrot said.

"Mmmmhmmm."

"But you're in love anyway."

"Mmmmhmmm."

"And doesn't that just figure." The parrot let out a disgusted squawk. "Now my ride has a pinup girl."

CHAPTER TWELVE

FORTUNATELY, LYNN REILLY WAS out back, enjoying the waning afternoon on her patio. Thus she did not see the mob approach and gather in her front yard. The crazy way things had been going, she might well have thought it was a lynch mob.

Not that there was any reason for anyone to want to lynch her, but then there was no reason for a lot of the things that had been happening lately. Life, she was beginning to think, needed no rationale at all.

The doorbell summoned her to the front, and her brief glance out the side window didn't warn her. Thus it was that she opened her front door totally unprepared for the sight that greeted her. She noted Jack instantly, but her eyes skipped immediately from him to the crowd of men behind him, none of whom looked at all happy. They clustered around the trench—some standing on the backhoe, which seemed to have become a permanent addition to her landscaping—and glared.

Her first instinct was to slam the door and flee. There weren't a lot of places to go on this island, but surely there was somewhere she could hide from the mob.

Visions of old westerns filled her mind, and she tried to imagine what a noose would look like hanging from a palm tree. Somehow it just wouldn't fit together.

Noose, mob, palm tree... No, it didn't fit together. Nor did it fit with anything she had yet done on the island, unless someone was morally opposed to the building of a terrarium. Or unless her neighbors were tired of the mess in her front yard.

"Hey," said Jack, drawing her gaze back to him. "It's okay."

"Okay?" Okay that she had nearly thirty angry-looking men standing on what was left of her front yard, glaring at her.

"We need you to settle a disagreement," Jack said. "That's all."

"That's all?" She gaped at him. "Are you nuts? These men are already furious. No matter what I say I'll be hanging from a palm tree somewhere!"

Jack looked startled. "What the...?" He didn't finish the sentence. Of course, he couldn't know he'd stepped into the middle of her imagination.

"Look at them," she said, pointing. "They want blood."

Jack turned and looked. He wagged his head slightly in a maybe-so gesture. "You guys don't want blood, do you?"

"Damn straight," one of the men said.

"Yeah," growled another. "Unfortunately, we're not going to get it." He turned and glared at another man.

"Of course not," Jack said, pitching his voice soothingly. "We just need a mathematical estimate, then everyone will go home happy. Right?"

"Wrong," another man said. "Nobody's gonna be happy, except maybe Carter. *Maybe.*"

Lynn shook her head and took a step backward. "I don't want to be part of this. It looks…dangerous."

"Relax," Jack said, facing her again. "Nobody's been murdered on this island in decades. People may feel like it sometimes—"

"Like right now," someone grunted.

"Like right now," Jack agreed. "But no one's going to do any such thing. Am I right?"

The question was a challenge, and it had an odd effect on the angry crew, causing them to shift uneasily.

He looked at Lynn. "We just want to know if it's

possible for the same person to get a royal flush twice in a row."

Lynn's jaw dropped. "You're kidding."

"See?" said one of the angrier men stepping forward and stabbing his finger into the chest of another. "I told you it plain just don't happen!"

"I didn't cheat!" the other man said, his face turning bright red. "It just happened!"

Jack turned on Lynn. "How could you say that?"

"Say what?" She was quickly developing the conviction that everyone *else* on this island was insane, while she was not.

"That they were kidding!"

Her jaw dropped. "I didn't mean *they* were kidding!"

"Then what did you mean?" Behind him the roar was growing again, and he wondered if he'd be able to regain control without the aid of Buster.

"I was just responding to the question."

"You call that a response?"

She bit her lip, suddenly wanting to laugh at the absurdity of all this. "I mean the question was absurd."

"Believe me, right now it is the *most* important question in the universe, at least as regards this island."

"I'm beginning to see that."

Jack turned before the rumbling behind him got too loud and raised both his hands. "Guys. Guys! Shut up and listen!"

This time, perhaps because they were in the presence of a lady and Treasure Island had some old-fashioned notions about how men should behave in the presence of ladies—notions which could appear at the oddest of times—they began to settle down.

"The teacher, Ms. Reilly, was not referring to the hand in question. She was expressing surprise at the question."

Eyes shifted from Jack to Lynn. Her mind seemed to have gone blank. "Umm, what was the question again?"

"Is it possible for one player to draw a royal flush in two successive hands?"

"Well, of course."

At that moment, Lynn could have sworn the entire island held its breath, so quiet did everything become.

Finally one of the men stepped forward. "It never happens."

Lynn shrugged. "You're talking about the difference between probability and possibility, sir."

"Dil. Call me Dil."

"Sure." She smiled. "It's highly improbable that

someone would draw a royal flush on successive hands, but it is *not* impossible. There's a difference there."

Some grumbling greeted her words.

Trying to settle things down a little since Jack looked genuinely concerned, she plunged in deeper. "First," she said, "it's a mistake to look at all the hands together."

"Why?" came a belligerent growl from the back.

"Because every time you reshuffle the deck, you're looking at a fresh set of probabilities. So every time you reshuffle, it's just as likely that someone will get a royal flush. Admittedly, the odds aren't high, but the possibility and probability are the same on every shuffle."

A long silence greeted her words. She waited, watching the men digest this rather difficult-to-accept notion. She knew how most people were accustomed to thinking, and while what they thought made a lot of intuitive sense, in the realm of mathematics things changed a bit.

"It's like flipping a coin," she said after a moment. "Every time you flip it, you have a fifty-percent chance of getting heads. Every single time. So while it is unlikely you'd flip twenty heads in a row, you could. It's possible. But every single time you make the flip, the odds are still fifty-fifty. Even if you've flipped ten heads in a row, that's no guarantee you'll get tails the next time. Because it's still a fifty-fifty chance."

"But…" The man called Dil scratched his head. "Teach, I don't get it exactly."

"I know. It doesn't seem to make sense." Enjoying herself now, she sat on the top of her two porch steps and wrapped her arms around her knees. "Wanna talk about it a bit?"

"Yeah," Dil said. Meanwhile, the man he had virtually accused of cheating was looking as if he had—barely!—escaped the gallows himself.

"It's all in how you ask the question," Lynn said to Dil. "It's in the way you look at it. That changes the math. Changes the probabilities. Changes the possibilities even."

"Try that again."

"Okay. If I asked you, 'Can I toss a hundred heads in a row?' you'd be justified in saying I couldn't. The odds are against it."

"Now that I get," Dil said.

"Right. If you look at a hundred tosses of a coin as a single unit, it would be all but impossible for me to toss heads a hundred times in a row."

"Unless you were cheating," Dil said, brow lowered.

"Ah, but you see, it might be all but impossible,

but it's still within the realm of chance that it could happen. It's *possible,* just not likely."

Dil nodded. "Okay."

"So that's the difference we're talking about here. If you look at individual flips of a coin, it's fifty-fifty every time. That's like reshuffling the cards. However, if you look at a hundred flips as one unit, the odds change dramatically, but it's *still possible.*"

Dil was brightening. "I get it." With that he turned to the man he'd been stabbing his finger at and stabbed his finger once again. *"But you better not do it again soon."*

"WHEW," JACK SAID AFTER the mob wandered down the dusty street back to their game. He sat next to Lynn on her step. "Thanks."

"You *better* thank me," she said humorously. "It's not a good feeling to open your front door and be faced with a crowd of angry men."

"Rather western, huh?"

"Those were the thoughts I started to have."

He grinned, one of those winning grins of his. "I knew you'd have the answer."

"How could you be so sure?"

"Well, two things. I knew Carter wouldn't cheat. That just doesn't happen on this island among the locals. And I vaguely remembered something from high-school math. I figured you'd know what it was."

At that she chuckled. "I'm glad I didn't draw a blank."

"Somehow I didn't think someone who worked with quantum physics would forget all that stuff."

A little sparkle filled her heart. "So you know something about it."

He held up a hand. "Layman's knowledge."

"Most laymen have no idea about quantum theory or physics. Most wouldn't even be able to recognize the name."

"Low opinion of your fellow man, eh?"

She shook her head. "No. It's just not important enough to most people to bother remembering."

His grin softened to a smile. "But to you it was everything."

She shrugged one shoulder. "It fascinated me. Endlessly. So many mysteries, so many questions. So many surprising effects. To me it's the world's greatest riddle."

"Almost mystical these days, to judge by some of the science programming I've watched."

She turned toward him. "What do you mean?"

"It's just…you listen to some of these theorists talking about the origins of the universe and they start to sound like mystics."

She nodded slowly. "I guess we do. I mean…frankly, Jack, I think you and I are coming at the same subject from two different directions."

"My thought exactly. So how could you give it up?"

She sighed and leaned forward, resting her chin on her knees. "It's stupid and sad. My fiancé stole my research and published it under his own name. Since I was a grad student and he was a professor, nobody believed me."

"Boy, that *sucks*."

"Big time," she agreed.

She was surprised to feel his arm wrap around her shoulders, giving her a comforting squeeze. "Some people do awful things. I'm sorry."

"I know people do awful things. I'm not stupid. It's just that I *trusted* him."

He squeezed her again. "I can identify with that, Lynn. There's something about any romance gone sour that harms our ability to trust. But what happened to you was at least a double whammy."

"That's one way of looking at it."

"Was that the reason you left Princeton?"

She nodded, pressing her chin harder against her knees because it kept wanting to tremble.

"You left the field of battle because of a single trouncing? Good heavens, woman! You should have hung around and proved with your future work that he was a jerk."

"I thought about it," she admitted. "But people were looking at me so oddly after I accused him of stealing my work. And they were ending the project anyway."

"So go to Stanford. MIT. Don't come hide out on a tropical island in the middle of nowhere."

All of a sudden her jaw quit quivering and she raised her head, giving him a faint smile. "Are you trying to get rid of me?"

He shook his head vehemently. "You just saved a man's honor. As far as Carter is concerned, destiny brought you here." He cocked his head to one side. "In fact, I'd be inclined to agree with him."

"But now that my mission is accomplished I should go back to the States?"

He shook his head, his gaze holding something hot and warm that made her quiver delightedly inside. "I hope not," he said quietly. "I hope destiny is still in play."

But even as she felt the faint touch of magic, she was swamped in utter fear. *Not again,* she thought. *Never again.*

CHAPTER THIRTEEN

SHE SHOULD HAVE INVITED him for dinner. Lynn stood just inside her front door, watching Jack walk back to his house, thinking that she had been totally rude. He had invited her to dinner after all and she had never reciprocated. And their parting just now had seemed awkward, as if something were unfinished.

But she didn't want to get involved again. Even with a preacher who was undoubtedly a pillar of moral rectitude. At least insofar as such a thing existed on Treasure Island.

Betrayal hurt way too much, and she was a long way from being ready to risk it again, if ever she would. But rudeness was something else, and she couldn't escape the feeling that she had been unforgivably rude. It wasn't as if she didn't have enough mac and cheese to feed two, or even three. And right now she could smell it bubbling in the oven, made with white cheddar and ham as she preferred. He had probably smelled it too.

He disappeared from sight, so she hurried back to her kitchen and looked out the side door. Here the aroma of her dinner was enough to make her mouth water. And there was Jack, pausing to look over his herb garden. He probably hadn't even started to make his dinner yet.

Before she could have any more second thoughts, she pushed open the screen door and called out, "Jack? Do you like mac and cheese?"

He looked back, clearly surprised. "Sure. Who doesn't?"

"Plenty of people. Would you like to join me for dinner? It's almost ready and I have more than enough."

He smiled. "I'd love to. Just let me wash up a bit."

"There's time. No rush."

She let the door flop closed and wondered if she'd slipped a cog again. And all of a sudden she wished Delphine were there to tell her she'd done the right thing.

For an instant she sighed and leaned her head against the doorframe. She wasn't, frankly, the most socially adept of people. She'd spent a lot of time among geeks and nerds who had a different way of dealing with one another. Delphine had always been on her about her social skills, and right now Lynn would have appreciated a little guidance.

She'd felt it was rude to let Jack go without inviting him in. So apparently she had some idea of the niceties. But now that she'd done what she sensed was the correct thing, she was totally at a loss.

Trying to remember the proper way to set a table, she brought out plates and flatware. Did the fork go to the left or right? Did she need to put out butter knives if there was nothing to use them on? Questions like these could drive her nuts.

Finally she settled for wrapping the flatware in a paper napkin and setting it on the plate. Since they did that in some restaurants, at least it wouldn't look totally stupid.

And she *hated* to look stupid.

The dinette wasn't in the best shape, but little on this island was. She didn't have a tablecloth. She'd never needed or wanted one.

It looked pretty sorry, she thought, staring at it. She hoped the mac and cheese made up for it.

Vegetables!

Good heavens, how could she have forgotten something so essential?

Rummaging in her freezer, she brought out a package of mixed vegetables, dotted some butter on them, then put in them in the microwave. Too early to start them, but they were ready.

Damn, she thought, using a paper towel to wipe her forehead, she was acting like a teenager getting ready for a first date. It was just a simple meal, nothing fancy. Jack knew that already. Nobody served mac and cheese for a fancy dinner. Then again, who served dinner at all when they had to wash up afterward in the bathroom sink?

He arrived about fifteen minutes later, smelling as if he had just stepped out of a shower…his only concession to the occasion since he still wore a Hawaiian shirt, khaki shorts and sandals.

But, oh, did he smell good. He smiled and held out a small cake. "From the bakery," he said. "I thought I'd contribute a little something."

"That's so kind!" She accepted the cake, sitting on a plate only slightly larger than it was, noting that the plate was chipped.

That chip hit her with a huge wave of relief. He wasn't expecting fancy. Nobody on this island was fancy. Her geekish ways were probably less noticeable here than anywhere away from a college campus.

She invited him to sit and offered him his choice of water or juice.

"Water, please."

"Unless you want coffee?"

He shook his head. "Not at this time of day. But thank you."

She sat on the other side of the table, glancing at the clock. Another few minutes and she would need to turn on the vegetables. And the silence felt awkward.

She looked back at him. "That was weird this afternoon."

"The guys getting so upset you mean?"

"Just the whole scene. It was unnerving."

He laughed. "Frankly, I was a bit unnerved, too. Poker is sacred around here. *Nobody* cheats. The whole basis on which this community is built would collapse."

"How so?"

"Everything is decided by card games, even who is on the city commission. So if somebody were to cheat, that would be the equivalent of messing with the polls back home. Only here it would be *really* bad because it's such a small community and everything is based on personal trust."

She nodded. "Once trust is sacrificed..." She didn't want to finish.

"Exactly," he said. "It takes forever to regain it. And around here, if one person were to cheat, then a lot of people would start looking askance at each other. Then we'd need the whole real-government thing, you know? Laws. Law enforcement. All the stuff nobody here wants."

She nodded, then popped up to take the mac and cheese out of the oven. The aroma of the bubbling concoction was absolutely wonderful.

"Man, that smells good," Jack said. "What did you make it with?"

"I use white cheddar and ham, and make it from scratch." She punched buttons on the microwave and the veggie bowl began to turn slowly.

When she returned to the table, she rested her chin on her hand. "This whole trust thing is huge. And I'll tell you, I kind of like the way this island operates. At first I couldn't imagine it, but now that I've been here for a while, I think it's pretty fantastic."

He nodded. "It's basically the way small tribes operate. But if the community got much larger it wouldn't work at all."

"I'm a little surprised that with all the cruise ships stopping here there hasn't been more development."

"That became a bit of an issue recently, but we stopped it. And you probably haven't noticed yet, but those are third-rate cruise lines. We don't have anything to attract the better cruises, and that's the way we like it."

"I made the mistake of visiting Key West during the cruise season." She shook her head. "It was awful. You couldn't enjoy it at all. It was better in the summer-time."

"Well, here, it's summer year round."

She smiled. "I like it." She popped up as the microwave dinged and began moving serving dishes to the table. She asked Jack to help himself while she refilled their water glasses.

"Wow, this is good!" he said, rolling the first bite around in his mouth.

"Comfort food," she admitted as she filled her own plate. "There are times when nothing else will do."

"I could develop the same feeling for this." He leaned a little toward her and winked. "Made with this recipe, at any rate."

She pretended to gasp. "Did you lie to me about liking mac and cheese?"

He pressed a hand to his heart. "Absolutely not. I like *some* kinds of mac and cheese."

A little laugh escaped her. "You're so good."

"That depends. I'm lousy at lying."

"But you can skirt the truth."

"Hey, that's called diplomacy! What was I supposed to do? My neighbor invites me for dinner. Am I supposed to question every ingredient she uses? Am I supposed to say, 'well, that depends'?"

Now she was giggling. "I guess not."

"I like mac and cheese. Just not every kind of mac and cheese."

"Fair enough."

He laughed. "It's like with those guys who followed me down here. I didn't know if you'd be able to convince them Carter hadn't cheated, but you were the best chance I had. They wouldn't have listened to *me*."

"Why not?"

"Because I'm the preacher. I'm supposed to smooth and placate and always say nice things."

"So they don't trust you?"

His eyes widened, then he set his fork down and put his head in his hands, laughing so hard that he shook. "You sure know how to undermine a guy."

She covered her mouth with her hand, but she couldn't stop the giggles.

When he lifted his head, his eyes were dancing. "It's also utterly against my position to lie."

"Uh-huh."

He laughed again. "Honestly. Disbelieve me if you want to." He lifted his hand in a scout's salute. "On my honor."

"Why did you think they'd listen to me? I'm newer than you are."

"You're also a brainiac and they know it. If you say the odds allow it, they'll listen. If I say the odds allow it, they'll just shake their heads, because I'm a preacher not a poker player."

"Don't you ever play?"

"Here and there. It's fun. But I can't quite get into it the way everyone else does. I don't know why. Well, yes I do." He picked up his fork, still smiling. "I feel guilty."

"But why?" The notion astonished her. "It's not as if you're gambling with church funds—are you?"

"I gamble for matchsticks, truthfully. I have no excess funds. But somewhere under this beach-bum exterior resides the remnants of a puritan."

"Ahh." She nodded her head wisely. "You ought to be doing something more important."

"Exactly. As long as I've been on this island, it still hasn't taught me how to relax completely. But I'm working on it."

"Why did *you* come here?" It was the question he had asked of her, and now she felt comfortable enough to ask him.

"I got tired of big-church-religion."

"How do you mean?"

He half-shrugged and devoured a few more mouthfuls of his dinner before answering. "I'm sure it's wonderful for some people. It just wasn't good for me. I didn't like having my strings pulled by the money people. I didn't like being told there were some things I couldn't sermonize about. And there was a kind of pride people had in going to a wealthy church, as if the buildings and facilities

somehow reflected their worth as human beings."
He shrugged again. "Which is not to say there
weren't a lot of very good people in my congregations, because there were. Anyway, I started to feel
guilty for my lifestyle—I was expected to live
well, you see, dress in suits, drive a nice car,
etcetera—and then I started to get royally frustrated that I couldn't establish some of the
programs I wanted or give the sermons I wanted,
and before I knew it, I was toe-to-toe with all of
the most important people—by important I mean
they gave the most money—and my presence was
no longer required."

Lynn nodded. "I'm sorry."

"I'm not, actually. I had one bad experience. I'm
sure that kind of thing wouldn't be the case at every
large church. But I wanted to be a pastor. A *real*
pastor." He flashed a grin. "Here I get to do exactly
that."

"How so?"

"These people, for the most part, seem to want
what I have to offer. And they have a great understanding of what it means to love your neighbor."

A smile flickered on her lips. "Even when they
think someone is cheating?"

His smile widened. "Well, I could have offered
to cast out the devils that possessed them, but I

somehow don't think that would have worked as well as your common sense and math."

"Thanks for the vote of confidence. You were looking so uneasy that I was feeling really scared for a few minutes."

"Well, I didn't want them to come to blows. If they had, they'd have made up eventually, but why get to that point in the first place?"

"Good question. So you're happy here?"

"Pretty much so."

"But no wife, no kids."

He looked away for a moment. "I was engaged," he said finally. "She dumped me when I dumped my six-figure job as the pastor of her church."

"But why?"

"Living poor didn't appeal to her. Plus, I lost all the prestige I'd had, at least in her eyes."

"So you're better off without her."

His gaze met hers. "That same could be said of you."

She flushed a little. "I've already figured that out. But it still hurts."

"Trust me, it passes. At some point you're going to thank God for your narrow escape."

"I may already be starting to reach that point." She toyed with her fork. "It still smarts, though."

"Of course it does. But look what you got in exchange."

She lifted a brow.

He spread his arms. "You've come to paradise!"

CHAPTER FOURTEEN

AFTER DINNER, JACK HELPED her clean up, then they moved out back onto her patio. The sky was reddening to the east, the setting sun reflecting off wisps of high cloud that looked almost like horses' tails.

"So we're both runaways," Jack said, leaning back on the chaise to look up at the heaven.

"In a way, I suppose so."

"Everyone here is a runaway."

She turned her head lazily so she could see him. "In what way? Haven't most of these people lived here all their lives?"

"Most of them, sure. But they've been off the island. They've seen the bright lights and conveniences. Some of the youngsters leave for the bigger world, but a surprising number stay right here or come back after they leave."

"They appreciate what they have."

"Must be. Lord knows there couldn't be any

other reason. Folks here work hard and don't have a lot of extras in their lives."

She nodded and joined him in watching the stars begin to appear. "Most seem pretty happy to me."

"I don't know if happy is the word I'd use. They have their ups and downs like everyone else, even their tragedies. What they are is content."

"I wouldn't undervalue contentment either. Happy, contented, pretty much the same thing."

"I guess so." He rolled onto his side and looked at her. "I suppose the thing I like so much about living here is folks expect to have to roll with life's punches. They haven't reached a point where they feel they should somehow be protected from everything."

"That's an interesting way of thinking about it." She paused, pondering. "You know, you might be right."

"How so?"

"Well, it seems like lately people expect to be protected from everything. Nothing should go wrong, and if it does, someone else should have to pay for it. I don't know. I mean, we don't even want to accept the fact that we die eventually. We worry about every new warning about food or drink or…or radiation from cell phones causing brain tumors."

"Does it?" He sounded genuinely interested.

"Research tends to indicate it doesn't."

"Just wondered."

"So did a lot of people. Reasonable question I guess. But you get what I'm saying."

"That I do. But life is inherently risky."

She chuckled. "There's only one way out of it."

"Well, we don't have cell phones on the island. We have a satellite uplink and regular phones. So no one ever worried about that. I haven't noticed people turning into vegetarians, either."

At that she laughed outright. "It probably would be healthier, but how could anybody do that on this island?"

"They'd break the bank trying." He joined her laughter. "I dunno. Since I got here, it's as if things have slowed down. As if sniffing the daisies is as important as anything else. And I know most other folks seem to feel the same way. They get up in the morning, most of them work brutally hard on those fishing boats, then they come home and have a picnic and play poker and hang out at the tavern and just generally..." He searched for the words he wanted.

"Just generally enjoy what they've earned?"

"Yeah, that's a good way of putting it."

She adjusted herself on her own chaise, resettling more comfortably. "That's what I need to learn to do. When I was at PEAR, I never stopped working.

Even when I went home, problems were running through my mind. I dreamed in math symbols."

"Now that *is* bad."

"Yeah. But it seemed normal at the time. Now I'm away from it and I have a variety of things to think about, and I'm having fun doing it. That terrarium was a blast to put together."

"How's it doing?"

"We had to add a little more water and remove a bug with an appetite that would rival Tyrannosaurus rex, because he was eating everything with leaves, but otherwise it's doing great. You ought to come see it."

"I will. I bet the kids check it every day."

She smiled. "That's such a good feeling to have so many of them stopping in before school to see how it's doing."

Just then a voice popped out of the darkness. Zed-the-Bait-Guy's. "Well, lookee who's here. Come on, Hester, let's go visit."

Lynn darted a glance at Jack and saw him do something close to an eye roll. "So much for quiet conversation," he said.

Hester and Zed made their way across Jack's backyard accompanied by the tinkle of glass and a few giggles. Moments later they were sitting in the other two lawn chairs with a bottle of wine and two glasses. Clearly Zed had won the poker game to ask Hester out.

"Want some wine?" Zed asked.

"No thanks," Lynn and Jack answered in unison.

"Good." Zed put the bottle down on the patio. "That was pretty neat what you done today with the royal flush business, teach."

"Thank you. It's just a matter of how you look at things."

"So it seems."

Hester spoke. "What did you do before you came here? Were you a math teacher?"

"I worked at the Princeton Engineering Anomalies Research Lab."

"Whoa," Zed said. "That's pretty fancy."

"We called it PEAR," Lynn said, almost apologetically. She didn't want these folks to think she was hoity-toity or something.

Zed laughed. "That's cute."

"Less of a mouthful," Lynn agreed.

"So what exactly did you do?"

She hesitated. "How much do you really want to know? I mean we worked with quantum physics."

"I've heard about that," Zed said, brightening. "Even saw some shows about it on TV. So you worked with that stuff? I could never understand much of what they were saying."

"Me either," Hester agreed.

"Nor I," Jack said. "But I'd like to hear something about what you did."

Lynn paused for a moment. "Are you really curious, or simply being polite?"

Jack seemed to study her for a moment. This was the point at which every man in her life—save one traitor—had turned tail and ran. "I'm curious, Lynn. I don't know much about science. I'll admit that. But I *am* curious."

His eyes bore no trace of dishonesty. "Okay, then. What do you know about quantum physics?"

"That's the really tiny stuff, right?" he asked.

Lynn nodded. "Exactly. Quantum physics is the study of phenomena at the atomic scale. What particles make up an atom? What are those particles made of? How do they interact? Things like that."

"I understand," Jack said. "So what does PEAR do?"

Lynn smiled. He remembered the name of the project, even for a couple of minutes. Far better than most men she'd talked to. "Well, once you get down to the quantum level—the tiniest pieces of space, time and matter—the universe gets a little strange. It becomes a universe of bounded randomness."

"Hmmm…" he said, considering her words. "You've lost me."

Lynn looked around. This was Treasure Island. Surely someone had a deck of cards. "I need a deck of cards."

Zed reached into his pockets and produced not one but three decks. "Never travel without them. Mind if me and Hester listen in?"

"Why would I?" Lynn asked. She selected ten cards—four Aces, three Deuces, two Threes and one Four—and shuffled them. She held the miniature deck out to Jack. "So what is the top card?"

"I don't know," Jack said. "It could be anything."

"Could it really?" she asked. "Anything? Could it be the Old Maid, or an UNO card or my business card?"

Jack laughed. "Of course not. You didn't put those in there. It's either an Ace, a Deuce, a Trey or a Four."

"But which is it?" she asked, looking at him intently, silently encouraging him to think through the problem.

"We don't know yet," Zed said. "But I play cards often enough to calculate the odds. Four times in ten it will be an Ace, three times in ten a Deuce, and so on."

"Exactly!" Lynn said, smiling wide. "We actually know quite a bit about that top card. We know the range of values it might have, and we know how likely it is to be this value or that value."

"Because we watched you choose the cards," Hester added, looking at Zed with a proud smile. "We know what's in the deck."

Lynn nodded. "Right. That's quantum physics in a nutshell. When you get down to the smallest bits of space and time and matter, it's like a deck of cards. Quantum physics is a set of equations which describes that deck, the range of potential outcomes and the probabilities for this outcome compared to that one. But, like the deck of cards, that all remains suspended as *potential* until a conscious observer looks at it…until the observer draws a card from the deck."

She turned over the top card, the Deuce of Clubs.

"So nothing exists until we look at it?" Jack asked. "That's not physics. That's Immanuel Kant…existential philosophy."

"Sort of," Lynn said. "I said 'a conscious observer.' That needn't be you or me or Zed or Hester, or any human, or even Buster. Anytime a quantum process needs to know, it draws a card. If two atoms try to bond, they have to know where their electrons are, so they can exchange them."

"Okay," Jack said, holding up his hands. "So you're saying every atom is *conscious?*"

"Every atom, every particle, every unit of space-time, yes. That's what the research seems to suggest."

"That makes no sense at all," Zed said. "How can something too tiny to have a brain be conscious?"

"That depends on how we define consciousness," Lynn said. "And right now, it has us all baffled. But we know, from experimental research, that the quantum field exists as waves of potential—like this shuffled deck—until a given event is observed. Only then do we get a particle, a card face-up, and even then we only know what that particle is or where it is...until it goes back into the deck. Then it isn't a particle anymore. It goes back to being a wave of potential in the quantum field."

"That's weird, teach," Zed said.

"That's just the start," Lynn said, smiling. "Now, what if I told you that, if this were a quantum deck of cards, when you drew the next card you would know *either* its rank *or* its suit, but never both?"

"Huh?" Hester cocked her head. "Now that part I don't understand. Can't you read the whole card?"

"Oh, it's not that simple," Lynn said. "With the quantum deck, it's not that we can't read the whole card. It's that the rest of the card *doesn't exist.* If I want to know the suit of the top card, I can draw a card and look, and it will *only* have a spade or a club or a diamond or a heart...but it *won't have* a rank. If I want to know the rank of the top card and I draw a card and look, it will have a rank...but *not* a suit.

Both the suit and rank are properties of the card, but the two properties don't exist at the same moment. It's one or the other, never both."

"My son was telling me about that," Hester said, leaning forward. "That's Heidi…Heidelberg…something…"

"Heisenberg's Uncertainty Principle," Lynn said.

Hester touched her nose as if she were playing charades. "Yeah, that one."

Lynn nodded. "What that tells us is that the universe is *aware,* even at the tiniest levels. If a quantum process needs to know the velocity of an electron, the quantum field potential wave collapses down to an electron with velocity. But if a process needs to know the exact position of an electron, the wave collapses to an electron with position. It's just as if—"

"Like you're drawing to a straight or a flush," Zed said. "If you're drawing to a straight, you don't care what the suit is, so long as you get the right rank. If you're drawing to a flush, you don't care what the rank is, so long as it's your suit."

"Bingo!" Lynn said. "And even the tiniest particles in the universe know whether they're being observed—if anyone is drawing a card from the deck—and the specific properties the observer needs to know at that instant."

She fell silent for a moment. And, amazingly for

this island, no one filled the silence. She looked at Jack, who was studying her intently.

"Wow," he finally said. "Don't take this wrong, but that sounds like science fiction. Is that fact or just theory?"

Lynn cringed. "It's fact, or at least so far as we understand our universe right now. In a few years, when bigger machines make it possible to look at smaller and smaller events, maybe we'll have to refine and revise it. But quantum physics makes astonishingly precise and accurate predictions of events that we can observe and measure, both in laboratories and in the real world. So it's not 'just theory.'"

"I didn't mean…" he began.

"No, it's okay," she said. "My students ask that kind of question all the time. So do most people. As it turns out, that question is precisely what science is about—can we make reliable predictions in the real world, using these equations in this model? If we can, scientists accept that theory as fact…until we get new evidence that shows our predictions aren't as reliable as we need. Then we revise the model. Tweak the equations. Or we find a new model, a new way to look at the problem."

"It's amazing," Hester said, leaning against Zed. "So even the tiniest piece of the universe knows what's going on around it?"

"It seems to," Lynn said. "It seems to even know what we're thinking about. That was my research at Princeton. How human thoughts can change the dimensions of the quantum wave potential. Like if you think about an Ace, will the top card be an Ace?"

Zed chuckled. "Not if I need one to win a pot."

"Oh, I don't know," Hester said, squeezing his hand. "You seem to win sometimes."

"Never feels like it," he replied.

Hester looked at Lynn. "So subatomic particles are aware, but men aren't?"

Lynn laughed. "That's an accurate prediction."

Much as physics was her passion, Lynn was glad that no one wanted to pursue the subject any further. She was quite sure she'd gone deeper into it than any of them really wanted, and for once in her life she was in a place where she *cared* what others thought of her apart from her brain.

"So tell me, teach," Jack said as they leaned back and resumed their study of the stars, so many more now than a few minutes ago, "do the stars look any different to a quantum physicist?"

"Not right now," she said. "I'm off duty. What I see is a majestic night sky."

And she could almost feel Delphine pat her on the back.

CHAPTER FIFTEEN

"WANT TO GO FOR A WALK on the beach?" Jack asked.

Hester and Zed had left a few minutes earlier, giggling like teenagers as they hurried across the lawn to Zed's house.

"Sure," Lynn said, stretching. The moon was beginning to rise, and the night couldn't have been more perfect. "Those two seem to be off to a good start."

"Yes they do." He rose and stretched out a hand to help her to her feet. Again that crackle of electricity ran through her. Not good, she told herself. But it wasn't something she could pull herself away from, either.

He released her hand and they walked side-by-side down the streets. With each passing step, the moon seemed to grow higher, silvering the world. From open windows they could hear voices talking quietly, or occasionally a TV blaring. The closer they drew to the beach, however, the more the sounds changed. Human noises disappeared in the gentle swishing of the surf.

They stepped barefoot into the sand, carrying their shoes, and walked down to the water's edge. The moon-dappled waters glistened, singing their song as they rolled toward shore. *The sea*, thought Lynn, *is alive.* Singing a timeless tune, following rhythms as old as the water itself.

Stepping forward, she let waves lap over her feet, sinking steadily deeper into the wet sand. Jack joined her.

"Do you hear it calling?" she asked.

"The sea? Yes. A siren's song."

She wiggled her toes as yet another warm wave lapped over her. "It's funny."

"What is?"

"I've devoted my whole life to empirical and theoretical science, but when I stand at the edge of the sea, all of that vanishes. I feel the call. I become small and insignificant, and I feel a yearning...." She stopped, not certain how to describe it any better.

"I know what you mean. I have a theory."

She looked at him. "Yes?"

"I think that all the reasons men have used over the centuries for building boats and sailing to far away lands don't explain why individual men become sailors."

She nodded. "I think you may be right."

He took her hand again, and together they began to stroll along the shoreline away from the docks. The shore breeze had begun to blow gently, a caressing touch. Nothing could be any more beautiful than this night.

Finally they were stopped by a rock outcropping, the remnant of one of the volcano's past eruptions. They could go no farther.

"Want to sit here for a while?" Jack asked.

"Sure. It's so beautiful out here. I'm in no hurry to get home."

"Me neither."

The dry sand was at once soft and hard giving just so much before it would give no more. Lynn sat with her arms looped around her knees, watching the hypnotic rhythm of water that appeared to be sprinkled with diamonds.

Then Jack's arm settled around her shoulders and her entire focus changed. The water seemed to recede, and in its place came an acute awareness of the man beside her.

She hovered on a cusp of anticipation so sharp that it hurt. Her limbs grew heavy and everything within her stilled. Even her breathing slowed and grew deep, as if she feared doing anything to jar the mood. A kiss. Was a kiss too much to hope for?

But her body was singing to another rhythm now, one as old as the sea. She pulsed deep within, and every cell of her being yearned.

A kiss….

The breeze stirred, catching her hair and brushing it against her cheek. It was a moment before she realized that Jack's fingers were also caressing her cheek, gently urging her head to tip back. With a sense of wonderful abandon, she let her head fall back, her eyes closed.

A shadow dimmed the moonlight that passed through her eyelids. She knew, in the instant before it happened, that he was about to kiss her.

The touch of his lips was at first gentle, a bee seeking nectar among fragile petals. It was so seductive that everything within her softened and melted. She would not be saying no this night.

He laid her carefully back on the sand, leaning over her as he continued to kiss her more deeply, letting her feel some of his weight on her. Nothing had ever felt so good or so right. Raising her arms, she looped them around his neck, willing him closer and closer.

His tongue found hers, warm and slick, a promise of things to come. She twisted her head, heedless of the sand, trying to bring them closer.

He broke the kiss, staying close enough for her to feel his breath on her face. "You're so beautiful," he murmured huskily. Had he not been so close, the waves would have drowned his voice.

She opened her eyes and saw one side of his face lighted by the moon, the other in shadow. This must be a dream....

Then his head moved, and he swept his eyes over her. The gaze was almost like a physical touch, causing her to tingle and ache all the more. Then his hand followed.

She caught and held her breath. First, the light touch of his fingers at her throat, a soft caress of skin on skin. She could have enjoyed that simple touch for hours, but his hand was sliding lower. She caught her breath again as he cupped her breast through the layers of her blouse and bra. The excitement that shot through her made the cloth seem irrelevant. A groan of sheer delight escaped her and she heard him chuckle quietly as if pleased.

He kneaded her flesh, heightening her arousal until he could find the nipple through the cloth. Then his touch became even more knowing, brushing back and forth until finally she could contain herself no longer and writhed against him.

He kissed her again, continuing his exquisite torture of her breast. Then...then...when she was as helpless as she could be, his slid his hand lower and cupped her between the legs.

Instantly she felt as if she were on a welder's arc, bowing upward and clamping her legs around his hand. Yes, oh yes....

He squeezed gently, then harder, driving her absolutely wild. His mouth left hers and closed over her peaked breast, through the cloth, sucking and nibbling.

The mindless drive for pleasure took over. Her fingers dug into his shoulders, her body reached toward him, everything forgotten but the need for culmination.

Now...now...now... It was a mindless chant as the wind and sea rushed in her ears, as she forgot every restraint and pressed mindlessly toward fulfillment. She thought she heard a laugh on the wind, his perhaps, a triumphal sound, but she didn't care...didn't care....

With a cry she surged over the peak, exploding in a shower of sparks. Arms closed around her, holding her tight as she slowly settled back to earth.

WHEN SHE RETURNED to herself, her head was buried in his neck, his arms held her tight, and she was vaguely aware that her back felt damp and a little cold. Sand had worked up into her shorts. All those troublesome reality things had returned, and she didn't want them. She didn't want anything to impinge on this interlude.

He seemed to understand, because he continued to hold her close, almost rocking her, cradling her head on his shoulder. Physics, she thought hazily, had proved that two objects never really touch. But they were touching. To hell with physics.

"Brawwwk!"

She jerked.

"It's just the bird," he said. "Ignore it."

She snuggled closer.

"Brawwwk!" came the cry again. "Storm warning, you idiots. Pay attention and get home."

"Right," Jack said, nuzzling Lynn's skin.

"I'll tell everyone what I saw!" the bird announced. "Every...last...detail! That will help to explain why they found your *dead bodies* on the beach after the storm!"

"Oh hell," Lynn said. "He'll do it, too."

There was no avoiding it. Reality returned with a resounding thud. She tipped her head back and looked up at Jack. "I think my aunt was less annoying."

"Idiots," said the bird. "Mating is good, but getting caught outside in a tropical blow is not. Get home now."

Jack trembled, then broke out laughing. "Okay, okay, birdbrain."

"The only birdbrain around here," the parrot said archly, "is you. I'm going back to Buster. He's smart enough to have already taken cover."

Suddenly feeling embarrassed, Lynn wiggled free and sat up. "The wind *is* picking up."

It was. Noticeably.

"Damn bird is right," Jack said, very unpreacher-like. "I can smell it. And look at the chop. We'd better hurry."

A pleasant tropical evening had suddenly turned wild. Jack helped her up, then hand-in-hand they ran barefoot down the beach toward town. By the time they reached the piers, salt spray was being flung up at them.

"This is coming on fast," Jack remarked as they helped one another to wash the sand from their feet with the dock hose.

Shoes on again, they continued running until they stood on Lynn's porch. She was just about to invite him in when he dropped a hard kiss on her mouth. "I've got to go put some things away at the church and at my house. The way this feels, you need to bring in your lawn chairs."

Then he was gone, dashing into a darkness that was no longer mitigated by moonlight.

Lynn stared after him, uncertain how to feel. Then a gust from the storm moved one of the potted plants on her porch a couple of inches. Sighing she bent to pick two of them up.

Deal with the tropical storm first, she told herself. Then there will be plenty of time to deal with the emotional storm.

THE RAIN WAS PRETTY heavy. When Lynn turned on her porch light, she could watch the hills of dirt to either side of her trench being washed away, both back into the trench and into the neighbors' yards. No question but what Harv Cullinan and his crew were going to have a time now filling that in. It gave her a sense of the most unholy glee.

How many days had it been since they'd torn up her house to fix a single pipe? She didn't even want to count for fear it would make her angry again.

She should go to bed, she thought as she listened to the wind and rain batter the house. But the entire evening had left her almost on edge in ways she couldn't quite put her finger on.

She supposed she was missing her work at Princeton, but it was more than that. Maybe Jack would come back tonight.

But she knew he wouldn't. Neither of them wanted to risk it. What had happened had...just happened. Things happened. Especially things like that. But it took a lot more than mere attraction to build a relationship, and she figured they both had enough experience and maturity to recognize that.

Having settled that with herself, she made a cup of hot chocolate, settled in her living room in the dark, and proceeded to remember each and every touch she had shared with Jack that night. Like a teen in the throes of a crush, she told herself, but no amount of argument could prevent her from remembering…reliving…savoring.

The embarrassment she had briefly felt was gone. She hadn't been alone on that beach. They had both shared the experience. How much further it might have gone except for the storm and the bird, she had no idea. Maybe she ought to thank the darn parrot for bringing the warning, because she didn't think she was ready to deal with the fallout from complete consummation.

What was it Auntie Delphine used to tell her? Be careful who you have sex with, because a woman's heart, unlike a man's, tends to fall in love with a sex partner.

A blunt statement, and after her last experience, she was fairly certain it was true. Her ex-fiancé couldn't possibly have loved her or he wouldn't have stolen her work. Of that she was certain.

But oh, had Lynn been in love. So in love that she'd been blind. In retrospect, as humiliating as it was, she could see the signs she had missed, some of them as big as road signs on the interstate.

Sighing, she curled up tighter and sipped her cocoa. She felt cold for some reason, something she hadn't felt since moving here. Must be the storm.

Then she knew otherwise, for faintly glowing in the dead-dark living room, she saw Delphine. At first merely a vague light, then the full apparition, this time in a purple toga-like thing, with purple hair. Funny, she never would have guessed Delphine had such an interest in wild clothing.

"You know," Delphine said sternly, "I've never seen anyone like you for throwing away an opportunity!"

Great, thought Lynn. Now she was in for it.

"Look," Lynn said as soon as her aunt was fully materialized, the only light in the otherwise pitch dark night, "I don't want to hear it. Some things are *my* business."

"What in the world do you think I'm going to say?"

Lynn could feel her cheeks heat. "Never mind." That last thing she wanted to do was to give Delphine an opening. "You're making the room cold."

"That's not me. It's the storm."

"Oh. I need to get a sweater."

"In a minute," Delphine said. "I just want to say one thing."

Lynn sighed and waited impatiently.

"When a man wants to be a knight in shining armor, let him."

"What in the world are you talking about?"

Delphine smiled. "It's really rather fun over here. No one would ever have let me wear something like this or dye my hair purple."

"They couldn't have stopped you."

Delphine leaned forward. "My point precisely."

Then, with a flicker, she was gone.

So what was that all about? Lynn thought. What had she done or not done to earn Delphine's disapproval *this* time? It wasn't as if she'd shoved Jack away. Quite to the contrary, she would still be lying contentedly in his arms, were it not for the rudely delivered storm warning. And once the warning was given, hadn't she done exactly what Jack had suggested: come home and clean her patio, moving potential missiles inside? So what, *exactly*, had she done wrong?

It was, she thought, very difficult to please Aunt Delphine. It always had been. Perhaps what was why Lynn had always been such a driven student, and later a driven woman. Even the slightest momentary lapse of diligence would leave her lagging behind Delphine's expectations, expectations that quickly became Lynn's own. The hour spent listening to Brahms, an hour she could have spent studying, became an hour lost.

In a ninth-grade history class, she had tumbled over Napoleon's maxim: I can regain a lost mile, but I can never regain a lost minute. In an instant, the world had come clear for her, or so it had seemed at the time, and that maxim had become her touchstone for the rest of her educational career. In the years since, she had lost many miles—transient opportunities to enjoy herself—but she had lost precious few minutes.

The one time she had lost minutes—she'd taken a week off for Delphine's funeral—her lover and research partner had seized the opportunity to steal every mile she'd ever won: her files and her research.

In a moment, her feelings came clear in a way that shocked and horrified her. At some level, she now saw, she had blamed Delphine for the loss of her work. If only Lynn hadn't had to leave work at that critical time, her partner would not have betrayed her. She'd still be at Princeton. She'd still be in love. She'd have received the credit and accolades and tenure she deserved.

Balderdash!

It was absurd. Delphine's death had merely provided the opportunity her two-timing lover had been waiting for. If it hadn't been Delphine's funeral, he would have found some other opportunity.

"I'm so sorry, Aunt Delphine."

The words were out before she really thought them. But Delphine did not answer. Or if she did, the answer was lost in the grinding, groaning, shuddering crash that built to a deafening roar.

Lynn was rolling out of her chair and crawling toward the door as the roof split open above her.

CHAPTER SIXTEEN

JACK HEARD THE CRASH as he was jogging back from the church. It was either his house or Lynn's. And because Lynn's house had been torn open by the plumbers…

He leaned forward into the wind, lifting his knees and driving harder as his jog broke into a sprint. Although he could not see through the rain-cloaked darkness, he had no difficulty visualizing what he would find. And what he saw in his mind's eye triggered a surge of adrenaline that, for the next two minutes, peeled away twenty of his thirty-eight years and twenty pounds and restored to him the body of his youth.

The wet *thwap-thwap-thwap* of his jogging shoes on the pavement merged with the rhythmic expulsions of breath and the hammering of his heart. He was aware of that peculiar warp of time that came from stress and exertion, where the world seemed to happen in slow motion, yet still just fast enough that he could not quite catch up to his fears.

As he rounded the final corner and peered into the darkness, those fears were confirmed. Lynn's house had nearly split in two, first sagging out and then falling in on itself. And she'd been in there.

He shouldn't have left her. He'd *known* that her house was weakened by the plumbing work. He should never have sent her home alone to put away her patio furniture. He should have gone with her, or taken her with him to the church. But he'd been so anxious to put distance between them—for his own emotional reasons having to do with his longings—that he'd sent her into danger.

He'd been a fool. And Lynn may have paid for his folly with her life.

His heart sank as his feet splashed across her lawn, and he remembered the existence of the trench—now submerged and invisible in the standing water on the lawn—in the split second before his right foot plunged into it.

The trench wasn't that deep, and he could stand in it. What he couldn't do, given the sodden ground of its walls, was climb out. Lynn was mere yards away, in that pile of rubble, perhaps even this moment crying out for him, and he could not hear her above the roar of the wind, nor could he reach her to try to dig her out.

He felt, rather than heard, the muffled splash at the far end of the trench, and recognized it from countless nature shows he'd watched. *Buster!* And in the darkness, Jack was no longer the mostly trusted human companion. He was simply an animal thrashing around in the water, which to a crocodilian brain was nothing less than ringing the dinner bell.

The phrase *Hobson's choice* came to mind. If Jack held still, perhaps Buster would ignore him, but he would stay in the trench while the weight of cinder block and water crushed the life out of Lynn. If he fought his way out of the trench, he would be in a race against the blinding *snap* of Buster's jaws, a race he could not hope to win.

"Brawwwwk!"

"Not now!" Jack yelled, waving at the fluttering gray form in front of him.

"Would you hold *still!*" the bird screamed. "We're trying to help you, you stupid human!"

He was, he realized, reduced to this: whether to trust a bird to both understand and communicate the intent of an alligator, so that he could, maybe, rescue a woman he had come to…love.

It was the word *love* that stilled his thrashing legs. No, not possible, he decided immediately.

And in the moment after he was still, he felt the hard, spiny form rise between his legs, raising him with what seemed effortless ease, propelling him toward the end of the trench and then depositing him onto the lawn.

"How did you *ever* get to the top of the food chain?" the bird demanded.

"Opposable thumbs," Jack said, scrambling to his feet. "They helped us wring the necks of lesser creatures."

"You don't have to get *personal!*" the bird said.

But he was already beyond hearing it, diving into the rubble, calling out Lynn's name. Did he hear a faint voice reply? Was it only his imagination? He had no training for such work, but he set himself to it with a vengeance, pulling at pieces of wall, lowering his head into crevasses to listen for sounds of life above the howling wind.

As he dug, he felt a growing, persistent tug at his leg. He turned to see Buster mouthing his foot. "Let go, Buster! She's in here! I have to find her!"

But Buster did not let go. Instead, his jaws squeezed harder, not quite to the point of penetrating skin, leaving no doubt that Buster could, and would, do exactly that if Jack did not comply.

"Buster, you don't understand!"

But Buster began to back away from the rubble,

still holding Jack's foot in his mouth, forcing Jack to follow or risk joining One-Hand Hanratty as the second island resident to lose a limb to the alligator's maw. Atop the pile that had been Lynn's house, the bird screeched, not in English but in what was apparently Alligator, for Buster looked up and seemed to nod, much to Jack's consternation as clamped jaws shifted on his foot.

"Ouch!" Jack yelled.

"Oooommmmm," Buster said, looking at Jack and obviously apologizing. He looked back at the parrot, who seemed to be dancing in and out of the pile, droplets of water flying from wing tips.

"There?" Jack asked.

"Duh!" the bird said.

The bird, Jack thought, must have learned its speech from the rudest person in history. Still, he and Buster went to the parrot and Jack set himself to work. His hands grew raw as he piled rubble onto Buster's strong back. The beast then crawled off of the pile and rolled over in the back yard, dumping one load before returning for another. All the while, the parrot offered encouragement, in words that would have elicited violence from any other sentient being.

They were, Jack realized, digging into what remained of Lynn's kitchen. But when finally they reached the floor and Jack was able to look around, there was neither any sign of Lynn nor any sign that she had been trapped here.

There was, however, a small box, which the parrot tore into with glee, spilling seeds across the wet floor.

"It'th abouth thime!" the bird said around seeds. It paused to swallow. "Saving your life made me ravenous! I might add that ravenous comes from my cousin, the raven, because while people talk about eating like birds, if you actually did eat like birds you would weigh three hundred pounds...."

"I was digging for *this?*" Jack asked, dumbfounded. "For...for *bird seed?*"

Behind him, Buster also let out a shuddering rumble, as if he too felt betrayed. If the bird had no fear of Jack, Buster's quiet bellow certainly got its attention.

"Of course!" the bird said. "I *told* you! Saving your life made me hungry! Don't you humans *ever* listen?"

"But...what about Lynn?" Jack asked.

"Mmmmhmmmmmm," Buster agreed menacingly.

"Oh, you were looking for *her?*" the parrot asked. "Sheesh. Why didn't you say so?"

"Grrrrrr," Jack said, beginning to believe that this bird might drive him to do something he'd never conceived possible: kill one of God's creatures.

"Oh, she's next door," the parrot said. "At Zed's, with Hester."

"She got out?" Jack asked, mouth agape.

"Duh!" the parrot said. "Now let me eat my dinner!"

"Urrrmmmmmmm," Buster growled.

"There's a chicken for you in her fridge," the bird said. "It's under *that* pile."

But Jack was already scrambling out of the rubble.

Lynn was safe?

"IT'S GOING TO COST me a fortune!" Lynn said, looking at the small stack of poker chips in front of her.

"It's only twenty to call," Zed said.

"I meant my house," Lynn replied. "My house is...gone!"

"But you're not," Hester said, sipping a glass of wine. "Lucky you heard the house begin to shift and got out of there. But it's still twenty to call, dear."

"But my house!"

"Will be good as new once Harv and his cousins get done with it," Zed said. "Better than new. And what's more, it won't cost you a cent, I'm sure. Harv will see that it wouldn't have happened if the storm hadn't hit you in the middle of repairs. Regardless, you can't do a thing about it right now. So…it's twenty to call."

He was right, of course. And Lynn knew she ought to be grateful for having escaped before the house collapsed. Still, she found it difficult to simply put the last hour out of her mind and focus on something so trivial as a game of cards. Then again, on Treasure Island, poker might be a form of therapy as well as a tool of politics.

Either way, she held the Ace and Jack of Hearts, and there was the Ace of Clubs on the table, along with two other hearts. If she had learned anything in her time here, top pair with a four-flush was a hand worth betting. "I'll rai—"

"Lynn!"

The voice reached her a split second after the front door slammed open, freezing her words in her throat. She looked up to see a creature from a bad 1950s horror movie in the doorway, dripping mud, caked over with cinder-block dust, striped by rivulets where water had run from his hair over his face.

"Jack!" Zed said. "Should we deal you in?"

The creature heaved. It shook. It made strangled sounds.

Lynn started to rise from her chair, afraid that Jack might be having some kind of stroke.

"I," said the creature, "just spent the last forty minutes digging around in the ruins of *your* house, trying to find your body before it was too late, being directed by the parrot from hell. And do you know what that parrot was directing me to?"

"Uh, no," she said, still half out of her seat.

"A damn box of freaking bird seed!"

She couldn't say anything. Apparently neither could Zed nor Hester, for the room was utterly silent save for the raging storm outside.

The creature moved, pulling out a seat at Zed's kitchen table. "Deal me in."

"Um," said Hester, "wouldn't you like a shower first?"

"Oh." Jack looked down at himself, then he rose and left by the way of the back door.

"Good heavens," Hester said. "Has he lost his mind?"

"I think," Zed said, "that he just faced a nightmare. Give him a minute to calm down."

It took five minutes, but when Jack returned, the storm had apparently scrubbed him clean. He looked at Zed. "Towel?"

"Sure, man," said Zed, hopping up. "And let me wipe that chair off before you sit again."

A couple of minutes later, wrapped in some riotously colored beach towels, Jack sat at the table with them. Zed re-apportioned all the chips so they were starting even, then dealt.

"Bird seed," Jack muttered as each of his hole cards slapped down before him. "Bird seed!"

Lynn reached out hesitantly and touched his hand lightly. "You're bleeding and cut up."

"Believe it or not, parts of your house were actually *nailed* together. Not that you tell by the way it looks now."

"I'll get some bandages," Hester said swiftly, leaving the table.

"I'll help her," Zed agreed. He scampered off after her.

"I'm sorry, Jack," Lynn said.

He looked at her. "Why should *you* be sorry? It's not your fault your house collapsed. Or that that bird led me on a useless chase when he knew all the while you were here."

Lynn gasped. "How awful!"

Jack cocked his head. "I think it might be wise to consider that conscience isn't a part of a bird's brain."

"That wouldn't be surprising."

"One of God's innocents," Jack said sourly. "He was almost one of God's *dead* innocents when I found all he was directing me to was bird seed."

"I can imagine," she said soothingly. Then, all of a sudden she remembered what Delphine said. "I'm so grateful to you."

He arched a brow. "To me? Why? I didn't do anything."

"Yes, you did," she said. "You tried to save my life. You risked your own neck delving into that heap of rubble to save me."

He flushed visibly. "Well, Buster saved *me* and helped me search."

"Admittedly," Lynn said, "it would have been far more satisfying to dig *me* out, rather than bird seed—"

"Stop right there," he said. "Not another word. I may be ticked off about spending forty minutes searching rubble for bird seed, but I am not the *least* disappointed I didn't have to rescue you. I thank God you weren't in there."

She smiled, then bent to kiss his battered hands. "Thank you," she said. "Thank you so much."

"Ahem."

Zed and Hester were back with a box of adhesive bandages, some tape and a few gauze pads. The cuts were easily dealt with, but the rawness of his palms proved a little more difficult.

"Hey," Jack said, "you keep that up and I won't be able to hold my cards."

Zed laughed, and the balloon of tension finally burst.

Moments later they were all laughing, though none of them could have begun to say why.

CHAPTER SEVENTEEN

A COUPLE OF HOURS later, Lynn was sleeping in Jack's bed, while Jack sprawled on his sofa. He wished he could sleep, but this night had been just too much to let him close his eyes. First he had to patch his heart, surround it in Kevlar, whatever was necessary to avoid the feelings he was beginning to have for Lynn.

And secondly... Secondly what? Oh, yeah, he was gonna take Harv Cullinan by his collar and give him a good dressing down. Lynn had lost everything tonight because that man had started a job he wasn't ready to finish.

And where the hell was she supposed to stay now? Other than the casino hotel, small and entirely too expensive, there was the town's one other motel. Whether or not people ever stayed there, Jack still didn't know. What he *did* know was that no one on the island ever saw a cockroach because they all lived at that motel.

And she couldn't stay with him. Preachers didn't do that stuff, even on Treasure Island. Plus, she was a teacher, and in a community this size, she was as much a role model as he was.

Or maybe not. At the moment he was tempted to blow all that stuff off and just explode into…into what?

Why did he feel like exploding? Everything was fine now, except one house. But every time he closed his eyes, all he could see was the rubble and a vision of Lynn's pale unconscious face suddenly appearing when he lifted a board.

He sat up. This would not do. The storm still raged outside, though he had the sense it was weakening a bit. He still had electricity which surprised him because Lynn had said her power had gone out shortly before the collapse. Probably because the house had shifted and broken the incoming power line or something.

Sighing, he went to his overflowing bookcase and looked for something to read. Books were his single vice. Apart from three copies of the Bible, he had both fiction and non-fiction, ranging from Bible history to the latest thriller. When things got too crowded, he gave a few books away, then went back online and ordered new ones.

He had a couple that had come in recently that

he hadn't opened yet. He reached for one that was sort of a sci-fi thriller cross and settled back on the couch.

He opened the book, skipped the acknowledgements for later and tried to read the first page.

And all he could see was Lynn's pale face. Dead or unconscious. It hadn't happened, but he kept seeing it.

Damn it.

He bent his head and forced himself to read. The book might as well have been written in Russian. Finally he slammed it closed.

He ought to be exhausted. The adrenalin should have worn off by now. But it hadn't. Not even close. If anything, now that things were comparatively quiet, having left Zed's poker game and with Lynn now asleep, all that remained was the adrenalin coursing through him, spurring the hairs on his neck to attention, his heartbeat now a drumbeat in his ears.

"Can't sleep either?"

He looked up to see Lynn standing at the end of the hallway, the T-shirt he had given her rumpled to her skin, pillow creases on her face. "No. I'm still too wired."

"So am I," she said. "That sound…"

He kicked himself, realizing that he hadn't even

considered what the collapse of her house must have been like for her. He'd been so focused on his own fear for her that he hadn't stopped to think of what she must have felt.

"I'm an idiot," he said.

"Why?" Lynn asked.

"All I can remember is looking for you. Until you said that, I'd totally ignored what you're going through."

"No, you're not an idiot," Lynn said, coming over to sit next to him on the couch. "There's a huge difference, and I'd rather have been in my shoes than in yours."

"How can you—"

"When the house started to shift," Lynn said, "I knew I had to get out. I knew where I was. I knew where *out* was. There was no one else to worry about. Just run-dive-crawl for the door as fast as I could. Zed heard it as it happened, and by the time I got outside, he and Hester were waiting for me. I knew I was safe. But you…"

Jack nodded. He took a long breath, trying to decide whether to say anything. Finally, he could no longer hold back the impulse. "I thought I'd lost you."

"I'm sorry."

"And it's almost funny. You might have lost *me*

if it weren't for Buster and that damn bird. Would you believe I fell in the trench in your front lawn?"

"That would explain the mud," Lynn said, smiling.

"I couldn't climb out. Then I heard Buster go into the water and I was sure he was going to attack. I mean, a thrashing animal in the water. That's prey, right?"

"Ordinarily," she said.

"But he hadn't come to eat me. He'd come to rescue me. Swam right up underneath me and once I finally held still for a moment, he lifted me up as easy as can be and dropped me on solid, if not dry, land."

"He's quite amazing," Lynn said, as if unsure how else to respond.

"He is," Jack said. "But do you know what finally got me to hold still? What finally got me to stop thrashing and trying to save myself?"

"The bird?"

He shook his head. "No. One word."

"Oh no."

"Oh yes."

"Jack…"

He held up a hand. "I know, Lynn. I don't want it either. I mean, I do…but…"

"Exactly," Lynn said. "Isn't everything crazy enough already without that, too?"

He nodded. "Yeah. Isn't it?"

"And yet…"

"Yeah. And yet. And you have this mess of stuff from back at Princeton to deal with. I won't even think of boring you again with my life story. Suffice it to say there's a reason I escaped to Treasure Island, and my escape wasn't entirely voluntary. Christians can be very…un-Christian."

She cocked her head, a faint smile brightening her face. "Let's just not go there. It's not a place either of us wants to go again. In the meantime, I'm homeless. I don't even have a change of clothing."

"We'll remedy that fast," he promised her. "I know this island. Once folks see what happened, you'll be showered with clothing and everything else they can spare. Admittedly, none of it might be to your taste…."

"I'm not picky about that kind of thing, honestly. For years I lived in neo-classic dorm style. The prettiest thing I've had in years was the furniture in my now-demolished living room, and that was only because I got a bug to recover the cushions and make matching curtains from some fabric I found in town."

"You know, that's actually kind of sad. All that work and it's gone."

"It's not the worst that could have happened, by far." She tried to smile, but to her evident horror, tears spilled forth instead. Despite their decision just moments ago not to get involved, he drew her into his arms and tried to comfort her.

"It must have been terrifying," he murmured, stroking her hair. "I know how scared I was, and I wasn't even in the house when it fell."

"I didn't have time to be scared until after I got to Zed's. Then it hit me. But before I could start shaking too badly, he pulled out the cards and started a game."

"It's the Treasure Island version of an English cup of tea."

A choked laugh escaped her. "I'm sorry. I'm being a baby."

"I don't think so. Not at all." He continued stroking her, making soothing sounds. She hiccupped a few times, and he could feel the shoulder of his shirt grow damp.

"Let it all out," he said. "Hey, I may not be a scientist, but I studied some psychology when I was in divinity school. You know what?"

"What?"

"In the last year, from what I can tell, you've been through four of the top five stressors in life."

"What?"

"Well, there's your aunt's death. I'm not sure how to rank her return on the scale."

An almost-laugh escaped her. "Make her number five."

"Fair enough, although I think she may get bumped. Where was I? Oh, yeah. Her death. Then your relationship with your fiancé blew up, in part because of betrayal, so that takes number two. Maybe number three as well, as I think about it."

"Delphine's return is going to get bumped."

"It's beginning to look that way." He was relieved to see her tears slowing.

"Okay, so we have death and the end of a relationship topped by a serious betrayal. But it doesn't stop there. No. You have a major job change *and* a major move to a strange place." He held up a hand, ticking them on his fingers. "Heavens, we've already reached five of the top stressors."

"That's why they tell you in public-speaking classes never to tell people you're going to give them a numbered list. They count."

"I screwed up."

"Royally."

"Nothing unusual in that. Okay, so we're at five, and Delphine's return is about to get bumped even lower."

"Yeah?"

"Yeah. Your house collapsed on top of your head. So Delphine's now down to seven."

"Maybe we can move her lower."

He gave her a quick squeeze. "I don't know if we

really want to do that. I mean, you've been through a real wringer in the past year. Enough to push most people over the edge and into the hands of a shrink with lots of pills. In fact, any *one* of those things can cause a major depression."

"I don't feel depressed."

"Which is amazing. But my point is, if you want to shatter for a few moments, feel free. You've certainly earned it."

"My house already did that for me."

He heard the feeble attempt at humor in her voice, and he wondered if she was still in shock. Or maybe she was just as amazing as he was beginning to think.

"Yeah," he said after a moment. "And just wait until I get my hands on Harv Cullinan."

He felt her shake her head against his shoulder. "He didn't know there was going to be a storm."

"He also shouldn't have ripped up things he wasn't ready to repair. Not only did he weaken your house by ripping out walls, but digging that trench undermined your foundation. Dirt that should have been under your house washed into the trench. I know because I was swimming in it."

She sighed, as if letting go of a major weight. "I was lucky tonight."

"Thank God. Because I sure was an idiot."

"What do you mean?"

"I should have thought of all that before I left you there and ran off to look after the church."

"What, you're required to be psychic now?"

"It was just a matter of common sense."

"In retrospect. Did *I* think of it either? Nope. So, don't beat yourself up. I was in a better position to realize the danger than you were. I was the one standing there watching the dirt wash back into the trench. I should have realized a collapse was possible. And when it comes to that, you're lucky Buster got you out of there, because the whole thing was probably ready to collapse in on *you*."

"I hadn't thought about that."

"So let's not beat ourselves up," she suggested.

"No," he agreed. "Let's save that for Harv." Besides, with every passing moment he was growing more aware of the woman in his arms, consequences be damned. Then she startled him.

She nuzzled his neck. "Come to bed with me please, Jack? If neither of us is going to sleep, we might as well not do what we're not doing."

"That," he said, "could *only* make sense to a scientist."

Lynn nipped at his earlobe. "So trust in science."

"Just for tonight," he said. "I am, after all, still a man of the cloth."

Her hand slipped down his belly to his shorts. "Then let's get the cloth out of the way."

CHAPTER EIGHTEEN

They got the cloth out of the way. They got it out of the way with an abandon Jack would never have believed himself capable of. Apparently Lynn was as astonished as he was, because when he was able to see again, she looked as stunned as he felt.

It was as if all barriers had fallen. Both of them strove to please the other in every way possible, exploring every conceivable sensitive place with fingers, then lips, then tongues. His entire body throbbed with an urge for completion beyond anything he had ever known. He became need, beyond which nothing else existed.

The only sounds in the room were heavy breathing, soft murmurs of "here" or "harder" or "please…"

He lost himself so utterly that when they at last collapsed onto the sheets, tightly entwined, he didn't know where he left off and where she began.

And then, just as the shudder that had racked him

began to ease and reality began to return, Lynn snapped upright and said, "Delphine, get out of here!"

Jack, astonished, scrambled to pull the sheets up over himself. "Where...what...?" Talk about a bucket of cold water.

"She's gone," Lynn said after a moment, slumping beside him. "I'm sorry. So sorry."

So was he, he thought as he cradled her close. So was he.

And what the devil was he thinking? A preacher couldn't have an affair with a schoolteacher, not even here.

But how could he possibly give her up?

Only one solution presented itself, but he had the feeling that if he offered it, she would probably run away in terror.

So he remained silent, holding her, waiting for the world to right itself.

And wondering if Delphine was always going to pop in like this.

Feeling glum, he stared into the dark.

CHAPTER NINETEEN

"SHE'S ON A MISSION," Lynn said, now propped on her elbows beside Jack in the sweat-drenched sheets. "She *says* it's a mission from God. That's your province, yes?"

"Umm…" Jack wasn't sure where this was going, nor was he sure he wanted to know.

"Well, it's supposed to be," Lynn said. "I do itty-bitty quantum stuff. You do God stuff."

"You do…more than that," Jack said, stroking her nipple, remembering what she had just given him. *Wow* did not begin to approach it.

"I'm serious," she said, nudging his hand away.

"So am I."

She grasped his hand in hers and kissed each fingertip. "I" (kiss) "promise" (kiss) "more" (kiss) "of" (kiss) "that. But first, we *must* deal with Delphine. I can't even have a toe-curling, mind-blowing climax without her being there. And whatever it might have seemed a few minutes ago, I'm *not* such a nymphet that I want to have a threesome with a ghost!"

"Umm…" Jack banished the thought as quickly as it came. This was not the time for universal male fantasies, even those he dared never to voice. "I…umm…"

"So she's doing God stuff and that's *your* job. You have to figure out what she's doing and make it stop!"

"Lynn, I'm not sure I can…."

"Ahem," Lynn said, her eyes fixing on his in a way that left him no doubt that she could not be dissuaded. "If we're going to do this sex thing, it has to be *us*. *Just* us. *Not* with my nosy spinster aunt sitting in the bed beside us."

"So how do you propose I handle this?" Jack asked.

"I've not the slightest idea," Lynn said. "That's your job. Like I said, I do itty-bitty quanta stuff."

"And you think I've figured out the God stuff more completely than you've figured out the quantum stuff? If so, I have news for you."

"Then you need to get busy and figure it out," Lynn said. She pointed to his groin. "Because we're not doing *that* again until I'm sure we have some privacy."

"From what you've said, I'm not sure that's even

possible," Jack said. "Delphine said they're not quite so concerned about privacy up there."

"*They* might not be," Lynn said. "But *they* aren't supposed to be letting us know they're watching, either. Delphine needs to learn her place. She's breaking the rules."

"Well, there is that."

"And God is all-powerful, right?"

"You mean as compared to Delphine?" he asked with a wink. That brought her up short. Her lips compressed as she seemed to ponder a new possibility. "Remember that the Bible was written pre-Delphine, Lynn. I'm not sure the prophets ever considered someone like her."

"Oh please!" Lynn said. "Don't tell me that Delphine has upset the entire power structure in Heaven."

He whistled innocently.

"Jack!" she said, thumping his chest gently. "Don't tease me like this. I'm not kidding. One moment I was so totally lost in you, lost in us, *consumed* in us. And then *she* burst in. It's maddening!"

"This is not a problem I've encountered before," Jack said. "It will require study."

"So study!"

"Okay," he said. He bent down and kissed her earlobe. "Let's start here...."

Lynn rolled out of the bed, fists clenched, and when Jack looked up he saw real tears in her eyes. "You don't get it! I'm not kidding! I felt…violated!"

His heart caught in his chest. No, she wasn't kidding. This was serious. "Lynn, I'm sorry."

But the words were lost as she strode from the bedroom, slamming the door behind her, leaving him alone on the bed, feeling like an insensitive boor.

Lynn Reilly was an incredible woman. There was no longer the slightest doubt of that. She was brilliant and charming and, not incidentally, a truly amazing lover.

She might also be nutty as a fruitcake. Either that, or they really had just shared a threesome with a ghost.

Jack wasn't sure which prospect he found more frightening. But somehow, he had to sort it out. Because he knew one thing for certain. He could never again look at Lynn Reilly without wanting her in his bed and in his life. If that meant sorting out God stuff with a dead aunt, then that's what he'd have to do.

But how?

THE EASTERN SKY WAS lightening, the storm gone as if it had never been. Instead of the usual stirring at the dock, however, the town had begun to gather at Lynn's crumbled house.

Thus, when she stepped out of Jack's, wearing the only clothes she had—one of Jack's T-shirts and a pair of shorts from last night—she came face-to-face with a goodly portion of the island's population.

She didn't know who she was madder at, Delphine or Jack. Regardless, she didn't want to be seen leaving Jack's house first thing in the morning…by everyone in town.

Too late.

A couple of hundred heads turned her way and she froze. But before she could react in any other way, a woman's voice called out, "Thank God you're all right, Lynn!"

It was one of the other teachers from the school, Pat Limon, and the crowd parted to let her through. Before Lynn knew it, she was wrapped in a bear hug.

"What an awful night you must have had, honey. I saw that house and I thought for sure you were dead."

"I got out in time," Lynn said, hugging her back. "Zed took me in and we played cards most of the night. Then Jack offered me a bed while he was kind enough to take the couch."

Too much explaining? Probably. But the questions were there on all those faces, and none of them likely believed her anyway.

"But what are you going to do?" Pat asked, standing back. "This is awful. Everything you owned was in there!"

Lynn grimaced. "Not everything," she muttered, thinking of Delphine. "But I wonder how much all that plumbing work had to do with that mess."

Pat turned and joined her in staring at the collapsed house. "From the look of it, the place slipped forward, probably because the trench weakened the ground underneath. And then with that rain…"

"That's what I'm thinking." She stepped off Jack's porch with Pat and moved closer to both the crowd and house. "I wonder if I'll be able to find any of my clothes in there." Then she laughed, feeling slightly hysterical. "At least the backhoe is already here to clean up the mess!"

To her surprise, her neighbors laughed along with her, and a few of them even patted her back as if she'd said something wonderful. But looking at the heap of tumbled house, with only small portions of it still recognizable as having been a dwelling once upon a time, she didn't feel much like laughing for real.

No matter how she tried to minimize it, the fact

remained that she was now homeless. Even the sparkle of the sun on the waterlogged wreckage seemed to highlight that fact.

Worse, what had been her home was now becoming something close to a shrine to the community spirit of this bizarre place. For while ordinarily she might be thrilled at the prospect of neighbors helping neighbors in time of need, on Treasure Island that became something altogether different than she would have imagined, as people she had never or only briefly met set themselves to the task of picking through the wreckage of her home to rescue her personal—no, make that her *most* personal—belongings.

"I found your bras," Zed said, emerging from the pile holding a bundle of dirt- and grit-stained fabric over his head. "I'm sure your panties are around here somewhere."

"Forget it," Lynn said. "I'll buy new ones."

"Nonsense," Zed objected. "No reason spending good money when you don't have to. We'll find them."

"Umm, Zed," Hester said, nudging him.

"Oh. Yeah." Zed looked down. "Sorry."

"I appreciate the help, really," Lynn said.

"Men," Pat said, as if that one word summarized the whole of the universe. "C'mon. Let's get you

something to eat and then we'll think about how to get your life back in order."

"I'm not sure my life will ever be back in order," Lynn said.

"Well, I'm sure your aunt will help."

Lynn turned to her. "What?"

"Everyone's talking about her," Pat said. "Apparently she made quite the impression at Buster's Café. She's such a charmer!"

"Oh, that she is," Lynn said, trying to hide her disgust. She was not about to have this conversation with someone else. Having it with Jack had been impossible, and he at least attempted to understand. She had no illusions about how it would go with anyone else. "Yes, breakfast sounds good."

Pat led Lynn to Buster's Café, which had added a breakfast serving to its repertoire. The tables were full so Pat and Lynn joined the queue of those waiting for tables and a chance to devour Mabel's amazing cuisine.

"Mabel sure can cook," Pat remarked. "If I ate this every day I'd *be* a house."

Lynn was past caring. After all that had happened, she was ravenous, and the food was at least making her feel a little better.

So was the camaraderie of the folks around her.

Overnight, she had become a full member of the Treasure Island community. The distance that had existed before had vanished. In her time of trial, she had been accepted.

Already others were discussing where she might live, and where they could get at least some furniture for her. Women were offering her clothes, mostly simple island garb of shorts and shirts, but welcome offers nonetheless. Before she had finished breakfast, she began to wonder if she were going to suffer from an embarrassment of riches.

At this point, just as a warm glow was finally replacing anger, fear and fatigue, the mayor walked into the café.

"Nobody told me there was a town meeting," Dan said.

A hundred heads turned his way and simply looked at him. Dan shifted, his eyes darting around. "Did I say something wrong?"

Mabel shoved a cup of coffee at him. "Where the hell have you been?" she asked.

"At home. Why? I'm retired. And this island rarely needs the mayor."

"*Too* retired if you ask me," she said sharply. "The teacher's house collapsed last night."

Dan Heilbaum's jaw dropped. "That's not possible!"

"Oh, it's possible," said a man on the far side of the room.

Lynn wondered if she would ever get to know everyone on the island. She should, she supposed, since there weren't *that* many people. But she had a limited number of brain cells left over from important stuff to devote to faces and names.

"But...but that house has stood for more than fifty years through every kind of weather! A little storm like last night couldn't knock it down."

Another man spoke, "Not unless Harv Cullinan had already knocked down walls and trenched the front yard. The dirt under her foundation slumped."

"Oh...my...God." Dan sank onto a chair that had been quickly vacated to make room for him.

Mabel put her hand on her hip and looked down at him. "Yeah, that's a bit of a problem, isn't it?"

He looked glumly up at her.

"I mean, part of what we pay schoolteachers here is housing. It's in the contract."

"I know!"

Lynn winced. She hadn't wanted to mention that part of it. Everyone was being so kind and sympathetic. Besides, it wasn't as if anyone had deliberately violated her contract. Had someone come in wielding a wrecking ball, that would have been different.

"Something needs to be done quickly," Mabel said. Murmurs of agreement came from all around. "She lost *everything*. Almost lost her life. And I don't know of another empty house on the island."

Dan cleared his throat. "I'm just the mayor," he said finally.

"Unfortunately," Mabel agreed.

"Hey! You know it's more an honorary thing. Who listens to *me?*"

"Nobody," came an unidentifiable voice from across the café.

"Exactly," Dan agreed. "Nobody. Not even my wife. What am I supposed to do?"

"Well, you could try the something truly revolutionary. You could…gee…*lead!*"

"How? Get a tent?"

"Get folks working on finding a solution, Dan."

Dan looked around the room. "You haven't started already?"

Mabel rolled her eyes. "We just brought Lynn back here. We're feeding her. We're talking about how to get her clothes."

Dan blanched. "It's that bad?"

"It's hard to tell it used to be a house."

"Oh, God."

"So we don't have a lot of time," Mabel continued. "She can't stay in that motel near the water. We all know that. Not unless you can fumigate it."

"The casino hotel," he started to say.

"And who here can pay for that?"

Dan hesitated, then puffed his chest. "I'll talk to Bill Anstin. He'll do it as a favor."

"Just don't give him the island in return," Mabel warned.

A chorus of agreement, sounding somewhat threatening, backed her up.

"I'm not that stupid," Dan protested. "I said he's going to do it as a favor, and he will."

"Umm…" Mabel said.

"Anstin owes me," Dan said with a flashing wink. "Last weekend he was convinced he couldn't lose. For a world champion, he's awful when he goes on tilt. I gave him a lesson, for which he hasn't yet paid. So now he can pay all of us by putting up our science teacher until her house is rebuilt."

Lynn, as usual, was uncomfortable at being the center of so much concern and attention. By nature she preferred the quiet, unnoticed life of an academic. Now she had a whole town, well most of them anyway, in a tizzy. And all about her. While part of her was warmed by all the caring, another part of her wished she could walk out the front door and solve all her own problems without inconveniencing anyone else.

At least at that point, however, everyone went back to eating, and conversations quieted and seemed to grow more personal, leaving Lynn pretty much alone with Pat.

Pat, however, was not exactly ready to let the subject drop. She reached out and patted Lynn's hand. "We'll take care of you. I'm just so glad you're all right. Do you want to come to my place after breakfast? I've got a shower you can use, we can wash your clothes and you can borrow some of mine, for as long as you need to."

"You're a sweetheart," Lynn said honestly. "I keep thinking this ought to be hitting me a lot harder."

"It probably will once the shock wears off."

"Is that what you think it is?"

"I'm sure."

Lynn forked a small piece of pancake and thought about that. It might explain a lot of her strange behavior last night. Gambling. Making love so desperately. To a preacher, no less! Doing things she ordinarily wouldn't do. It had been as if she'd blown off her shell.

And now she felt utterly naked and defenseless.

Discomfort crept along her nerve endings, verging on paranoia. Never in her life had she allowed herself to become exposed in so many ways. Her ex-fiancé, despite their relationship, despite his theft of her work, had not left her feeling as utterly exposed as she did now.

For a few moments she considered just going up to the airport and leaving. Flying back to Princeton. Finishing out her doctorate. Doing new research. Hiding in her math and her mind. It had always been a relatively safe place.

In abandoning her work, she had abandoned part of herself and she knew it. She could still pursue most of it right here with nothing more than a white board and markers. Her research happened more in her mind, in the crafting and rearranging of complex formulae, than in the laboratory. She could use the school's Internet connection to confer with colleagues if she needed to, and she still had friends at PEAR who could check her data. Even if the project was being shut down, they already had a wealth of data simply waiting to be weighed against theory.

She didn't really need Princeton. But at the moment it sounded like a haven, despite all the bad things, and she wished desperately that she were back in her cozy little apartment, watching the autumn foliage slowly give way to winter.

CHAPTER TWENTY

LYNN SHOWERED AT Pat's house, borrowed a light cotton dress while her clothes were being washed and set out for school without books, lesson plans or any of the other props she usually carried.

This is going to be an interesting day, she thought. Her concentration was scattered all to hell and she had hardly any idea how she was going to follow a lesson plan she only vaguely remembered. In fact, remembering it was proving to be difficult when her mind kept drifting back to the collapse of her house. Her house and Jack. Jack and Delphine's intrusion.

The urge for a primal scream nearly overwhelmed her. She stopped mid-stride, considering it, then gave up on the idea. The whole island probably thought she was utterly crazy already. No need to confirm it.

She finally made her way to her classroom. No one had arrived yet, so she sat at her desk with her chin in her hand studying the terrarium. Maybe today's lesson should be about the formation of landslides and sinkholes.

Yeah, it would fit in with earth science and all the stuff they'd been covering in a general sort of way. How does the earth swallow a house without an earthquake? It was not an uncommon phenomenon, and especially on the steep slopes of Caribbean islands, many of which were little more than volcanic cones that had attracted flora and fauna. The firm, igneous rock gathered a layer of decayed plant and animal material, in the form of soil, which served as a rich matrix for the brilliantly colored flowers and hardy trees that helped to stabilize it.

But hurricanes or any heavy rainstorm could lubricate the underlying surface of that rock, leaving the soil and trees and flowers to skid down into the ocean. That was, in fact, the most deadly element of tropical weather in the Caribbean Basin, far more than the winds or even the storm surge. Floods and landslides killed more people, destroyed more farms and businesses and uprooted more communities.

Yes, that would be today's lecture.

As the students entered the room, Lynn propped one end of the terrarium on a book. The slope was not severe, and during the first hours of the morning the students seemed to grow confused, for nothing was changing. On the other hand, she had to answer sixty-three questions about her house collapsing.

"Who knows what the temperature is outside?" Lynn asked. For a moment no one answered, as they considered why she had asked the question and what it had to do with the day's project. Lynn realized she couldn't expect them to read her mind. "Okay, is it hot outside right now or just comfortable?"

"It's okay," Jane Keppler finally said. "But the radio said it would get hotter during the day."

"Right," Lynn said. "Now, will we get hot here in the classroom?"

"We better not," one of the boys said. "The school is *supposed* to have air conditioning."

"And it does," Lynn agreed, pointing to the vent that was directly over the terrarium. "What will happen to our little ecosystem when the A-C kicks on?"

"Cold air blowing on it," Jane said. "So it should get colder."

"And what happens when humid air gets colder?" Lynn asked, walking them through the previous day's lecture.

"Precipitation," Tom Miller said, his face bright with the pride of understanding. "The inside of the glass will fog up as water condenses."

"And where will that water go?" Lynn asked.

"It runs down the side," Tom said. "Into the dirt."

"And then?"

"It soaks through the dirt to the bottom," Jane said.

Lynn nodded. "And then?"

No one answered for several moments. Lynn heard the muffled thump, followed by the hum as the school's central air conditioning kicked on, as if on cue.

"Let's just watch and see," she said.

The students gathered to watch the process unfold. Exactly as the students had predicted, the cold air from the vent began to chill the terrarium, and the moist air within it began to shed its water in little droplets on the walls and lid. Soon the water was trickling down the sides and dripping from the lid, soaking the soil. Lynn broke a glow stick and put it beneath the bottom of the terrarium, and within minutes there was what appeared to be a pale, glowing, yellow film along the bottom.

"That's the water," Jane said.

"Exactly," Lynn said. "And what happens if you're running outside and you step in a puddle?"

"You ruin your clothes," Tom said, laughing along with the other kids.

Lynn rolled her eyes. "What else?"

"You make a splash," Jane said, then punching Tom on the shoulder, she added, "Idiot."

Stifling a giggle, Lynn said, "Yes, if you're ready for the puddle, and you come straight down, you make a splash. But what if you don't see it until you step in it?"

"Then you probably make an even bigger splash," Jane offered.

"Yes," Lynn said. "Because the water acts like a lubricant. Instead of your shoe sticking to the surface of the ground, it slides." The elementary schoolers she was now teaching drew closer to the terrarium.

At that moment, the dirt in the terrarium seemed to break loose from the glass base. Slowly at first, as if pushed by an invisible hand, it began to skid away from the raised end. Within seconds, it had settled, burying some of the tiny plants and mosses the children had placed.

"Did you see what happened?" Lynn asked.

"Yes," Tom said. "Pretty cool landslide."

Lynn smiled. "Exactly what happened. We saw a landslide."

"I've seen those on TV," Tom said. "There was a big one in Mexico after a storm. Is that how it happened?"

"Yes," Lynn said. "The storm sucks up moisture from the ocean, making the air very, very wet. When that air gets pushed up a mountainside, it cools, just like the air in our terrarium did when the air conditioner turned on. That causes—"

"Precipitation," Tom said, interrupting and clearly impressed with himself for remembering the word.

"—yes," Lynn said. "Rain. And because our island is basically a volcanic cone, like most of the islands in this part of the world, the volcanic rock acts like the bottom of our terrarium. First the dirt grows heavier as it soaks up water. Then when the rain soaks through the dirt, it builds a film of water on that rock, and…"

"And the dirt slides off the hill!" Jane said.

"They're really bad," Tom added. "The one I saw took the houses with it and everything. Oh…wait…that's like…"

It was as if the seed of the idea sprouted in all of them at once. Their eyes turned to Lynn.

"That's what happened to your house," Tom said.

Lynn nodded. "That's exactly what happened to my house. But in my case, it was because my front lawn had been dug out, so when it started to rain, the dirt that was under my house—dirt that had been held in place by the front lawn—slid into that hole."

"Okay," Tom said. "So, how could we keep that from happening again?"

"That's an excellent question," Lynn said. "And

that's what I want you all to figure out. What can we do with our terrarium so the dirt won't slide to the lower end once the water starts to condense?"

"Take the book out," Tom said. "So it's level again."

"That's silly," Jane objected. "We can't make the whole world level."

"She didn't ask about the whole world," Tom said. "She just asked about the terrarium!"

"But she's obviously *talking* about the rest of the world," Jane said, pointing out the window. "Making the terrarium level would be pointless if it doesn't show us what happens out there."

Tom's jaw jutted out. "I'm not stupid, you know."

"Then don't *act* stupid," Jane replied.

This had obviously gone too far, Lynn thought. She was just about to interfere when another student spoke up.

"They're practicing for when they get married."

"It sure sounds like it," Lynn agreed.

At once everyone else started giggling, and the combatants looked embarrassed. But then Jane shook her head, silencing them all. "It's not good to be married if you argue like that. It's better to be nice."

Tom's truculence quickly disappeared. "Sorry," he said.

"I'm sorry, too," Jane said, then looking Tom up and down she added, "Besides, no way, no day!" Tom made a face and everyone laughed.

She turned to Lynn. "Are we talking about fixing the aquarium or fixing your house? Because I don't think we can fix the whole island."

Lynn nodded, pleased by the girl's assessment both of relationships and what was feasible.

"Well, let's fix the terrarium while we talk about it. But what would you do if we decided to keep the terrarium on a slant?"

The solutions were creative, some wildly impractical, others simple and relatively easy, but every one of them showed an understanding of the dynamic she had demonstrated.

Finally Tom turned to her and asked, "Which idea would be best for your house?"

Lynn pursed her lips. She hadn't expected to be asked that question. "I haven't really thought about it," she admitted. "I suppose it would be smart of me to go look at the land before I say anything."

Jane nodded wisely. "Collect your data."

Lynn smiled, actually feeling good as a teacher. These kids were learning by leaps and bounds. "Exactly, Jane. That's the first thing to do."

"So why don't we all go do it?" Tom demanded. "After school."

Lynn shook her head. "I'm not sure it's a safe place for you to be right now. In fact, I'm pretty sure it's not."

Tom shrugged. "We're gonna go out and look anyway."

Lynn felt certain that they were going to do exactly that, regardless of what she might say. She certainly had no authority outside the classroom. "Just promise me you won't get near the wreckage. It might slip some more."

Though she hadn't intended to return to the rubble at all that day, that's what she ended up doing. Someone had to keep an eye on the kids who came to look at the mess. At that time of day, there might not be a lot of adults handy.

She reached the ruins before the kids did, but not to find a deserted mess. As she rounded the corner and gained her first full view of the wreckage since that morning, she gaped.

Harv Cullinan and his crew were back. So were some of her neighbors. And in the street in front of the remains a collection of her personal items was growing. Undamaged or salvageable furniture, baskets of clothes, waterlogged books… Even some ceramic knickknacks that she would have written off.

Amazed, she slowed and approached. Harv was

the first to see her. At once he pulled his ball cap off his head and began to work it with his fingers, looking every inch the abashed eight-year-old, rather than a man in mid-life.

"Sorry, teach," he said, mumbling. "But this ain't my fault."

She gaped at him. "How do you figure that?"

"The storm. We wasn't supposed to get one."

"Well, we did."

"But if we was supposed to get one, we coulda put tarps over the trench and stuff."

"Why didn't you do that to begin with, seeing as how you dug the trench then stopped working."

He scratched his head. "Cuz we was having a *drought!*"

"Oh, that explains it all."

"Damn straight," he agreed, turning to look again at the house. He crammed his hat back on his head. "Wanna be sure we save what we can before I clear the crap out of the way."

"I'm surprised so much has been saved."

"Waste not, want not," he said.

Oh, thought Lynn, that was priceless, as if she'd tossed her home on to a rubbish heap on purpose. She managed, however, to bite her tongue. Then a thought occurred to her.

"Mr. Cullinan?"

"Harv, please," he said.

"Harv, some of my students are on their way over here. We were talking about landslides in science today, and they want to come assess the situation here."

He looked at her, his eyes bigger than usual. "The kids want to *what?*"

"Assess the situation," she said pleasantly. "You know, see what needs to be done to the ground to make sure the next house doesn't collapse like this."

He scratched his head. "Now what in the hell would kids know about that?"

The answer came from behind them. "More than you, apparently."

Lynn swiveled her head and saw Jack standing there. His face was utterly rigid, an expression that made her at once feel about two inches tall.

"What do you mean, Jack?" Harv demanded.

"I mean that while I'm no construction genius, it seems to me you should have left a jack under the slab where you dug."

"We didn't go that far under."

"Really." Jack stuck his hands in his pockets, looking from Harv to the house. "Results would say otherwise."

A squawk caused all three of them to turn. Buster was lumbering down the street with the African

Gray parrot on his head. The bird squawked again. "Buster's pissed at you, Harv."

At once Cullinan took a backward step, away from the gator. "Why should he be pissed?"

"Because he had to dive in that muddy trench and save the preacher last night after the house collapsed. Because it's your fault the house collapsed. Because he's fond of the teach."

At that Harv seemed to boil over. "Wasn't my fault the storm came through."

"No," said the bird. "But the storm didn't knock over anybody else's house."

"Hey!" Harv objected.

"Mmmmmmmmmmmm," Buster said, his voice thrumming deeply.

The bird hopped a little on Buster's head, fluttering his wings. "Always tickles my toes when he does that. Don't ever make him do that again." One dark bird eye peered directly at Harv.

By this time everything had been forgotten by everyone there except the bird, Buster and Harv. And the way Buster was grinning at Harv looked more feral than friendly.

"I'm working on it," Harv finally said. "Gotta clean up first."

The bird spread a wing and spent a moment or two pecking around for a flea or something. Then it raised one talon and scratched its own head. "Yeah," said the bird. "Clean up."

"Then what?" asked Jack.

"You stole my words," the bird said.

"I'm gonna fix it," Harv said. "Good as new."

Jack stepped closer. "And the cost?"

Harv hesitated. It was clearly a painful moment for him. Buster slithered closer. Lynn suddenly thought of the crocodile that followed Captain Hook everywhere.

Apparently Harv had a similar thought. "Nothing," he finally said. "I still say it ain't my fault, but I ain't gonna leave the teacher here without a house."

Jack turned and walked away, without ever saying a single word to Lynn.

CHAPTER TWENTY-ONE

"COME ON," DAN HEILBAUM said to Lynn as he pulled up beside her in a Cadillac so old it should have been in the Smithsonian. "We're gonna talk to Bill Anstin and get you a room at the casino."

"I can't go. Some of my kids were talking about coming out here to look at the damage and decide what needs to be done to make the earth more stable."

Harv Cullinan harrumphed. "Like they would know."

The bird squawked. "They obviously would know better than *you*."

For an instant Lynn feared the bird was going to wind up served for Harv's Sunday dinner, but Harv got a grip. "Stupid bird," he muttered.

Lynn bit her lower lip, not because she wanted to laugh, but because she wanted to cry. And the whole reason she wanted to cry was the sight of Jack's back as he walked away. He hadn't even looked at her.

"Great move," Delphine said. She was sitting on the wreckage, wearing a black beaded evening gown, carrying a feathered fan.

Lynn fought down the urge to reply. Matters were bad enough without standing here talking to thin air in front of dozens of people.

"You hurt that man," Delphine said.

Lynn ignored her.

"Look, we have to go now," Dan said. "Bill Anstin is planning to fly to Vegas tonight."

"Can't you do it without me?"

"I need the sympathy factor."

"But the kids…"

One of the women stepped forward. "Don't worry, teach. I'll make sure they play scientist without getting too close."

"Thank you!"

The woman smiled. "I have a feeling one of those kids will be mine."

Lynn gave her a quick hug, then climbed into the ancient Caddie with Dan. The engine purred like a happy kitten, even though the seats looked leftover from the Jurassic age.

"Will I still be able to walk to school from the casino?" Lynn asked Dan.

"Yeah. I can have somebody show you the way. This end of the island isn't all that wide, and there's a direct path. Maybe five minutes longer than you're walking right now."

"Thank you."

"Least I can do," Dan said, puffing a little. "Besides, I've been looking for a way to nettle Anstin after Saturday. It's not every day a guy like me gets to beat a World Series of Poker winner."

"Is that what he is?"

Dan gave her a pitying look. "You got a lot to learn, teach."

"So it appears."

She turned to look out through the front windshield and was appalled to see Delphine playing hood ornament. She closed her eyes, refusing to look. She was still mad at Delphine for this morning, and it occurred to her that if she ignored her aunt, maybe she'd go away. At least for a while.

Sunlight flickered through her eyelids as they drove along a rather bumpy road through a thickly forested part of the island. She would have liked to see the view, but Delphine all but blocked that.

At last they came to a halt, with a jerk, and her eyes popped open.

The casino, which she had only briefly seen before, still looked like a haphazard collection of very large tiki huts running up the side of a gentle hill. At the moment a lot of people were busy moving machines and tables back into place under the woven roofs. Apparently the storm hadn't caught *them* by surprise. She almost snorted.

But at least Delphine was gone for the moment.

"There's Bill," Dan said, giving a toot with his horn.

For an instant it seemed Bill Anstin, whom Lynn knew only by sight, was about to dart away, but then, with a squaring of his shoulders, he started walking their way. Dan climbed out to greet him, so Lynn did, too, although the purpose of this visit was making her feel distinctly uncomfortable.

"Hey, Bill," Dan said with entirely too much good cheer.

"Hey," said Anstin. "And this is?" He looked at Lynn and his expression changed to one she didn't at all like. It occurred to her she might be safer sleeping on the beach, and that Bill Anstin was a crocodile of a different stripe. His smile widened, showing perfect teeth, and he gave her the once-over.

"This is our new teacher," Dan said. "Lynn Reilly."

Anstin held out his hand. "Bill Anstin. It's a pleasure."

Lynn shook his hand, but said nothing in return. She barely managed a dubious smile.

"So," said Dan. "Ms. Reilly's house collapsed last night."

Anstin arched his brows. "I know it was a bad storm, but *that* bad?"

"Well," Dan shrugged. "There was a little added problem in that Harv Cullinan had trenched her front yard."

"What on earth for?"

"He took one look at the plumbing and decided the place was a mess."

Anstin shook his head. "It's more of a mess now."

"Just slightly," Dan said. "She lost everything."

Anstin turned to look at her again, his smile a bit...oily, Lynn thought. "That's tragic. I'm so sorry."

"I've lost more in the past," she said, trying to put him at a distance.

"That too is tragic."

Dan cleared his throat. "Thing is, she needs a place to stay. And after our game last Saturday..."

Anstin's brows knit. He apparently didn't like being reminded of his losses. For an instant, there was nothing handsome about Handsome Anstin.

"I thought," Dan continued almost gleefully, "that you'd like to step up and offer her *free* accommodations."

Lynn wished the ground would open up and

swallow her. This was even more embarrassing than she had anticipated. And regardless of what might be going on between these two, she didn't like standing right in the middle of it.

She turned and started to walk back to the car. "I'll sleep on the beach," she said. "I'll use a pew in church."

"No!" It was Anstin who called after her. "Please don't. I'd be more than happy to give you a room. After all, that's part of what this island promises its teachers, yes?"

She turned slowly and looked at him. Suspicion filled her, but his face looked entirely sincere.

"Be sure to lock your door at night," Delphine said without materializing. "He's a womanizer."

"Seriously," he said. "This is a terrible tragedy and I'd be a terrible person if I didn't do everything in my power."

"He's also a poker player," Delphine continued. "Don't believe that face."

Lynn wished she could elbow her aunt. She hesitated, hating to be a charity case, certain that Delphine was right, yet having no other immediate option. "Thank you," she said finally.

"There, that's settled," Anstin said, looking purposefully at Dan.

"Completely," Dan said cheerfully. "Completely

settled. Now I need to show her the shortcut to the school from here."

"I can do that," Anstin offered.

Dan looked him over, then shook his head. "I'll do it. You're evidently busy putting the casino back together, and if I'm not mistaken, there's a cruise ship on the way in."

Lynn looked to the right and saw that the mayor was correct. "How does it dock?" she asked. She'd never thought about that before.

"It doesn't," Anstin answered. "They anchor in the harbor, then use their lifeboats as shuttles to bring passengers ashore. We'll probably see the first of them in about an hour."

"So you need to stay here." Dan smiled. "Thanks, Bill." He took Lynn's arm and began to walk her toward the woods. "This is a wonderful walk," he said loudly, then more quietly, "That man is a shark. If I had my way, I wouldn't leave you alone within a hundred yards of him."

"I was getting that impression."

"Just lock your door."

Two Aunt Delphines, Lynn thought. Could life possibly get any more troublesome?

But just then it did. Anstin appeared beside them, smiling. "Let *me*, Dan," he said smoothly. "You know your wife will start wondering why you were gone so long. Besides, your car is *here*. You'd have to come back to get it."

At that, Dan hesitated visibly.

Lynn, taking her future in her hands, told him it was okay. "You drive home, Dan. I'll be fine."

Dan paused only long enough to look suspiciously at Anstin, then nodded almost abjectly and returned to his Caddie.

Anstin was still smiling. "His wife *will* be all over him if he doesn't get back soon. She's as jealous as they come."

"Does she have a reason to be?"

Anstin looked at her, cocking a brow. "What do *you* think?"

There was nothing about Dan Heilbaum to suggest he could be a womanizer even if he tried, but Lynn caught herself in time to maintain good manners. The laugh that almost burst from her would have been rude in the extreme, and *not* something she would want to get back to Dan.

Instead of answering, she turned toward the path and began to walk. It was actually quite well-cleared, apparently often used.

"A lot of my employees walk this way to and from work," Anstin said. "It's almost a super highway for feet."

"That's convenient."

"It's also a lovely walk. Birds and butterflies, mainly. It also avoids Bridal Falls, and thus the tourists. They can be enough trouble in the casino. My people don't need to be meeting them on isolated trails."

"Well, that's a thought!" Lynn said.

"You never know how someone might react to a big loss at the tables or slots."

She couldn't argue that. Butterflies and birds, huh? And Delphines, a series of them, one after another, perched in trees or standing beside the trail. Lynn gritted her teeth so as not to demand of her aunt just what she thought *she* could do if Anstin got out of hand. It wasn't as if a ghost could pick up a weapon.

But Delphine continued to appear at points along the trail, smiling as if she knew something Lynn didn't.

Then two real people showed up, two women walking briskly in the other direction.

"Hi, Bill," said the older of the two. "Is the ship in?"

"We should see the first customers in about forty-five minutes."

"Great. Hi, teach."

"Hi." Lynn tried to place her, but couldn't. The younger woman, maybe twenty, simpered a little, as if trying to catch Anstin's eye. If Anstin noticed, he didn't let on. "Hi, Belle," he said. "Better hurry there. I'll be back at the casino in about twenty minutes."

Twenty minutes, Lynn thought. Good. She couldn't get into trouble in twenty minutes.

"It's safe to come this way after dark," Anstin said as the two women passed. "But you should bring a flashlight if you need to, just so you can see your way. I'll make sure there's one in your room."

"Thank you."

He touched her elbow. For an instant she felt as if her skin was trying to crawl in every direction away from the spot of contact. Then he dropped his hand. "Let me buy you a drink later," he said, pleasantly.

"Um, thank you, but I don't think so. It's been a horrid day and I'm just going to want to collapse."

He nodded. "I can understand that. But perhaps you'll feel differently later."

Not bloody likely, she thought, quickening her pace. As they came around a curve, she suddenly saw Delphine again, this time hanging upside down like a bat from a palm limb. Oddly, her clothes remained perfectly in place. Gravity clearly did not affect her anymore.

The sight, however, was enough to make Lynn

close her eyes in disbelief. Which then made her stumble.

At once Anstin reached out to catch her, and before she could react, she was pressed to a hard male chest.

She gasped and her eyes flew open.

"What—"

"Just steadying you," he said, although his eyes said something entirely different.

"What are you up to, Anstin?"

Lynn jerked away from Anstin and turned to see an angry—very angry—Jack staring at the two of them.

"Ms. Reilly stumbled," Anstin said smoothly.

"You wouldn't have had anything to do with that?"

"Oh for God's sake," Bill Anstin said disgustedly. "She tripped!"

"I tripped," Lynn said swiftly, not wanting to see the violence she could read in Jack's gaze. "Really. My foot caught."

Jack eyed her coldly. "I'll take you the rest of the way."

Anstin apparently decided retreat was the better part of valor. "Thanks. I've got a ship coming in." He took off for the casino.

Jack stared at Lynn, who suddenly felt as small as an inch worm.

"Really," she said in a small voice, and hated her for it. "I tripped. I saw Delphine hanging like a bat in the tree and I tripped."

The savagery faded from his face. "Hanging like a bat?"

Lynn crossed her heart.

"I'd have tripped, too," he admitted.

"And her dress was still hanging to her ankles as if she were standing upright."

"I'd like to learn that trick." Reaching out, he took her elbow. From his touch, she decided it wouldn't be wise to pull away. "You can't stay at Anstin's casino."

"Where else am I supposed to stay?"

"You can stay with me."

"Right. I want everybody on this island talking about us."

"They're already talking about us. It's a small island."

"How delightful."

"Your choice. They can talk about you and Anstin or you and me."

She tightened her mouth and glared at the path in front of her. "Lovely. Preacher and schoolteacher. Aren't we supposed to set a better example?"

"That's another world, Lynn. Here folks make allowances for people being human."

"Delightful." Now she did pull her arm from his grasp. "I have to go to Pat's to get what's left of my clothes. Maybe she can put me up."

"Fine! Have it your way."

How had this become an argument? she wondered. But what difference did it make? She'd never understood people anyway.

"Thank goodness," she said, "that tomorrow I'm going out to Empty Island."

"You are? Who's taking you?"

"I'm going by myself." She turned to face him. "I *am* capable, you know."

"I don't doubt it."

She turned to continue along the path, seeing a welcome hole of daylight ahead of her. At some level she realized he was no longer following her.

Good.

CHAPTER TWENTY-TWO

LYNN FOUND HER STUDENTS at the wreckage of her house, ten of them, all of them discussing the slump and taking notes. Harv Cullinan looked harried, and the crowd around the place had grown rather than shrunk. Apparently this was one of the most interesting things to have happened on the island in a while.

Her salvaged belongings stood alongside the road, looking pathetic. Anywhere else they'd have been consigned to a rubbish heap.

A new man had joined to group—tall, handsome, clad in work khakis. He was quickly introduced to Lynn as Buck Shanahan, owner of the island's airport.

"We're discussing what I need to get first from Aruba," he said to Lynn. "We want to get your house rebuilt as quickly as possible."

"Thank you."

"Best way to go is cinder block," said another

man. "It's all well and good to talk about building it the old way, but the teach needs a place to live and we haven't got forever."

"Cinder block is heavier," Buck Shanahan pointed out. "I'll have to make more trips."

That seemed to cause several moments of reflection among the gathered men. That was when Lynn realized that except for her students, all the females had vanished.

Men's work here now, she supposed, with a touch of annoyance.

Harv, looking utterly dyspeptic now, shook his head. "Wood frame," he said finally. "We'd have to order a bargeful of cinder blocks, and God knows when they'd get here."

"All right then," said Buck. He turned and smiled at Lynn. "I'll go out tomorrow and get the wood. I should be able to get most of it back in one flight."

She was beyond guessing how accurate any of this might be. Nor did it seem to matter.

As Buck strode off and climbed into an open-top Jeep, the kids who were still there crowded around her, trying to show her the notes they'd made on the destruction, and their suggestions for improvement.

Any hope of conversation vanished as Harv Cullinan made a motion with his hand and the

backhoe roared to life. Moments later, the last of her
house was being shoveled into a dump truck headed
for the island landfill. Peeking from one corner was
a shred of curtain, the bright colors she had chosen
with so much hope only a short time ago.

Everything, she thought, *everything* was ephem-
eral.

SHE SPENT THE NIGHT on a cot on Pat's porch and in
the morning, clad in her washed shorts and T-shirt
from the night of the disaster, headed out to the
docks to get the boat she had been promised for the
day. To her surprise, no one was there. A note,
however, had been tacked to the wheel.

*Fueled up, keys in ignition, a snack in the cooler.
Have fun, Teach.*

She had to smile. Nowhere else in the world, she
thought. Nowhere else.

She turned to cast off the lines and discovered she
wasn't alone after all. Jack Marks was standing at
dockside, working the lines to cast her off.

"Thanks," she called.

"Not necessary," he said. As he cast off the last
of the two lines, he jumped aboard. "You're not
going alone."

Now would have been a great time to throw a
screaming hissy fit, she thought. Stomp her feet,

jump up and down and just generally tell the world what she thought of it.

Instead, maintaining her dignity, she turned back to the wheel, started the ignition and sailed for Empty Island.

Jack left her alone, so she pretended he wasn't even on board. It was a beautiful day, one of those days that reminded you the best things in life are free. The sun hadn't been up that long yet, so the light was still golden and the water had an almost metallic look to it, the Caribbean blue less green than usual.

She had planned to dawdle on her way to the island, pausing to look down at the sandy sea floor which wasn't that far away, maybe ten meters, but Jack's presence acted like a goad. Get to the island, check it out and get home. Such as home was.

Even at half speed, reaching Empty Island took less than half an hour. When she pulled up as close as she dared to the beach, she dropped anchor, essentially stapling the boat to the sea floor within at most fifteen feet of the beach. She'd consulted the tide charts last night and knew they were at low tide, which meant as the day progressed the boat would float higher, not lower.

"Want the dinghy?" Jack asked.

Reluctantly, she turned toward him, realizing she wasn't going to be able to ignore him all day.

"We don't need it now," he said, "but later when the tide rises…"

"Sure," she agreed. Getting the word out was like getting molasses past her lips. Hard.

The dinghy hung from transoms over the rear of the boat, and lowered easily with one man's touch. Lynn went to help to make sure it didn't swing against the boat and do some damage.

Just as the dinghy settled into the water, there was another splash. The two of them turned instantly around and heard an all-too-familiar squawk.

"Ack! I told you you'd get me wet," said one angry African gray.

Jack and Lynn rushed to the bow of the boat and, as one, groaned. The sight of Buster swimming to shore with that damn bird perched on his head was almost too much to bear.

"How did he get on here?" Lynn said.

"Damn if I know," Jack answered. "One thing for certain, we've got to get him back. Folks on Treasure Island will kill us if we lose that gator."

"He can't survive on this island anyway. And he'll kill the ecology."

They looked at one another, then ran back and jumped into the dinghy. It took them a minute to release the knots that secured the small wooden boat so it couldn't slip away, then Jack paddled like mad for the beach. When they got a little closer, Lynn threw caution to the wind and jumped out, wading for the beach.

"Awwwwk!" came the parrot's voice, as the alligator vanished from view into the thick undergrowth.

Lynn paused, still up to her ankles in water as Jack arrived in the dinghy.

"Oh. My. God," she said.

"I'm not sure God has anything to do with any of this," Jack replied. Straining, he pulled the dinghy far enough up the beach to tie it to a palm tree in case it floated when the tide came in.

Lynn looked at him, for the first time truly allowing herself to see him since the night they had spent together. And darned if she knew one thing to say.

Jack brushed his hands on his shorts, wiping them free of sand and grime. "Okay," he said. "You wanted to explore the island. We're going to do that regardless. If I recall correctly, there's only one pool of fresh water. When we find that, we'll find Buster, because he can't drink anywhere else."

She nodded. "I'd still like to know what he was doing on the boat."

"You're not the only one."

"Oh! I left the lunch on the boat!"

Jack half smiled. "We may need it later for bait. If not, I'll swim out and get it."

She nodded slowly, wondering why she felt a need to apologize to him. She hadn't done anything wrong. Not really.

Slowly she turned around to look, because after all, seeing this island was the entire purpose of the trip. The beach was small, a patch of white against the water, surrounded by mangroves and a surprising amount of rock.

"I guess this was volcanic at one time, too."

Jack wiped his forehead on his sleeve. "You'd have to ask Edna to be sure, but that would be my guess."

Lynn pointed at the basaltic rocks. "If this were a mangrove island, you wouldn't see anything except sand and earth caught by the mangrove roots. Those rocks tell a different story."

"I didn't know that." He sounded impressed. "Teach me, teach."

She looked at him, saw his mouth trembling with suppressed laughter, and in spite of herself, she laughed, too. "You know about mangrove islands, don't you?"

"Not really."

She was off to the races. "Mangroves are trees that can grow in salty water. The natives used to call them walking trees because their roots come up so

high it looks like they have legs beneath the trunks."
She walked over to one and patted its legs. "See?"

Jack nodded. "I like that: walking trees."

"Anyway, those roots capture sand and silt, and
over time, if you have enough trees, enough silt and
so on, other plants begin to grow among the trees.
Eventually, plants die, the decaying plants combine
with sand and silt to create soil and bigger things can
grow. These trees make islands."

"That's fascinating!"

"But that rock over there," she pointed, "indicates
at least part of this island is volcanic in origin. It's
not pumice, which would be light enough to float and
get caught here. It's too heavy. So while we're here
we should look for the remnants of an old volcano."

"You know what?" he said, and for the first time
since yesterday morning, his gaze was actually gentle.

"What?"

"The kids are going to absolutely love this tour.
Walking trees. Volcanoes. I'm enthralled."

She blushed, realizing he meant it.

"And Buster," he said after a moment as if to
break the awkward spell. "Damn gator. I wonder
what got into him."

"Maybe a bird," she said, feeling able to move
again. "But he can wait for a little while." Dropping
to her knees, she began to dig in the white sand.

"Looking for something?"

"Shells. Crabs. Anything that might live here or die here."

He squatted nearby. "It's just sand."

"It's an ecology in its own right. I'm surprised there's no sign of seaweed washing up. That would have been one of the first things to nourish soil and plant development here."

But as she dug, she found it. At once the pristine shoreline began to smell like a seashore.

"Ah, there it is. The storm the other night must have washed up sand to cover it."

"So all is right with the world."

His tone was gently teasing, so she smiled. "Apparently."

"Well, could you cover it back up? Rotting seaweed stinks."

"The smell of the coastline," she agreed and she pushed the sand back into the hole. "It always amazes me that out at sea there's almost no smell at all. Yet we all identify the coastal smell as being the sea."

"Well, it tends to be there the world over."

She laughed. "True. Maybe I was the only one surprised to find that out."

"I doubt it."

She remained kneeling, taking in everything,

making mental notes. Between the legs of the mangroves, some small red flowers blossomed. She supposed she should take a sample and see if she could identify it, but she really didn't want to disturb things at all. Inching over, she touched the rocks, looking closely and running her fingers over it.

"Definitely basalt," she said. "Eroded. It's been here a long time. I need to bring Edna over. Will you introduce me?"

"Sure. If you're positive you want me to."

She looked at him. "Why wouldn't I be?"

He shrugged. "Edna drives a lot of people crazy around here. And she's a bit catastrophic in her approach to science. Hey. How did you learn all this stuff about rocks and islands?"

She laughed. "I have to keep ahead of my students. Study, study, study. Besides, I've always been fascinated by anything science and math."

"Kinda like me and theology."

"Just theology?"

"Well, philosophy in general. That whole kind of thinking. But now you've got me interested in your stuff. Who could resist walking trees?"

She smiled at him and thought, *at least he isn't mentioning Delphine.*

"I wonder which would be the best way to go," she said, looking around.

"I'd suggest following Buster. He probably nosed out the path of least resistance right away."

"Do you suppose that bird is an instigator?"

"Of course it is!" Jack laughed. "Haven't you been listening to it?"

"Of course. But…why would they want to get on the boat and come over here?"

"Beats me. Maybe the two of them know something we don't."

He rose to his feet, shook off sand, then helped her up. She brushed herself off, and together they started in the direction Buster had taken. It wasn't long before she was wishing she'd worn jeans or brought a machete.

"Well," she said, "I've learned one thing."

"What's that?"

"Tell the kids to wear jeans."

"Yeah." He looked back over his shoulder. "Annoying as the stuff is, though, it's not cutting me. You?"

"Not yet."

As they traveled farther inland, the ground became rockier and the mangroves completely disappeared, as was to be expected.

A whole habitat had grown up here thanks to the volcano and the mangroves, and Lynn felt as if she'd just been given something priceless.

"Eden," she said.

"As close as we'll get," he agreed.

They emerged into a small clearing where rock rose up high enough to prevent the deep rooting of plants. The place was awash in flowers, however, and to no one's surprise, bees seemed to have discovered Eden as well.

Because of the rockiness, the growth was smaller and sparser, and Lynn spent some time examining rocks. To her delight, she found a fossil shell.

"It's not all volcanic," she told Jack excitedly. "Look at this. Sedimentary rock, a fossil. This island has been around for a while."

"You know what I'm curious about?"

"What?"

He waved his arm, indicating the entire island. "There are birds, bees and a whole bunch of plants. Why no animals?"

"Maybe there's not enough for them here." Her brow furrowed. "The rain pool would have to dry out sometimes."

"True. It may be dry right now."

She nodded.

He flashed her a grin. "Actually, this island isn't a whole lot bigger than the terrarium you have at school."

She laughed again, feeling something deep

within her begin, at last, to relax. "Maybe it's an artifact."

"What do you mean?"

"Maybe Big Mouth—and who the heck named that volcano, anyway?—threw off a huge lava bomb or two that landed over here sometime in the distant past. Maybe this island was never a volcano in its own right."

"Now that's a reason to get Edna over here. And sorry, I don't know who named the volcano."

"Probably One-Hand Hanratty. He sounds like the type."

"Descended from pirates by all accounts."

"Of course," she giggled. "It adds more romance to the tale."

"Well, it wouldn't surprise me," Jack said more seriously. "The entire Caribbean was a huge area for pirates. Still is by some accounts."

She turned to face him. "Is that why you came with me? Pirates?"

He shrugged. "Let's just say that no one, man or woman, ought to go to some isolated and abandoned place alone. It's just not safe. What if you twisted your ankle and couldn't walk?"

She looked down a moment then looked at him again and said sincerely, "Thanks, Jack."

He shrugged it off. "Just common sense."

Now that was a phrase calculated to light her fuse. "Are you saying I have no common sense?"

"No!" He held up both hands. "Absolutely not. No way."

"Yeah? Well try to explain what you just said, okay?"

CHAPTER TWENTY-THREE

JACK STARED AT LYNN. For long moments he remained silent, unsure of the best tack to take in response to that comment. And finally he knew that he was in an impossible situation. Nothing he said or did was going to make this one better.

So he went on the offensive. "Why do you have to take everything I say wrong? I didn't make any reference to your intelligence. Not one. All I did was brush away my own decision to accompany you as being merely common sense, hardly worthy of a thank you. But can you understand that? Hell no! You want to turn it into an insult directed at you, and what's worse, make it world war three."

With that he turned and stomped out of the clearing. Enough was enough. He couldn't please that woman to save his life. He'd go back to the boat, and if she didn't show up by dark, he'd assume she'd fallen into a hole and needed help. But damned if he'd do one more little thing to be helpful.

In fact, let Delphine help her!

Crazy woman with dead aunts hanging like bats in trees. God, the amazing thing was that for so much as one second he thought she might be seeing something real. He should have known that she needed commitment papers. The sooner the better.

High dudgeon worked better when you headed off in the right direction. He hadn't gone ten yards when he realized he was heading inland, away from the boat. Muttering under his breath he turned around and headed back. He expected to find the clearing long since empty, but instead he found Lynn sitting on a piece of rock with her head in her hands.

He stopped stomping and froze. Then, with a lighter step, he approached. He hated it when women cried.

"Lynn?"

She looked up, revealing as he had feared a tear-stained face. "I'm sorry," she said.

Those words stuck a pin in the balloon of his anger, and he deflated. "It's okay," he said, helpless to know anything else to say.

"No, it's not. It's like the whole world has crashed in on me, and I'm not thinking clearly. I'm not even being nice anymore. I used to be a nice person. I shouldn't have gotten mad at you. If I were myself, I would have understood perfectly that you weren't insulting me."

He couldn't drag up a piece of rock to sit beside her—they were too heavy—so he settled for sitting on the leafy stuff growing all over the ground.

"I'm sorry I blew up," he said.

"I blew up first," she reminded him.

"Well, we can argue about that if you want."

She sniffled and dashed at her eyes. "I don't want to argue at all."

"Good. Neither do I. Let's relax a minute and get back to exploring. I was having a great time."

"So was I," she admitted in a small voice.

He patted her knee. "So once we've calmed down, you can tell me more fascinating stories."

She nodded and wiped at her eyes again. He had the worst urge to rise on his knees and hug her close, but he remembered where that had eventually gotten him only the night before last. He wasn't ready for another round.

So he sat quietly, waiting for her to regain control. She sniffled more than once, and kept wiping at her eyes. He had to admit the last couple of days *had* been pretty hard for her. Homelessness, their lovemaking followed by a huge fight, being thrown on the mercy of Bill Anstin....

That was enough to crack anyone up by itself.

And she'd had it all hard on the heels of equally tough stuff, as he'd already mentioned to her. He wasn't being fair to her, to expect her to be perfectly normal.

The Delphine thing…maybe it was real, maybe it wasn't, but what did it matter if it helped Lynn through this time? She was certainly making a good impression on the children she taught, and most of the island for that matter.

So to hell with it all. He decided to just leave it in the category of "God works in mysterious ways." There seemed to be no other alternative.

At last she wiped her face one more time and rose. "Come on," she said. "Let's explore. I still need to find the rain pool."

"And Buster," he reminded her. "I don't want to face the lynch mob back home if we don't return with that stupid gator."

"People wouldn't do that, would they?"

He shrugged. "They might not lynch me, but that gator is part of the local community. Part of the lore. Part of everything. Losing him would be like stripping the island of half its identity."

"We can't allow that."

"No, we most certainly cannot."

"I wonder which way he went." Lynn looked around the clearing as if she expected to see some sign.

"There," Jack said suddenly. It looked to him as if the undergrowth had been pressed down in a long trail.

"As long as there's nothing else on this island as big, it's gotta be Buster," she agreed.

The two of them set off in that direction, taking care as the growth grew thicker.

"That bird would come back to us to tell us where he is," Lynn said.

"Are you sure of that? The bird might find this island hospitable."

"I don't think that critter would be happy if he didn't have people around to make feel stupid."

"You might be right."

At that she giggled, filling him with a huge sense of relief. "I can't believe how he talks to people. And what's even funnier is that he understands everything he's saying."

"I'd read about that in some science magazine, but I'd never expected to see it outside a laboratory. I mean, you think of birds as mimics, not independent talkers."

She chuckled. "Not anymore I don't."

"Me neither," he admitted. "I'd hate to get on his wrong side. I really *don't* want his honest opinion of me."

He was glad to hear her break into a peal of

laughter. "Me neither," she agreed. "That's the last thing I want to know. He doesn't seem to have a very good opinion of the human race in general."

"I haven't heard him give us a compliment yet."

Following what they believed to be the gator's trail led them deeper into the island. It was such a small island that Jack assured her they'd come out on the other side soon unless they walked in circles.

"Maybe that's what Buster is doing."

He shook his head. "Don't give me nightmares."

They paused often to drink in the beauty.

"The thing that amazes me," Lynn said, "is how thick everything grows. Just imagine for a moment that you're a settler, coming here for the first time, determined to carve out some kind of life. I can't imagine how you'd deal with all this."

Jack swatted at a mosquito. "I can. You'd burn it down."

"No!"

"Yes. How else could you clear it to grow things? Set fire to it and sit out on your boat waiting for the fire to die. Then you've got cleared, fertile soil, ready for planting."

"I don't like the way you think."

"I'm aware that our ancestors didn't ever think about conservation. That isn't *my* thinking, but it would make a good subject for your students.

Contrast and compare." He paused, wiping sweat from his brow. "Okay, so you don't burn it. What do you do then?"

"Good question." She turned slowly, looking at the dense foliage. Moving in any direction other than the one taken by Buster would be difficult and back-breaking. "But a lot of these islands were settled by natives, weren't they? And then you look at Central America, even Florida. They moved into jungles like this."

"And probably clear-burned as they went."

She sighed. "Okay, okay."

"But nowadays we don't want to do that. So how could we make this island habitable with the minimum of destruction?"

"I don't know frankly. I wasn't thinking about that. I just wanted the students to see nature virtually untouched."

"This is sure a good place for that. But I think Treasure Island was a little different, teach."

"How so?"

"It's my understanding that the town started where there was nothing but beach and rock to begin with. It's expanded obviously, but the first settlers didn't come and slash and burn. They fished. I think a lot of the original natives did the same."

Buster's trail led them right to the rain pool. Rain

from the other night must have filled it part way, for it wasn't dry, but Buster was nowhere to be seen.

Hot, sweaty and getting sick of mosquitoes, Lynn found herself a seat on a rock. "Everything here depends on this pool," she murmured.

"Makes you think," he agreed.

"There's such a thin line between survival and non-survival. It's not always apparent."

"WELL ALL HAIL the brilliant scientist!" the bird squawked. A moment later, the flutter of wings preceded a *splat* on Lynn's shoulder. "I guess you were on the wrong side of *that* thin line, huh?"

Lynn rose and whirled angrily. "What did you do that for?"

"I did it because my bowels were full," the bird said. "I thought you were a *scientist*. A *scientist* would know why birds poop."

Lynn clenched her fists and glared at him. Or was he a she? Him a her? Whatever. "Look…whatever your name is. You have a severe attitude problem."

"*I* have an attitude problem?" the bird asked. "Was *I* talking about whether to clear and burn entire forests just to make somewhere to live? Noooo. Do you have to give *me* classes on reducing carbon emissions? Noooo. Are *my* kind busy making war with the birds over the next pond over who gets the juiciest worm fields? Noooo. *I* have an attitude problem? Sheesh. You humans should hear yourselves! You are an embarrassment to the animal kingdom!"

"Now hold on," Jack said. "We were given dominion over the world. That's in the Bible."

"Brawwwwk!" Another *splat,* this time on Jack's shoulder. "Oh *do* lecture us about God, Mister Preacher Man. Do tell us about your higher morality and your special place in the ecosystem—bet you never thought you would hear a parrot say *that* word!—when you're busy messing it up for the rest of us. Oh please, I sooo want to hear this explanation."

Then, impossibly, the parrot folded its wings over its breast as if crossing its arms in defiance.

"I don't think I should have to defend myself to a bird," Jack said.

"Fine!" the parrot said. "You're too boring anyway. Plus you can't even see her dead aunt Delphine!"

Lynn gasped. "You can?"

The bird cocked its head. "Duh! Just because you humans have decided to ignore most of the world around you doesn't mean the rest of us have. Why do you think Buster's always around where he's needed? Come to think of it, why do you think I showed up?"

"To annoy us," Jack said.

"True," the parrot said, nodding. "But apart from that? Why am I here? And oh, don't I sound neo-Kantian, dare I say neo-Aristotelian, with that comment?"

"Okay," Lynn said. "Did you just say neo-Kantian? Neo-Aristotelian? Did I hear that correctly?"

Another *splat,* this time in her hair. "What does it *take* to wake you up? Do you need a treatise from on high, carved on stone, to make the simplest things clear to you? Oh wait, your people already got that...*and you still act like idiot humans.*"

"Oh great," Jack said. "A parrot that knows about the Decalogue."

"Did you think you had a monopoly on that?" the parrot said, turning to Jack now. "What, you thought God would only deign to talk to *your* kind? Didn't you pay attention to that passage about God clothing the lilies of the field, and feeding Saint Beaker."

"Who?" Lynn asked.

The parrot shook his head again. "Wow, you all are *really* uninformed. You've never heard of Saint Beaker, the sparrow mentioned in the Sermon on the Mount?"

"I didn't realize he had a name," Jack said.

"You wouldn't," the parrot replied. "You were

too busy thinking about the people in that sermon. I bet you never stopped to ask yourself *why* God clothes the lilies and feeds the birds."

"I always thought it was metaphor," Lynn said. "I mean, I'm no theologian, but…"

"No, you're not," the parrot answered. He pointed a wing at Jack. "Neither is he, really. All he does is…well…human the things he was taught to say in school."

"'Human' the things?"

"You think I would disparage myself by saying you *parrot* them? Oy vey!"

"So, font of all wisdom," Jack said, finally seeming to have had enough, "enlighten us. Teach us how we're soooo stupid and you're soooo smart."

"Okay," the parrot said. "I'll do that. Look around. Really *look* around. I'll wait."

And, true to his word, the parrot waited while Lynn and Jack looked around at the rain pool, at the riotous swirls of color in the flowers at its edge, at the thick, leafy canopy above it. Lynn smelled the rich, loamy scent of fresh earth and the tangy crystalline clarity of the sparkling water.

"Did you look?" the bird asked.

"Yes," Lynn said.

"Is it beautiful?"

"Very much so," Jack said.

The bird leaned forward. "Do you think it cares whether you think it's beautiful?"

Lynn pursed her lips for a moment. This had all of the earmarks of a trick question. "Umm...no?"

For an animal with no irises, the bird did an amazing imitation of rolling its eyes. "No? *No?*"

"Yes," Jack said.

"Pah!" the bird said, ignoring him. "He's just saying that because he knows 'No' is the wrong answer. But he has no idea *why* it's the wrong answer. So, Ms. Scientist, why is 'No' the wrong answer?"

"I have no idea," Lynn said.

"'And God saw that it was good.'" Jack crossed his arms and stared down the bird. "I'm right, aren't I?"

"Even a blind squirrel finds an acorn sometimes," the parrot announced as if he were John Houseman, the contracts instructor in *The Paper Chase*. "Of course this pond cares whether you think it's beautiful. It wants you to *notice* that it's beautiful. Buster wants you to *notice* that he's cute. I want you to *notice* that I'm annoying!"

"I'm one for three anyway," Lynn said off-handedly.

"The problem with you humans is that you *don't* notice anything. You think about what you want,

what you can get, how you can get it, who you can
get it from, who won't give it to you, how much it
will cost, why you want it, how long you've wanted
it, how long it will take to get it and how long it will
last once you have it...*and you never notice what's
happening around you.* Or you do it so damn rarely
as to make it a cliché about stopping to smell the
roses, which by the way the roses resent because
bees and dogs and parrots don't think it's excep-
tional to stop and smell the roses, *but you do.* You
barely notice one another most of the time. You two
have lived next door for *months,* and if it weren't for
Delphine and Buster and me, you'd *still* be oblivious to each other. 'God saw that it was good.' But
people don't. And *that* is why the rest of us sit
around thinking up ways to eat you in your sleep."

"You don't," Lynn said.

"Well, no, not really," the parrot admitted. "But it
sounds impressive, doesn't it? And some of us...not
Buster, don't get all paranoid about him...but some
of his cousins would gladly make a meal of you.
Because you are so damn oblivious that you don't
recognize you're screwing up your world until a hur-
ricane sweeps in and floods one of your cities and
suddenly everyone wonders if maybe the humans
have finally gone too far. Well, *yes,* you have. And
that you could even *talk* about how to clear this island

to make it habitable—when it's already habitable for everyone else!—shows just how little you've learned."

"He's got a point," Lynn said.

"He does," Jack agreed.

"Except for one thing."

The bird squawked and glared. "What thing?"

"If you'd been listening," Lynn said sweetly, "you'd have realized we were talking about what people *used* to do. And that neither of us would want to do any such thing to this island."

"Used to do? *Used to do?*" The bird screeched loudly and flapped until it was hovering over head. "Look around the world, teach. It's still being done everywhere!"

"But I can't…" Lynn began.

"*Brawwwwwk!* You can't. You *can't*. Pah. I'm done teaching you morons. I'm going to go talk to Buster. At least he makes sense!"

With a last *splat* that left Lynn wondering exactly how such a small animal could store so much waste, the bird disappeared into the trees.

CHAPTER TWENTY-FOUR

"I THINK I OFFENDED HIM. Or is it her?" Lynn said as she knelt by the pond and tried to clean her hair and shoulder with a corner of her shirt.

"I don't care," Jack said frankly. "I'm enjoying the relative quiet."

Lynn sat back on her heels and looked around. "He was right."

"We already agreed to that."

"No, I mean *right*."

"There's a difference?" He arched a brow, waiting.

"It's hard to explain. It was part of the reason I wanted to bring my students over here. To see an ecosystem untouched by humans. But it was the other part that really got to me. I've spent most of my adult life peering at things too small to see, thinking about things that could be represented only by obscure math equations. They're real, yes, and they're wondrous, but they're not *this*." She spread her arms, indicating everything around them.

"Yes, but," he said, smiling slightly. "We're not the lilies of the field. We *do* have to toil. And what's more, the things you were studying and thinking about give rise to all this."

"True."

"From what you've said to me, I gather your studies were also about beauty, just on a different scale."

"I guess you could say that." She unfolded her legs and scooted back until she could lean against a rock. "I was wrong about this island."

"In what way?"

"It *was* a volcano. Without a basin of granite or basalt, that rain pool wouldn't exist."

He sat nearby and looked. "Makes sense."

"I think that's an old caldera. A very small one. I guess I should get Edna over here after all. She could say for sure."

"That'll be interesting."

She sighed, then chuckled. "That bird is way too much. I would dearly love to know who he lived with before he arrived here."

"My guess is he lived with some kind of teacher or professor. Where else would he learn all that stuff?"

She shook her head. "Maybe he reads."

Jack immediately broke out in laughter, and she couldn't help but join him.

"Shh," she said, shaking with laughter, like a kid who didn't want a parent to hear. She waved her hand. "Shh. He'll come back and lecture us again."

"About what? Our levity?"

That sent her off into fresh laughter, and the two of them didn't even begin to quiet until their sides hurt. When they did, however, they were leaning against one another, shoulder-to-shoulder, and gradually relaxed back against the rock. Idly, Jack took her hand, squeezed it and held it. She didn't fight him.

"So the bird sees Delphine," he remarked. "Now I feel left out."

She started to laugh again, but it hurt too much. "Shh," she said once more. "She might hear you."

"You think I'm afraid of her?"

They laughed again, but more quietly. Gradually, though, their humor gave way to something quieter and more serious.

Presently Lynn said, "I never liked that part of the Bible."

"Which part?"

"About being given dominion over the earth."

"Ah. Well, I was just arguing with Birdmouth for the sake of argument. Too many people misinterpret that line."

"How so?"

"Being given dominion doesn't mean we can do whatever we want. A shepherd has dominion over his flock, and he spends the better part of his life looking after them. Keeping them healthy, making sure nothing hurts them, rescuing them if they get into trouble. That's the kind of dominion we were given. To be good caretakers."

She laughed. "Okay, I cede."

"Our problem is one of scale. And heedlessness."

Lynn nodded then tried to smother a yawn. "Sorry, I guess the last few days are catching up with me."

"Then take a nap. I'll keep an eye out."

His shoulder somehow turned into the most comfortable pillow she had ever enjoyed. Moments later she slipped away into dreamless sleep.

"THAT WAS A GOOD lecture," Delphine told the bird.

He preened. "I thought so." He had resumed his station on Buster's head, and the alligator hummed agreeably.

"Where *did* you learn all that?" Delphine asked.

"I read," the bird answered.

"Oh, really?" Delphine arched a carefully penciled brow.

"I sat on some man's shoulder for thirty years while *he* read. Of course I caught on."

"Oh." Delphine nodded. In an instant she shed her beaded gown for a more practical outfit of slacks and shirt, bright pink of course. Her hair settled into a color somewhere between violet and blue. "We've got work to do."

"No thanks," the bird said. "We've already done our work for the day. We'll just watch, Buster and me."

"Buster and *I*," she corrected him.

"English teachers!" the bird said disgustedly. "Picky picky picky!"

"Of course. If we aren't picky, who will be?"

The bird cocked its head, looking at her from one dark eye that appeared almost accusatory. "What are you going to do?"

"Make sure they don't leave this island tonight."

At that the bird hopped with glee and let out a few happy squawks. "Yeah. Let them experience nature unfettered."

Delphine rolled her eyes and kept moving toward the beach. She could have gone there instantaneously, but out of regard for the sensibilities of the alligator and the bird, she kept pace with them.

"Your part, you two, is to make sure they don't find Buster."

An agreeable rumble from the aforementioned alligator caused the bird to dance from one foot to another. He batted the top of Buster's head with a wing. "I keep *telling* you that tickles."

Buster didn't seem to care. He just kept pushing forward through the thick growth.

"Unfettered nature," Delphine reminded the bird archly. "Buster is unfettered."

"Oh, go suck eggs," the bird said irritably. "I'm still not sure how I got caught up in all this. I was on a cruise ship. Why did I ever get off that ship?"

Buster rumbled something.

"You numbskull," the bird said, batting the gator's head again, "I *can't* just 'get on the next boat.' I have to know where it's going. I got on the next boat this morning, and look where it's landed me."

"Mmmmmmmmmhmmmmmmmm."

The bird hopped again. "Dang it!"

"You *could* fly," Delphine suggested.

"Too much work." The bird settled its feathers, stroking them back into place. "Of *course* I had to befriend an alligator." He looked up from preening. "A stupid alligator that doesn't properly appreciate having someone to speak English for him!"

"Mmmmmmmmmmmmmm."

"Aaaaccck!" This time the parrot lifted a full foot off Buster's head. "You did that one specially to make it tickle more."

This time Buster didn't answer.

Delphine spoke. "You need some 'nice' pills, bird. You catch more flies with honey than with vinegar."

"Why would I want a fly?"

"Don't be so literal."

"That's my stock in trade."

This time Delphine groaned.

"Okay, okay," the bird muttered. "I'll try. But it won't be easy. I've never had much patience for stupidity."

Delphine halted mid-float and looked at the parrot. "Who are you calling stupid?"

The bird looked down, possibly indicating Buster, but possibly not. "The persons to whom I refer shall remain nameless."

"Wise. Very wise."

The journey to the beach resumed.

The parrot spoke again. He seemed constitutionally incapable of silence. "I get the keeping them over night here. But do you really think it'll do them some good?"

"You *did* give the lecture about not seeing what's right under their noses?"

The bird's chest puffed. "Of course. In magnificent detail if I do say so myself."

"Well, that's the point, isn't it?"

"It is?"

Delphine sighed. "Have you ever had a girl-friend?"

"Of course." A surprising silence followed that revelation. Then the bird said wistfully, "There was this lovely red-breasted Abyssinian. I thought we'd be together forever."

"What happened?"

"Her stupid human left the boat. When I tried to follow, my human chained my talon to the perch and clipped my wings." The parrot shuddered. "Never again. I escaped at the first opportunity."

"And then?"

"And then I found that silly man who spent all day every day reading books. At least he didn't chain me up. But I never met another parrot, only humans."

Buster rumbled sympathetically, but this time the bird didn't hop.

"Well, all water under the bridge," the parrot said with a shake of its feathers. "Life goes on."

"Indeed it does," Delphine replied. "A lesson we all have to learn."

"But I still don't understand," the bird said, "why we're interfering with those two. Are they *that* stupid?"

"No," Delphine said sharply. "But neither am I,

and I was given orders directly from Herself. I can't go back until I fix this. I want to be on my way."

"Oh." The bird cocked his head as if this explained everything.

"And will you do me a favor?" Delphine asked.

"If I can."

"Give me a name to call you by. I can't keep thinking of you as birdbrain."

The parrot clacked his beak unhappily. "Names are meaningless to my species."

"But not *mine.*"

"Oh, all right. But I refuse to be called by the names that either of my humans gave me. I hate them."

"Fine. I don't care. Pick anything you like as long as it's something I can use."

"Let me think." The bird lifted one leg and chewed at a claw while Buster continued to make his steady way through the thick growth. Suddenly the claw snapped down and the bird's head lifted. "I have it. Pita."

"Pita?"

"You know, acronym for pain in the—"

"I get it," Delphine said quickly, cutting the bird off. "I never liked that word. Please don't use it."

"I'm not," the bird argued. "Pita is also a bread. Live with it."

"Easily," Delphine said with a sniff. "It fits."

"I thought so." And which point the parrot began to whistle *The Colonel Bogey March,* from *The Bridge On the River Kwai.*

"I got sick of that years ago," Delphine remarked. Pita just kept on whistling.

CHAPTER TWENTY-FIVE

WHEN LYNN AWOKE, the sun had just passed zenith and the day had turned unbearably warm and humid. As she stirred, she felt Jack stroke her hair gently.

Part of her wanted to remain right there, but she felt overheated. Sitting up, she pushed her hair back from her face and said, "God, it's hot."

"No breeze because of the jungle," Jack offered. "I'm trying to decide whether it would pay to take a dip in the rain pool. The water would have to be cooler than the air though, because my sweat isn't even drying."

Right above water, any water, there was a humidity layer where evaporation was taking place. Over a glass of water or a very small pond it was hardly noticeable. Over this island, surrounded as it was by a body as large as the Caribbean, they were literally inside it.

Darn, what was that layer called? She'd have to look it up.

Pushing her hair back again, she inched toward the pool and stuck her hand in the water. Skin temperature. All she could feel was the slight prickle on her skin as she broke the surface tension.

"We'd be better off going back to the beach if we want to get cool. There's probably a breeze." She turned and looked at him and felt her heart leap. She still wanted him, and no amount of telling herself otherwise was going to stop the feeling. She had to swallow before she could speak.

"What about Buster?"

"My thought is this," Jack said. "We've got food at the boat. If we can't entice him with that by sundown, we'll have to go back to Treasure Island and mount a rescue."

"What a thought!" She shook her head. "I really don't want to go back there and tell everyone I lost their gator."

"You didn't," he said soothingly. "The gator lost himself."

"Right. That's why you were worrying earlier about lynching."

A short laugh escaped him. "Okay, so we won't be popular. But it's still not *our* fault he stowed away."

"It wouldn't surprise me if it was that damn bird's idea," Lynn remarked.

"He does seem like a provocateur."

Lynn sat staring at the pool, thinking. "That water may be too warm."

"What do you mean?"

"Well, it rained just the night before last. And the sun doesn't shine directly on the pool. That's a lot of water to heat up just from ambient air temperature. Plus the rock underneath would have to be warm or it would just suck the heat out of the water."

"What are you saying?"

She turned and flashed him a grin. "I think I need to get Edna out here. Dollars to doughnuts we've got us a dormant baby volcano."

Jack looked at the pool with new respect. "Wow. Maybe we're sitting too close."

"I think we'd hear some rumbling or something if it were active right now. And I could be all wet."

"You already are," he said with a wink.

Looking down, she realized sweat had pretty much plastered her clothes to her. "Be a gentleman. Don't look."

"Oh, gentlemen look, they just do it discreetly."

She pretended to scowl at him, but merely made him laugh. He laughed so easily, she thought. It was a trait she really liked.

"Come on," he said, rising to his feet and reaching for her hand, "let's get back to the beach.

At least there we can cool off in the water and wait for Buster to come to his senses."

"You're pinning a lot of hope on that alligator."

"No, I'm pinning a lot of hope on that bird." He pulled her up and they began following their path back to the boat.

"What do you mean?"

"I mean," he said with a twinkle in his eye, "that I never saw a bird with a greater desire to live amid civilization. Who the heck would listen to his tirades out here?"

"Good question," she admitted.

"That fowl needs an audience, and if he's not careful, his audience may sail away without him."

"Devastating."

He nodded. "Believe it. He couldn't stand it. Trust me, he won't let us escape without him."

BY THE TIME THEY REACHED the beach, the tide had risen noticeably. Ignoring everything else, they dumped clothes and shoes and jumped naked into the surf. The gentle breeze proved a godsend, and the water was a few degrees cooler than their bodies.

"Oh, this is heaven!" Lynn said.

"Refreshing," Jack agreed. Apparently a strong swimmer, he took off along the shoreline with long, powerful strokes. Lynn, who'd never had the benefit of a swimming lesson in her life, stayed where she was, balancing with her arms, keeping her feet safely on sand.

Looking back at Empty Island, she soaked in the beauty and wondered why it was she couldn't just build herself a hut here and ignore the rest of the world. But as soon as she had the thought, she laughed at herself.

Yeah, she'd be happy eating roots and berries for the rest of her days, cut off from the Internet and her colleagues with whom she discussed the problems she was working on. Yup. Just her and a pad of paper.

Get real.

But Treasure Island was the next best thing, she admitted. Life followed an easier, slower rhythm, and despite her usually reserved geekish nature, it had drawn her out of herself, giving her more acquaintances than at any time in her life.

She even got invited to beach parties.

Tipping her head back, she let the water play with her hair. So soothing and relaxing, a lover's caress. In fact, she felt caressed all over by the water, even in places she rarely thought of. Little currents licked and lapped at her, teasing her, reminding her of nerve-endings long ignored.

Everything became so elemental here. So

removed from daily cares. A new kind of appreciation grew in her, one far removed from science and close to her primal nature. She wanted to sink into the feeling and let it possess her forever.

"Hey, look what I found."

Jack's voice caused her to raise her head, and for an instant she had to fight for balance. He was walking toward her in the chest-high water, holding up a huge shell.

"Nothing's living in it?" she said uneasily as she eyed it.

"Not as far as I can tell." He reached her and held it up admiringly. "I'll put it back, just in case, but you don't get to see shells this big very often."

She reached out a wrinkled fingertip and touched the mother-of-pearl on the outside. "Do you see how symmetrically it grew?"

He almost smirked. "Somehow I knew you'd see the science."

"But it's beautiful science. It grows according to the Fibonacci Sequence."

"Please don't explain, at least not now."

"Later," she promised. "But the Fibonacci Sequence is fundamental to nature. It covers the way shells grow, the way leaves emerge on a branch...." She trailed off, letting go of the numbers and paying attention to the shell. "What an exquisite creation."

"Now those were *my* very words," Jack said. "The marvelous, ineluctable beauty of creation embodied in this shell."

"On that we agree."

He passed it to her and she held it gently in her hands. For once in her life she didn't ask what kind of shell it was. She didn't care about the taxonomy. It was enough that it was there and it was beautiful. The sun struck fire off it in places, almost like a diamond.

Reluctantly she passed it back. "You'd better return it," she said. "It feels a little too heavy to be empty."

He nodded, cradling the shell carefully and wading away.

Again she stood alone, staring at the island, and all she could think was: Empty Island was a very bad name for that place.

Which brought to mind what the troublesome bird had said earlier. Humans were blind. Only a certain kind of blindness could call a place bursting with so much life "empty."

A little shiver went through her as she felt a major shift happen inside her mind and heart. This day had changed her, and it had changed her for good.

How and why she couldn't say yet. She wondered where it was going to lead her. Only time would tell.

Then she put her head back and let the water play with her hair again, thinking that this must be how a porpoise or whale felt as it swam through the water.

Caressed. Immersed in life. Immersed in love.

"Umm, where did we leave the boat?" Jack asked.

So much for immersion, Lynn thought.

"IT WAS RIGHT HERE," Jack said. They had left the water and stood side by side, looking up and down the shoreline. "I remember that big tree with the Y in its trunk. I know we anchored it here."

"It does look familiar," Lynn agreed. "But there might be another tree like that around the island, no?"

"No," Jack said. "I was always good at this. My dad called it a built-in sense of direction. We left the boat right here."

He studied the treeline again, measuring it against his memory of where they'd landed. Nothing seemed out of place. Except, of course, for the boat.

"The tide rose," he said. "But that was a heavy anchor. The tide couldn't have set the boat adrift."

Lynn shook her head. "No, I don't think so. Besides, we'd pulled the dinghy up into the sand and tied it to a tree. The tide couldn't have taken that too."

"And it *was* here," Jack said, walking a bit closer to the trees. "See, here are the tracks where we dragged the dinghy up."

"Yes, I see," Lynn said. "What I don't see are any tracks where someone dragged the dinghy away."

"Right," Jack said. "Which makes no sense whatever."

"Oh, it makes perfect sense," Lynn said. "Delphine took our boat."

"Lynn…"

She turned to him, and he saw no hint of overreaction or fantasy. Instead, her face was that of someone who was completely assured of what she was saying. "Jack, don't. It was Delphine. It had to be Delphine."

And she was, essentially, correct. Much as he hated to admit it, he could think of no other explanation for the missing boat. "Okay, so what does she want? And how do we get our boat back?"

"I would guess that the first question is the answer to the second," Lynn said. "And since Delphine is spirit, and you do the spiritual stuff…"

"So you're putting it in my lap?"

"Maybe, just maybe, that's what Delphine wants," Lynn said. "For me to put it in your lap. The 'it' being…"

"You," Jack said.

She nodded with a playful wink. Maybe that was what Delphine wanted. Maybe not. But here they were, stuck on this island, still naked, with no way to leave and nothing else to do. So…why not? Why not, indeed?

He sat on a rock. "The lap is now open."

Lynn giggled and straddled him, placing a forearm over each of his shoulders. "The lap is now occupied."

"Shall we conjure up Delphine?" he asked, brushing her nose with his.

"We could do that," Lynn said, nipping at his lower lip. "She might not show up for a while, though."

"It might take…intensive conjuring, then."

The tip of her tongue trailed over his lips. "Yes, it might. Very…intensive."

"What a shame," he said. "That's a lot of work."

"Yes," she agreed, now trailing kisses along the curve of his jaw, sending little shudders through him. "But such is the life for working conjurers."

"We need a conjurer's union," Jack said between moans.

"Oh yes," Lynn said. "Let's make a conjurer's union. Right here. Right now."

CHAPTER TWENTY-SIX

"THEY MAKE BAD PUNS," Pita said.

"Shhhhhh," Delphine replied. "If they know we're watching them, Lynn will freeze up again. Not that I can blame her. I remember what it was like. People are so repressed about their bodies."

"I never cared who was looking," Pita agreed.

"Uhhhmmhhhmm," Buster agreed.

"Ahem," Pita said. "You've never done it, Buster."

"Urrrggghhhh."

Pita gently patted Buster's head with a wing. "I didn't mean it that way. And I know it's been tough for you. But hey, at least you have the statue at the café."

"Urmmmmuuuhh?"

Pita shook his head. "I can't. We mate for life."

"That's sad," Delphine said, stroking the feathers at the back of his head. "There's no reason you should be alone the rest of your life."

"Tell that to my DNA," Pita said.

"You mean…"

Pita nodded. "It's programmed into my genes. One mate. Either it was an evolutionary advantage, or Herself decided we were better off that way. Regardless, I had my love for life. And she's gone."

"Uhhhhhhurmmmm."

Delphine scratched beneath Buster's chin. "True, he has you. But you're not exactly Pita's dream date, kiddo. And I know he's not yours either. But hey, at least you're friends."

"So what about you?" Pita asked. "Are you getting laid up there in heaven?"

If Delphine had ever been capable of blushing, and she never had been, she'd have done it then. Instead, she laughed, gaily and joyfully. "Ohh, Pita!"

"WHAT WAS THAT?" Lynn asked.

The sound seemed to have come from far away and right next to her, at the same moment. And this was not the time for such distractions. Oh no, not when Jack was thrusting so perfectly, in that smooth, easy, flowing rhythm that beckoned her to clench down each time he began to withdraw, both holding him in and intensifying the sensation of his movement, sending sparkling shudders through her body.

If Jack heard the question, he didn't answer. He simply shook his head, his stubbled chin brushing over her cheek, the briefest momentary pause in his rhythm the only clue that he'd heard her at all.

Exactly as it should be, Lynn thought, pushing the sound from her mind, focusing on the muscles of her vaginal walls, willing them to release…and clennchhh…release…and clennchh…feeling the burn intensify with each contraction as her exertions generated lactic acid, the burning muted only by the shimmering, sparkling shower of endorphins that carried her deeper, deeper into the passion of the moment.

Every driving thrust of his hips was met with a thrust of her own, every grunted breath in perfect synchronicity, fingernails digging into each other's backs. Lynn sought his tongue again and again with hers, their kisses broken only by their need to breathe, to draw in oxygen to fuel their seemingly endless mutual quest for the perfection of their needs, desires, hopes and dreams.

For, once again, this moment went beyond simple physical pleasure. Lynn had experienced physical pleasure before. But never, ever in her life had she known this…this completeness…this wholeness…the reification of love itself.

Her toes grasped at the sand, squeezing it in an

outward expression of the movement within her, the random firings now spreading to her calves, causing her feet to tap-tap-tap against the warm, soft sand as if she were swimming. Now her thighs joined in, flicking against his hips and legs, almost lifting her from him. She clutched hard at his back as the muscles along her spine arched, her head falling back, mouth open, primal sounds rising up with his as oh…oh yes!…the contractions began, twitches of absolute bliss, driving out every other thought except the white-hot intensity of the moment, the shared joy as he pulsed within her, flooding her cervix with liquid heat, filling her with the purest love she had ever known.

Again and again the waves crashed through her, her grunts shifting to growls and then to cries that would have made the parrot proud….

The parrot!

"Wow, he's good!" Pita said from a branch above her. "Let me take notes in case I ever find my true love again."

"What the…?" Jack stammered, obviously shaken out of his orgasmic reverie long before his mind was ready. "You were watching us?"

"Of course!" Pita said. "Someone had to be on the lookout for predators and such."

Lynn broke out in a laugh, still holding Jack

within her. "Right. You were looking out for predators."

"That's my story and I'm sticking to it," Pita insisted.

"So did you get a nice view?" Jack asked.

"Oh yes," Pita replied. "Great breasts, huh?"

Jack cleared his throat.

Pita spread his wings. "Puh-*leeze*. You just finished the horizontal mambo and you're still going to act like you didn't notice? That train has left the station, preach."

Lynn laughed and leaned back. "He's right, Jack. So, what do you think?"

Jack could blush. And did. Then he nodded. "Umm yes. You're beautiful."

"That's rather pallid," Lynn said, with mock consternation.

"Okay, okay!" Jack said, laughing. "Yes, you have beautiful breasts. Amazing breasts. Breasts I could spend the rest of my life waking up next to and burrowing into and…oh, my, yes…you have great breasts."

Lynn looked at the parrot. "What do you think?"

"That sounded sincere enough to me," Pita said.

"I think so, too," came another familiar voice.

Lynn swiftly crossed her arms over her chest. "Delphine!!!"

"You *did* want to conjure me," Delphine said. "I heard you. So you succeeded and now you complain that I'm here?"

"At least let me get dressed first!" Lynn said.

"And cover those great breasts?" Delphine said. "I'd never dream of it. Jack's enjoying the view, aren't you, Jack?"

"Umm, yes ma'am," Jack said, lowering his eyes, not from her chest, but from...

"You can see her?" Lynn asked.

He looked at Lynn. "Umm, sort of. I think. Yes."

The feelings that flooded through Lynn were so contradictory that she leapt off Jack's lap and began to pull on her sandy clothes. "Enough. A nosy bird is one thing. A nosy aunt is another!"

Pita made a *tsking* sound. "My lovely red-breasted Abyssinian never felt the need to cover up."

"She was already covered," Lynn said between her teeth. "In *feathers*."

Jack, too, was pulling on his shorts. "I hope this isn't a sign of things to come," he remarked.

"It's not," Delphine assured him.

He whipped around and stared in the direction of her voice. "Uh, Lynn?"

"Yeah?" The answer was short, disgusted. Sand was grating against her skin all over, and the only solution she could think of was to march back into the water and hope most of it rinsed out.

"Is your aunt a flapper with a long cigarette holder?"

Lynn turned to look. "Right now, apparently. She's been getting more outrageous every time I see her."

"So…" Jack hesitated. "I'm seeing a ghost?"

"Tsk," Delphine said. "I'm not a ghost. Although I guess by your terms I'm a spirit."

Jack gaped. "There's a difference?"

"Significant."

"Oh." He appeared flummoxed.

Delphine floated toward him, changing into a flowing white gown. As an afterthought, at the last moment, she added wings. "Does that help?"

His astonishment only grew more pronounced.

"You see?" Pita said to Buster. "When they want to look holy, they add wings. What does that tell you?"

Buster harrumphed, causing the bird to screech and dance on his head. "Stop that!"

Delphine looked at the bird. "Will you just be quiet for five minutes?"

"Hmmph," Pita said and folded his wings, dipping his head down beneath one of them.

"That's better," Delphine said. She was still floating in her angel garb.

"Auntie Delph," Lynn said desperately, "where is our boat? Why did you move it?"

"The boat will return when it's time for it to return. To everything a season, you know. In the meantime, you two still have some experiencing to do. I'll take these two away, and I promise you, *none* of us will bother you again."

With that, Delphine *poofed.* The bird screeched as if nudged, and Buster began lumbering back into the undergrowth.

"Should we let him escape?" Lynn wondered.

"Are *you* going to wrestle with an alligator?" Jack sank down on the sand and stared out over the water.

Lynn sat beside him. "What's wrong?"

"What's wrong? What's *wrong?* I just saw a ghost."

"A quantum wave collapse," she corrected him. "Not a ghost."

"Semantics," he muttered.

"Well, I should think you'd be excited. You just got proof for everything you believe in."

"Hmmm."

"You don't sound happy."

This time he didn't answer at all. Giving up, she waded back out into the water and tried to get rid of the sand that was abrading her everywhere. She supposed she should feel vindicated, since now Jack had seen Delphine, too, but instead she felt vaguely worried.

It was a lot to handle, even for a man of faith like Jack. And then there was something else....

She closed her eyes, allowing the water to gently lift and drop her. Something else...

A reason, she thought. A reason bigger than a day trip to see an island. A reason bigger than a talking parrot, a missing alligator and an apparition.

She was overlooking something. A purpose. A message. A lesson. The certainty grew in her with every lift of the gentle waves.

In her study of quantum physics, the absolutely chaotic underpinnings of the universe, the place where, as Einstein had put it "God played dice with the world," she had discovered a beautiful order and symmetry. Everything was entangled. Linked. The chaos proved to be a beautiful kind of order. Like the old line about how a butterfly flaps its wings in Australia and you get a storm in Florida, or whatever it was.

But that was something she already understood. Why did she have the feeling there was another understanding just beyond her grasp. One that was the real reason for Delphine's appearance in her life.

Oh, yes, she said she wanted to encourage Lynn to have a romance with Jack, but that wasn't it. At least not in total.

Sighing, she leaned her head back and let the water rinse her hair again. It would come to her. It always did.

And then maybe Delphine would give the boat back.

JACK, TOO, RINSED OFF, but then he sat on the beach, keeping an eye on Lynn as she savored the water, and thought about a lot of things, not the least of them the way his entire world view had taken a good shake today. The worst of it was that he couldn't quite say why Delphine's appearance upset him so.

He believed in the afterlife. So why should seeing Delphine rock him to his core? Because this life and the afterlife were never supposed to meet?

That was a ridiculous notion, he decided the more he thought about it. After all, he prayed all the time and believed he was heard. Sometimes even answered.

Drawing his knees up, he rested his chin on them and watched Lynn bobbing on the waves. It would be dark soon, and he wished they could build a fire. It would make them feel safer, although there didn't seem to be anything on this island to worry about.

A fire would also be helpful if anyone on Treasure Island thought of looking for them.

Why did he think no one would bother? Because the preacher and the teacher had gone out on a boat together, and why wouldn't they stay overnight?

The islanders had that kind of view of love and sex. Far more open than he was used to, but in a nice sort of way. Nothing salacious about it. But he still had to return early enough in the morning to hold Sunday services.

Just the acknowledgement that men were men and women were women and desires were normal and healthy.

So okay, no rescue party likely before morning. Besides, even if one tried to come, Delphine would probably find a way to divert them. She seemed to be determined to keep Lynn and him on the island for a while.

And darn it, she had all the food on the boat.

The sun was glistening gold on the water now. It seemed to gild Lynn, making *her* glisten like precious metal. He stood up. "Lynn?"

She didn't seem to hear him, so he called louder, cupping his hands around his mouth. "Lynn?"

Her head lifted at once.

He motioned her back in. "You need to get dry before dark."

She waved and began to move toward him. The sight of her rising from the water, naked, made him think of Venus rising from the waves.

He sat back down, filling his eyes with the view of Lynn and thinking that he was trembling on the edge of something significant. Something transcendent. If only he could grasp it....

Lynn emerged from the water, dripping. To his surprise, she moved away from him then flung out her arms and began to whirl in circles. It had nearly the same effect as a wet dog shaking, and he had to duck a few times as water flew his way. She laughed, though, apparently enjoying herself. When she had shed as much water as she could, she sat on a boulder and grinned at him.

"I'm not minding our incarceration as much as I should," she admitted.

"Me neither. Other than the fact that it's not my choice, anyway."

"Maybe," she said, looking serious all of a sudden, "surrendering control is a good thing sometimes."

He thought about that. "Yeah. Maybe it is." It was certainly something he didn't like to do as a rule. But right now he had no choice. "My kingdom for a fire," he said, by way of taking them away from dangerous areas.

"I'd ask Delphine to make one, but she promised to leave us alone."

"Could she do that?"

Lynn shrugged. "At this point, I'd believe almost anything."

The thought tugged at him, pulling him closer to something….

Finally he got up. "I'll be right back. I want to find something to make a bed with. The sand is soft enough, I guess, but we'll rub ourselves raw every time we turn over."

"I'll come with you."

He shook his head and smiled. "Do me a favor and sit right here. That way if someone comes over from the island looking for us, you can holler and wave."

"Okay."

Besides, he needed some thinking time, and from the look on her face, she did, too. And after a bit more thinking, maybe they could talk.

Because something told him this was going to be an earth-shattering night.

CHAPTER TWENTY-SEVEN

As THE EVENING BREEZE strengthened, Lynn dried off quickly. Her clothes seemed stiff and a little damp, but the sand was gone, for which she was grateful. As she sat staring out over the water, she became aware of the waves steadily lapping at the sand, much higher now than this morning when they had landed.

But it was the rhythm of that motion that captured her mind, so steady and soothing. Again she felt that shift within herself, and half-closing her eyes, listening to the waves, she thought of how that water encircled the globe and that everywhere someone stood on a shore they could hear the same sound, of the same water. That perhaps the water called to humans because its rhythms still resided in their blood.

Or maybe she was just thinking too much. She sighed, then drew in the myriad scents that filled the air, heard the sound of the breeze in the palms, a gentle clatter, the whoosh of the waves reaching shore.

She began to let go.

Just then she heard a loud rustling and turned to see Jack emerging from the jungle with what appeared to be banana leaves.

"I figure a couple of handfuls of these will be all we need."

"Thanks."

"My pleasure." He donned his shorts and disappeared again, and she realized the moment was lost.

Later, she promised herself. Later she would reach for that feeling again.

For now she rose and went to start spreading the leaves into a bed that might keep out most of the sand.

By the time Jack and she had finished, the bed was large and several layers deep. He even surprised her with the gift of some bananas to eat. While they were barely just past green, they were delicious and filling.

"I guess the bird was right," he remarked. "Everything you need is right here if you look."

She smiled. "Maybe so. To a point, anyway."

He grinned. "Hey, I was just trying to be nice to him. Being stranded on a tiny island isn't exactly my idea of paradise."

"What *is* your idea?"

He paused, thinking, half-eaten banana in his hand. "Heaven. Being one with God. What's yours?"

She leaned back, stretching out on the bed of large soft leaves and looked up into a sky full of reddening clouds as the sun began to set. "Maybe we're already there. It's hard to...oh, forget it."

He stretched out beside her, head propped on his hand. "Tell me."

"I've told you how I worked with quantum ideas. As you probably know, Einstein never accepted quantum theory."

"God wouldn't play dice with the world, or something like that, right?"

"Exactly. And at first blush it *does* look horribly random and chaotic."

"But then?"

"But it's not. It's like the example I gave about the deck of cards. There's order there. It's not one-hundred percent predictable, but neither is it utterly random. Or look at the waves out there. What is the *exact* depth of the ocean in any given place?"

"It changes all the time," Jack said. "The tides, even just the ripples."

"Right. And yet, we can sit here, reasonably confident that the ocean isn't going to rise right up over top of us and drown us both and this entire island. When something like that does happen, it's a catastrophe because it's so unpredictable, so totally out of line with our expectations, and it catches us unprepared."

"The South Asian Tsunami."

She nodded. "Every once in a while, Mother Nature rises up and gives us a good hard kick, to remind us of our place in the universe."

"And that place isn't nearly as exalted as we'd like to think," Jack said. "I find myself questioning my own beliefs, after what the bird said. Why couldn't there be a Saint Beaker? Why do we assume that God only revealed himself to human beings?"

"I didn't know religions assumed that," Lynn said.

"Neither did I, until the bird mentioned it. Then it all came clear. My own beliefs, my faith, what I've given my life to…suddenly there's a big gap that I've only now seen. Angels aren't supposed to be like Delphine, and birds aren't supposed to tell me how short-sighted I am. It's not that it doesn't fit the Bible. The serpent talked to Eve, a fish carried Jonah to Ninevah, and a talking donkey was God's messenger to Balaam. And as for angels, they appear in countless forms in the Bible. So why do that parrot and Delphine shock us?"

"We're not used to miracles anymore," Lynn said. The thought she'd been searching for was crystallizing. "They happen, but we don't see them. We go out of our way *not* to see them."

"You may be right," Jack said. "But we cry out for them all the time."

"Oh sure," Lynn said. "But we really don't *want* them. What we really *want* is to control things ourselves, for the universe to be perfectly orderly and predictable, so we can manipulate it with total confidence. We want to *be* gods, and miracles remind us that we're not."

"That's quite an indictment. And not very scientific, I might add."

"Science is organized observation," Lynn said. "It's not magic and it's not about white lab coats and equations on a whiteboard. At its core, science is nothing more than organized observation…offering an explanation for what we think we see, then testing that explanation to see if it holds up. So call this a hypothesis. Given a choice of some random possibility of reward, with an attendant risk of loss, or some much smaller but almost certain reward with little or no risk, which will we choose?"

"A bird in the hand," Jack said.

"Yes." Lynn paused to organize her thoughts. "Some recent research in economic cognitive theory supports that. It turns out that we, as individuals, don't weigh risk and reward very well. We make 'bad' economic choices all the time, but we do it in very consistent ways, overvaluing the risk of loss, undervaluing the potential rewards. Large corporations, that often do make more detailed and rigorous risk-to-benefit analyses, maximize their profits by relying on ordinary consumers to make those *bad* choices in those predictable ways."

"Like professional poker players rely on the *fish* to misplay their hands," Jack said.

Lynn laughed. "Exactly. In Treasure Island terms. So we, the fish, want to believe things are orderly, that is, precisely predictable, because we think that's in our best interests. We avoid risks. We avoid uncertainty. So we reject miracles."

Jack paused. "Like love."

Yes, that was it. Lynn nodded. "Like love. I don't know if we're going to like each other a month or a year from now. I don't know if you'll get sick of me being lost in my equations, or I'll get sick of you explaining that I need to trust some divine mother to take care of us. And maybe all we're feeling is just the effect of neuropeptides triggered by incredible, passionate sex. What happens when one of us gets sick, or depressed, or distracted? Will we lash out at each other? Once we know each other's most sensitive, most vulnerable feelings, will we push those buttons to get what we want? That happens in relationships…a lot more often than happily-ever-after." She sounded almost desperate.

"It does," Jack said.

"If I had to bet on a quantum wave collapse, it's at best a fifty-fifty bet that we stay together."

"That's the statistic," he agreed.

She turned to him. Taking a deep breath, she said, "And I still want to hope for a miracle. Because even if Einstein is right and God really doesn't roll dice with the universe, I've already rolled the dice with my heart. And it's landed with you."

"Lynn…"

She froze. There were a million ways he could respond. A lot of those ways began with "Lynn…" And almost none of them had happy endings. Her breath caught in her throat, and for a moment she felt an utter fool, caught up in another fanciful chain of reasoning that, in the end, led only to heartache and loss.

"Lynn Reilly…"

Could it be? Was it possible? She dared not hope, dared not look at him in this moment, lest by her mere act of observation she might change the quantum field and push one probability aside for another. Or perhaps would she do that by *not* looking? Wasn't the act of non-observation an act of observation itself? If everything she'd studied at PEAR were true, her mere thinking about the possibility was shaping its probability. But how could she turn off her mind and simply let the universe bring what it would bring?

"Lynn Reilly, would you marry me?"

Stephen Hawking theorized that a black hole has an "event horizon," the point beyond which all matter will, inevitably, collapse upon itself, infinitely, vanishing into the singularity. That gave rise to the Hawking Paradox, for if matter and time and space could vanish into the singularity at the heart of a black hole and remain undifferentiated, regardless of how much matter and space and time were sucked in, was that not the same as saying that matter and space and time were being sucked out of our universe altogether?

Lynn Reilly did not know how to resolve the Hawking Paradox. Not even the great Hawking himself had resolved it yet. The greatest minds in the world still fell short at the threshold of such a fundamental question.

But she knew this.

In those words, Jack Marks offered her an event horizon. And the whole of her heart and mind and soul, the whole of her universe, perhaps the whole of the universe itself, was poised at the precipice of that singularity. Poised at the precipice of oneness. A oneness she had never known before. A oneness she would never have dared to imagine, but for this amazing man, whose eyes even now rested on hers, kind, hopeful and anxious.

"Yes, Jack Marks. I will marry you."

EPILOGUE

BOTH BOAT AND DINGHY had miraculously reappeared by dawn. Lynn and Jack sat together, embracing, watching the new day being born. Magical, mystical, an incredible moment of unity.

Until Pita squawked. "Hurry up," he called from the fishing boat. "We're waiting and Buster is getting hungry enough to look at me as if I'm a fat chicken."

Lynn looked at Jack, and found laughter dancing in his eyes. He kissed her again. He must have kissed her a million times in the course of the night. "Should we keep them waiting?"

"As long as we want."

But they didn't keep anyone waiting too long.

"We'd better get back," Lynn said finally. "I know a man who's probably worried to death about his boat."

"Yeah." Jack sighed. "And I need to get to church. We're going to come back to this island very soon. I promise."

"With or without my science students?"

"Both," he answered.

He rowed them back out to the fishing boat and helped Lynn aboard. Buster was in plain sight, lying on the deck as if waiting for the sun to hit him. Pita perched on the edge of the wheelhouse.

"You'd better feed him," the bird said. "There's no telling what he might snap at."

While Jack drew up the anchor then started them toward Treasure Island, Lynn poked around in the ice chest and found the peanut-butter sandwiches. She tossed a whole one to Buster who took it in one snap.

Then she fed a small piece to the bird, and laughed aloud when the peanut butter made his bill stick shut. The bird hopped around angrily for a minute before getting rid of the stickiness. "Are you trying to kill me?"

"It's all I have. Eat it or shut up."

The noisome beak clacked pointedly closed. Buster ate the other two sandwiches and groaned happily.

Of course, they couldn't just slip into town quietly, tying up at the dock and hurrying away. No, it seemed every living soul was out waiting for their reappearance, and as they pulled in, resounding cheers greeted them.

"Don't be embarrassed," Jack said as he eased them up against the dock.

"Why should *I* be embarrassed. I'm not the preacher, and it's Sunday morning."

"Oh, yeah." But then he laughed and switched off the motor. Minutes later they were safely tied up with only one small problem.

Buster. A crowd gathered trying to figure out how to lift him out of the boat. Quite a few mentions of One-Hand Hanratty accompanied the discussion.

"He'll get out on his own," Pita finally said. "Lead me to some bird seed."

But no one moved. Every eye settled on Jack and Lynn until finally one guy cleared his throat and stepped forward. "Set a date yet?" he asked.

Jack looked at Lynn. She looked at him.

Jack spoke. "As soon as possible."

Surrounded by cheering neighbors, they kissed again.

Dazzled, Lynn Reilly knew for absolute certain that she had finally found the thing that lay behind everything:

Love.

REQUEST YOUR
FREE BOOKS!

2 FREE NOVELS
FROM THE ROMANCE/SUSPENSE
COLLECTION PLUS 2 FREE GIFTS!

YES! Please send me 2 FREE novels from the Romance/Suspense Collection and my 2 FREE gifts. After receiving them, if I don't wish to receive any more books, I can return the shipping statement marked "cancel." If I don't cancel, I will receive 4 brand-new novels every month and be billed just $5.49 per book in the U.S., or $5.99 per book in Canada, plus 25¢ shipping and handling per book plus applicable taxes, if any*. That's a savings of at least 20% off the cover price! I understand that accepting the 2 free books and gifts places me under no obligation to buy anything. I can always return a shipment and cancel at any time. Even if I never buy another book from the Reader Service, the two free books and gifts are mine to keep forever.

185 MDN EF5Y   385 MDN EF6C

Name	(PLEASE PRINT)	
Address		Apt. #
City	State/Prov.	Zip/Postal Code

Signature (if under 18, a parent or guardian must sign)

Mail to **The Reader Service:**
IN U.S.A.: P.O. Box 1867, Buffalo, NY 14240-1867
IN CANADA: P.O. Box 609, Fort Erie, Ontario L2A 5X3

Not valid to current subscribers to the Romance Collection,
the Suspense Collection or the Romance/Suspense Collection.

Want to try two free books from another line?
Call 1-800-873-8635 or visit www.morefreebooks.com.

* Terms and prices subject to change without notice. NY residents add applicable sales tax. Canadian residents will be charged applicable provincial taxes and GST. This offer is limited to one order per household. All orders subject to approval. Credit or debit balances in a customer's account(s) may be offset by any other outstanding balance owed by or to the customer. Please allow 4 to 6 weeks for delivery.

Your Privacy: Harlequin is committed to protecting your privacy. Our Privacy Policy is available online at www.eHarlequin.com or upon request from the Reader Service. From time to time we make our lists of customers available to reputable firms who may have a product or service of interest to you. If you would prefer we not share your name and address, please check here.

Sue Civil-Brown

77114	HURRICANE HANNAH	___ $6.99 U.S.	___ $8.50 CAN.
77076	THE PRINCE NEXT DOOR	___ $6.99 U.S.	___ $8.50 CAN.

(limited quantities available)

TOTAL AMOUNT	$ _____
POSTAGE & HANDLING	$ _____
($1.00 for 1 book, 50¢ for each additional)	
APPLICABLE TAXES*	$ _____
TOTAL PAYABLE	$ _____

(check or money order—please do not send cash)

To order, complete this form and send it, along with a check or money order for the total above, payable to HQN Books, to: **In the U.S.:** 3010 Walden Avenue, P.O. Box 9077, Buffalo, NY 14269-9077; **In Canada:** P.O. Box 636, Fort Erie, Ontario, L2A 5X3.

Name: _____
Address: _____ City: _____
State/Prov.: _____ Zip/Postal Code: _____
Account Number (if applicable): _____

075 CSAS

*New York residents remit applicable sales taxes.
*Canadian residents remit applicable GST and provincial taxes.

HQN™

We *are* romance™

www.HQNBooks.com

PHSCB0807BL